Gone!

"How bad is it," Bell asked.

"It was the Tracs, sir. Twenty-seven incoming ships appeared out beyond Saturn twenty hours ago, closing at close to point four of light, dropping down to point one by the time they reached Mars' orbit. Colonial forces took out all but five of them. We finally got the rest of them, but you saw what they did."

"What'd they get?"

"Nearly half the orbital power grid, the Kenya Skyhook, thirty ground hits. I guess you saw Atlanta go."

He nodded, looking off to the south. The dark cloud was still roiling over where Atlanta used to be. . . .

BAEN BOOKS by WILLIAM R. FORSTCHEN
1945 with Newt Gingrich

Also in this series:
Star Voyager Academy
Article 23

The Wing Commander Series
End Run
by Christopher Stasheff & William R. Forstchen
Fleet Action
by William R. Forstchen
Heart of the Tiger
by William R. Forstchen & Andrew Keith
The Price of Freedom
by William R. Forstchen & Ben Ohlander
Action Stations
by William R. Forstchen
False Colors
by William R. Forstchen & Andrew Keith

PROMETHEUS

WILLIAM R. FORSTCHEN

PROMETHEUS

Copyright © 1999 by William R. Forstchen

A Baen Books Original

Baen Publishing Enterprises
P.O. Box 1403
Riverdale, NY 10471

ISBN: 0-671-57795-6

Cover art by Gary Ruddell

First printing, February 1999

Distributed by Simon & Schuster
1230 Avenue of the Americas
New York, NY 10020

Printed in the United States of America

✧ Chapter 1 ✧

TO: JUSTIN WOOD BELL
FROM: UNITED SPACE MILITARY COMMAND
SUBJECT: REACTIVATION TO ACTIVE DUTY
STATUS

YOU ARE HEREBY ORDERED BY ADMIRAL
WILLIAM MAHAN, COMMANDER USMC, TO
PRESENT YOURSELF WITHIN TWENTY-FOUR
HOURS OF RECEIPT OF THIS NOTIFICATION
AT USMC UNITED STATES REGIONAL
COMMAND HEADQUARTERS WASHINGTON
DC FOR REACTIVATION INTO ACTIVE
SERVICE WITH THE RANK OF CAPTAIN.

Justin Bell reached into his pocket and pulled out a
lighter. He flicked it to life, then held it to the bottom
edge of the printout and watched, expressionless, as the
paper flared. He dropped it to the ground when the flames
finally licked up around his fingertips.

Sitting down, he pulled a pipe out of his pocket, lit it
and then picked up the triple scotch he had been nursing
ever since the message had arrived more than an hour
ago. With a single gulp Justin downed the drink and then

sat in silence, watching as the order from the old service to which he had given so much of his life flickered and collapsed into charred dust.

"Screw 'em."

He reached down to the ground by his chair, lifted the bottle and poured another triple, resolving to nurse this one through the sunset.

Funny, sunsets never really bothered him. Sunrises, however, were something different—memories of Matt and himself trapped in the ruined station on the asteroid Lucifer, waiting for the sun to come up and fry them. *Strange, they both look the same though.*

Matt Everett.

He tried not to think of his old friend, if he could still be called a friend.

"It may be for years and it may be forever . . ."

The song, "Katherine Mauvareen," still haunted him. He and so many of the old cadets from the Academy had suddenly made it popular when the Civil War between Earth and the United Colonies started. It harkened back to the old traditions of West Point on the eve of their Civil War and the legend of brother officers North and South who had sung the same song together before departing to their destinies—where more than one helped to kill the other.

Where was Matt now? Last report was Mars, at least the last time he checked three years ago. Justin knew he could find out easy enough, but what the hell for? That friendship ended at Bradbury Station. It was best to forget, forget all of it.

He sighed and looked back through the open door of his cabin to the small cramped study. An antique of a computer that looked like it belonged to the early 21st century rather than the '80s was half-buried beneath a mound of papers on a desk made out of a heavy oak door. Piles of books and holo memory cubes were scattered on the floor around it, along with half a dozen empty bottles. The illusion of writing a book about the history of Star

Voyager Academy and its founder Thor Thorsson was just that, an illusion. But it gave him a purpose, a fantasy to hide in, to make believe that he was still doing something.

The illusion had kept him going for three years now, ever since he had resigned his commission after Bradbury. He sipped his drink.

The old argument of "only following orders" no longer provided a way to cover over the guilt. Article Twenty-three of the service code clearly stated there was a moral obligation to resist illegal or immoral orders. *Should have invoked that, knew I should have, and made a stand but I didn't. I accepted their arguments that Bradbury would end the war and thus save lives rather than losing them.*

He stared at the pattern of lights flickering from his heavy crystal glass, which caught the setting sun. *So I balm my soul afterwards, resigning as if that would ease my conscience.* Yet he knew there was more—it was simply that after the death of all too many comrades from the old days, on both sides of the fighting in that campaign, resignation of his commission was a blessing and an escape.

He looked at the ashes at his feet. *What could they do— arrest me? That would be a joke. Medal of Honor winner arrested for refusing a recall to service. They got twenty-one years out of me, take someone else.*

The phone on his desk beeped, and he blearily looked over at his only connection to the outside world. He let it ring until the computer finally clicked into the line and took the message. Gulping the rest of the drink down, Justin went into his office and hit the message delete button, not even bothering to read what it was, and then shut the system down so no more notes or officious demands could come through.

He spared a quick glance around the room. The walls were covered with too many memories, many of them class photos from the Academy. *Ghosts, I've wallpapered my world with ghosts.*

His gaze lingered for a moment on the holo image of his first command USS *Francis Marion*, flanked by USS

Ethell—she was a beauty of a ship, now bits and fragments orbiting Mars. And then there was the last ship, USS *Gagarin*, lost at Bradbury. Letters of commendation were clustered in dusty frames around his Medal of Honor citation; the more dead you harvested the more medals they hung on you.

He had never signed into the service for that task. Back then, before the Civil War, it was maintaining the peace, protecting civilians and saving lives that they were trained for. There was always the threat of the alien Tracs, but it had been over twenty-five years since they had last been seen.

The Civil War between Earth and the Colonies had changed everything. Granted, in the overall scheme of things the war had been relatively bloodless; far more had died in the settling of the Colonies than in their fight to free themselves from United Nations rule. Both sides respected the rules of engagement against attacking nonmilitary targets—at least most of the time—until Bradbury.

No, not much of a bloodbath for a system populated by ten billion souls. Except, of course, if you were in the USMC or the CFF, the Colonial Free Forces. All right for us to die while the civilians of both sides cheered. How many out of my graduating class? A third, half maybe. And how many by my own hands? He pushed that thought away as he took another sip.

Admiral Mahan managed to cover the real reason for Justin's resignation, trumping up a press release that Medal of Honor winner Captain Justin Bell had resigned due to injuries sustained in service. Justin had been willing to keep the myth alive and retreat to this hiding place in the North Carolina mountains. It would not have been popular at all to make a public announcement that the great war hero had told the commander and his government to go to hell.

He looked back at the ashes still scattered out on the front deck.

What the hell do they want now? Could it be that the new government is looking for an excuse to arrest me, when I refuse to return?

He pondered that thought for a moment. The coupist government had seized control of the United Nations in the wake of the war's end. The seizure had been a popular move, since they took power with the claim that the war could have been won if only the USMC had fought with a will for victory no matter what the cost. They were backed by the EDF, the Earth Defense Forces, which had been created during the war as nothing more than a rear-guard unit in case Colonial forces ever attempted a landing.

Justin snorted with disdain at the thought of the EDF. The possibility of a Colonial offensive to ground sites was in itself inane. They were fighting a protective action in their own systems and the defensive lines the USMC maintained out beyond lunar orbit were simply too strong. The real reason for the creation of the EDF by Lin Zhu, who had been head of ground defense in the old administration, was now obvious. He had created a military force loyal to him as a counter to the USMC. It was also a nationalistic move since the USMC was increasingly American, European, Japanese and Russian of late, while the EDF was more Asian and Southern Hemisphere in makeup.

That national separation bothered Justin. The dream of the USMC's creator, Thor Thorsson, was to make it a truly international force, but Zhu had managed to subvert that ideal by playing on old nationalistic lines. The USMC still existed, it still was responsible for transatmospheric defense of what was still Earth's out to lunar orbit, but it no longer had authority over controlling the peace back on Earth.

What the hell is going on? Why are they bothering me now? Justin wondered, fighting back the haze of alcohol for a moment.

Justin turned and went back to the doorway. The sun was drifting behind the Smokey Mountains and he went back out onto his front porch to watch. Shadows from a spur of the Black Mountains stretched out across the valley and blanketed the village below. On the faint breath of the westerly breeze a church bell chimed. Overhead the last birds of evening were winging in, coming to rest, weaving through the flaring orange, red and yellow leaves of autumn.

He sniffed the breeze. The sky to the west was crystal clear; the distant ridge of the Smokies fifty miles away stood out sharp, silhouetted by the shifting indigo and scarlet.

The air was cold, crisp, carrying with it the faint aroma of woodsmoke.

Better put a fire on tonight, he thought. *Frost by morning. Good, maybe hike up the old toll road to Graybeard Mountain. Need it to clear the hangover I'm prepping up for now.*

A breeze stirred through the trees, a scattering of leaves drifting down, rustling, like a curtain of fiery rain, the pile of ashes on the front deck swirling away with the wind. He poured another drink, starting it out as a single but deciding to make it a triple again.

Justin fought with a momentary temptation to turn his computer on, tap into the news service and see what might be up. The last time he had bothered to check in, the Titan Colony was rebelling against the United Colonies government over its decision to honor all pre-war debts to various corporate investors in Colonial development. It was a sound move on their part to insure the reestablishment of credit, but he could well imagine that more than one Colonial thought the whole thing was a denial of what they had fought for. Perhaps that was leading into some sort of crisis.

The hell with them! If they want someone to fly in another war, go find them, but I'll be damned if I'll serve again, Justin thought coldly.

He looked up. The sky was dark enough that the first beads of light appeared—the orbital solar power stations, catching the energy-rich light of space. He studied them for a moment. Funny, Alpha Three wasn't showing, nor was Alpha Four. Curious, were their panels turned edgewise?

Ah, the hell with that too, he thought glumly. *If there's a problem it's not my worry . . . the world could do with a little less juice, make people think twice about wasting so much of it.*

Justin slipped back into his cabin for a moment, stepping over the piles of books. He went into his bedroom and pulled a blanket off his unmade bed. Stopping in the kitchen he discovered a ready-to-eat meal in a cluttered cabinet, ignored the dirty dishes piled high in the sink, and went back out onto the front porch.

The stars still called . . . he knew he'd never really get that out of his blood and it was comforting on a cool autumn night like this to simply sleep outside.

He sat down in his lounge chair; the dinner of shrimp and noodles heated up once the lid was snapped open. Most everyone aboard a service ship had come to despise the ready-to-eats but they were so damn convenient, and besides food was nothing more at this point than a means of keeping himself going. Finishing the meal and still holding what was left of his drink he cranked the lounge chair back, turning it into a cot.

A chill wind slipped down from the mountains and he pulled the blanket up around his chest. Through the haze of drink he noticed that his arm and right leg throbbed slightly. Ever since *Gagarin* the wounds were a daily reminder. He closed his eyes for a moment. The piercing alarm still haunted him, the signal to abandon ship.

If only I had stayed, he thought almost wistfully. *None of this would be here to bother me now. Or was it the other way around?*

Sighing, he opened his eyes and watched as the stars slowly traced their graceful arcs across the heavens.

Damn, I still miss it, he thought, *still miss the silent watches, the sea of stars to guide my ship.*

Give me a ship . . .

*How I miss it all, but I'll never go back . . . too many
ghosts float out there.*

It may be for years and it may be forever . . .

The drink slipped from his hand.

He awoke, the old dreams becoming, as they so often
did, too painful to bear. Sirens . . .

Siren down in the valley, reminded him of battle alerts.
The tone wavered, sounding as if it was coming from the
old highway. Some damn fool most likely wrecked.

Dawn. Damn, how I hate dawn, always have.

Groaning, he sat up and rubbed his temples. *Single malt
will still give you a hangover if you drink enough of it,* he
thought ruefully.

It was cold, frost coating the leaves on the ground, the
half-empty bottle of scotch by his recliner rimmed with
an opaque sheet of silvery crystals.

They always said space was cold, unless your suit cooling
winked off and you were out in the sun. Suspended between
fire and ice and all so silent, deliciously silent.

The morning birds were astir, calling, fluttering through
the trees overhead. *I always did miss that,* he thought,
looking up at them. They reminded him of waking in the
early light to do the farm chores when he was a boy in
Indiana. Somebody on *Gagarin* had tried to pipe birdcalls
in through the PA when the morning watch started; it had
lasted only a couple of days before he had put a stop to
the absurdity.

He watched the birds for a couple of minutes and finally,
with a groaning sigh, Justin stood up and went back into
his cabin. He hit the electric heater while going into the
kitchen. Putting a cup of water into the microwave he
pulled down the instant coffee and then threw several
spoonfuls into the steamy cup of boiling water.

Damn dream, Mars on fire below, half a dozen nuclear
warheads bursting above Bradbury, his ship on fire, the
eject alarm screaming. Outside the siren still trilled.

"Stereo, Wagner, *Gotterdammerung*, final scene," he said quietly, and the sound system in his living room turned on.

It was Tanya Leonov who had cultivated his interest in classical music and introduced him to the one piece that, more than anything he had ever heard, epitomized the tragedy of a world being destroyed.

Wagner echoed through the cabin, the nightmare still lingering . . . the first an airburst, EMP nailing down the comm links, the second a penetrator groundburst right on the target, the third, fourth and fifth in a triangle pattern around it, slamming down any interceptors coming up. Mushroom clouds soaring up through the thin atmosphere . . . Wagner.

Should listen to Pachibel, Vivaldi, or even Copland for dawn, not this stuff. It's an exercise in self-pity that will leave me depressed for the rest of the day, but what the hell!

Justin stepped out onto the porch. To the west the Smokies were catching the first light of dawn about to break behind him.

He sipped the coffee as the music thundered, reaching its climax as Valhalla was consumed in flames.

A snap of light flashed across the mountaintops.

Strange.

Justin stepped to the side of the porch to look back to the east. The sun was breaking over the eastern spur of the Black Mountains behind him. And yet to the northeast, far away, another sun was rising, a brilliant fiery yellow-white ball of light. Another flash ignited near the first, and instinctively he covered his eyes and turned his head away.

The stereo shut off. The computer chirped, signaling a power interrupt, and then died.

EMP burst, Justin realized.

He spared a quick glance up, covering one eye just in case. Flashes of light winked overhead and to the south. Geosynch orbital defense and solar power grid, they were all going. He lowered his head, glad that he did a second later when there was another brilliant flash that etched the mountain tops with a crystalline white light so sharp that their image burned into him even while he closed his eyes and looked away.

Still no sound of course, not above the atmosphere.

Justin retreated under the eaves and sat down.

He picked up the bottle of scotch, poured a shot into his coffee and put it back down, his fingerprints burned into the frost that coated the bottle.

The Colonies?

No. Nothing to be gained. They'd won the war, they needed Earth now for trade and for immigrants. No, not the Colonies.

Terrorists then. He mused over that for a moment, averting his eyes when a ground strike missile erupted far off to the southeast, flaring for an instant as bright as the sun. Must be the base at Jacksonville. Another sparkle of lights raced overhead and he looked up at the tracer of fire coming down.

A ship burning up, cutting through the atmosphere at high speed. It flashed overhead and then disappeared beyond the Smokies. Two more flashes followed, more ships out of control, diving in, one exploding silently above, the other streaking off to the north to disappear over the horizon, breaking up as it entered the upper atmosphere.

Couldn't be terrorists, far too coordinated. At least a dozen hits so far; besides those were fighters going down. Terrorists wouldn't have the hardware to take them down.

There were two more flashes, and then a white streak of light slashing down from the fiery heavens . . . air-to-ground strike missile on booster.

To the south pulsing arcs of light shot up, point-defense Shrike missiles . . . they detonated short of an intercept as pulses of light snapped from the incoming laser countermissile suppression attached to the missile, he realized as he watched the incoming drop down. *Damn, that's cutting edge equipment, who's doing this?* He saw the booster flare again, streaking in to its target.

He instinctively dived out of his chair and hit the ground as the airburst ignited over Atlanta two hundred miles away. He waited for the dazzling light to subside before coming back to his feet.

"The Tracs," he whispered.

Justin Bell sipped down the rest of his coffee, the ground beneath his feet trembling, the birds in the trees silent, as humanity finally confronted what was waiting for them among the stars.

He was not surprised when the helicopter started into a deeply spiraling turn, coming to hover over his cabin like a vulture examining its prey; the USMC insignia emblazoned on its side. The copter turned slowly and then edged in between the towering hickory and oaks to land nearly at his front door.

He had been waiting. His uniform barely fit anymore, hanging loose. Drinking too much usually affected people one of two ways; in his case it had peeled off the tight conditioning, leaving him thin and haggard. Hoisting a small flight bag he ducked low, ran up to the copter and pulled the door open. The pilot looked out at him, then down at a photo, then back up, a curious look in her eyes.

"Captain Justin Wood Bell?"

He climbed in, nodded an acknowledgment, and slammed the door shut, blocking out the noise.

"You've got him."

"I need to ID-check you, sir."

She held an ID unit up to his right eye and flashed the laser beam on. An affirmative on cornea match beeped on her unit.

"Captain Bell, you are under arrest for failure to report for duty as ordered."

"Cut the bullshit, young lady, and let's get out of here."

He watched her features deflate. She'd most likely been gearing up for this on the flight out. The backseat was empty. If Mahan couldn't even spare a couple of MPs to help her things must be really bad.

"I'll note, sir, that you came of your own volition."

"Thank you, Lieutenant, now could we kindly get a move on?"

She pulled back on the collective and the copter started to rise. Justin spared a quick glance back out the window. He had not even bothered to close the door to the cabin. *What the hell, I'll never see it again anyhow*, he thought dryly. Chances were some refugees would move in; as the copter turned and circled up over the Black Mountains he could see the old interstate highway below, jammed with vehicles, panic-stricken civilians pouring out of the cities in anything that would still move after the EMP bursts. They were heading to what they hoped would be the safety of the mountains. Within a matter of days they'll be starving, and then they'll turn on each other. Hell, it might be safer in the war after all.

"How bad is it?" he asked, looking at her nametag, "Lieutenant Graham."

She spared him a glance.

"I guess you wouldn't know."

"Hell, I'm not even sure who did it yet."

"It was the Tracs, sir. Twenty-seven incoming ships appeared out beyond Saturn twenty hours ago. They were closing at close to .4 of light, dropping down to .1 by the time they crossed into Mars' orbit. There was a hell of a fight over Mars late yesterday, Colonial forces taking out all but five of them. They then did a drop down towards the sun, slingshot around it, and then came straight in on us. The damn Colonials broke off the pursuit once it was obvious the Tracs were closing in on Earth."

"Can you blame them?" Justin asked quietly, "Hell, defending us isn't their job anymore."

Graham looked over at him angrily.

"And what the hell did we do?" Justin asked.

"Not much, sir. Remember, the Colonials have antimatter drive; we're just starting to come online with that and we've got nothing flying yet that's combat-worthy. We tried an intercept but they were just too damn fast. Beyond that, sir, it was weird! They can maneuver like hell, almost like they have aerodynamic reactive wings in the vacuum of space. They ripped the hell out of us and three made it into near-Earth space.

"We finally dropped the three of them, but you saw what they did."

"What'd they get?"

"Nearly half the orbital power grid, the Kenya Skyhook, thirty ground hits. I guess you saw Atlanta go."

He nodded, looking off to the south. The dark cloud was still hovering. Firestorm.

"Near miss to the northeast of DC, another one bracketing to the west."

"What about regional command?" Justin asked, surprised at his own anxiety.

"Top personnel evacuated out to Wallops ground-to-space launch station, outside the fallout path where the new headquarters is being set up. I heard Washington's in chaos. You can kiss most of Maryland and Baltimore good-bye, though. The Cape, Star City in Russia," she hesitated for a moment, "and the northern part of New York City are all gone. The EMP bursts knocked out most of the communications grid around the world, it'll be months before we're back up. A number of orbital units are gone as well. Fortunately the yield on the weapons was low, half-a-meg range, but still we've got at least several million dead."

"The Academy ship?"

He was almost afraid to hear.

"That's where we got one of the bastards. A cadet squadron took it down as it closed in on the Moon after dropping its load here," Graham said fiercely.

"Mars got hit too," and he could detect a cold sense of satisfaction in her voice. Old hatreds die hard, he realized, even when there is something new to hate.

"It's a mad panic downwind from the hit sites. This area

is gonna get a good dusting from Atlanta by tomorrow when the wind shifts to the southeast."

He noticed they had turned north, already clearing Mount Mitchell. The Blue Ridge Parkway was jammed with traffic, both lanes heading northeast, away from the fallout.

He looked back at Graham. Her jaw was set tight, her eyes red-rimmed, dark and sunken, her jaw quivering.

"You want me to take over flying for a couple of minutes?" he asked.

She looked over at him fiercely, her eyes filling up.

"Where the hell were you?" she snapped. "All of you space defense bastards. Where the hell were you?"

"Who'd you lose?" he asked softly.

"My parents, my kid sister were in New York, what was New York."

"What's our course, Graham?"

"Tactical Lift Station at Wallops Island."

Justin checked the nav system. The course was already locked in, the copter's retractable wings deployed for standard flight mode.

"Stand down for a couple minutes, Graham. It's all right."

She buried her face in her hands and started to sob, and Justin sat beside her in silence. He felt as if he should somehow cry with her as well. To pray Kaddish for a world that was once more at war. But he had long ago forgotten how to pray for his dead, for there were far too many to mourn.

As he swung out over the Chesapeake Bay he nudged Graham awake. Like a child she had cried herself to sleep, curled up in her seat. It wouldn't be very good for her career, however, if the prisoner she was responsible for called into the tower for final clearance.

"We're here," he said softly.

She rubbed her face, embarrassed, trying to put on a tough professional demeanor and failing miserably.

"Any news on the radio?"

"Usual confusion."

There was no sense in upsetting her. There was a firestorm fifty miles square blazing in New York. Even from here he could see the smudge of smoke on the northern horizon.

She called in for final approach and expertly brought the copter in low and fast, weaving through the traffic. At the north end of the island's runway an old heavy-lift military transport roared down the runway, banked up sharply, swung out over the ocean, then pointed its nose up. It punched through the clouds and disappeared.

He felt a tightening in his gut at the sight of it. Nearly everything went into space by way of the Skyhooks, but emergency and high-priority payloads still used the old chemical rockets.

Lost in thought, he barely noticed as Graham touched down. Two MPs came up to the side of the copter and looked in. Justin ignored them.

"Take care of yourself, Graham," he said quietly, extending his hand.

She tried to say something but couldn't. She quickly shook his hand and then looked away. He could understand; she allowed herself to be vulnerable and now just simply wanted him out of her life.

He popped the door open and the MPs saluted.

"Captain Justin Wood Bell?"

"You've got him, sergeant."

"Come with me, sir."

The second marine took Justin's flight bag and the three set off at a brisk pace towards one of the bunkers that lined the edge of the flight line. Behind them another *Aldrin*-class surface-to-space transport turned onto the runway, its boosters roaring to life, the ship leaping forward in spite of its thousand tons of mass, the air crackling with the roar of engines.

The noise was blocked by the double doors that opened into a long flight of stairs leading down into the underground bunker. At the bottom of the stairs was another set of doors;

these were made of polymer-weave steel. The entry was guarded by two heavily armed marines, who checked IDs then let them pass. A marine officer was waiting on the other side and Justin was passed off to him.

"Glad you could join us, Captain Bell," the officer said coldly. "Admiral Mahan is waiting."

Justin wanted to ask what the situation was but knew better than to try. There was nothing more sanctimonious than a staff officer, especially when the person he was escorting was obviously due for one hell of a chewing out from the big boss.

They wove their way down a crowded corridor that seemed choked with a palpable sense of panic, Justin was led into a small, paneled office and the door was closed behind him.

Even from the back Justin could tell that Mahan had aged in the three years since they had last met. His shoulders were stooped, his graying hair gone white. Mahan was hunched over a holo display, examining it intently, dictating an order in a soft voice. Finished, he came erect and turned around.

Mahan looked at him coldly, his eyes dark, filled with exhaustion, his full lips compressed in what Justin knew was a look of barely suppressed rage.

"You son of a bitch, I wanted you here yesterday!" Mahan snarled.

"I'm sorry, sir."

"Sorry isn't good enough, mister. You got my order . . . I needed you yesterday. God damn it, Bell, you knew the Tracs were coming!"

"No, sir, I didn't. I haven't heard a news report in weeks."

"Don't bullshit me, mister."

"Honest, sir." He paused for a moment. "Let's just say I was having an extended conversation with Mr. Glenfiddich."

"You got my order to report in, didn't you?"

"Yes, sir, but like I said, I didn't know why."

"So what did you do?"

"I burned it and got drunk, sir."

Mahan paused and walked towards him. He was a good six inches shorter than Justin, and as he approached he looked up into Justin's eyes.

"Son, you look like one godawful mess. What the hell you been trying to do, kill yourself?"

Justin didn't reply. There was no sense in explaining. And beside, Mahan had seen just as much combat in the Civil War. If he couldn't understand, then the hell with him.

Mahan shook his head and turned away, walking back to the holo display.

"Come over here, Bell."

Justin came up to his side and Mahan pointed at the display, a projection of Earth defense systems. Justin knew them all by heart, as he had helped to build more than one of them. A scattering of flashing green dots still circled the globe in geosynch, high-polar, and lunar orbits. But flashing yellow dots now outnumbered them, meaning damaged, and flashing red, meaning that they simply no longer existed. On a side panel was a tote board listing the various commands and wings deployed in space; again, a number of them had yellow or red dots beside them.

"Did Graham brief you on what happened?"

"Yes, sir."

"Bell, we've had three encounters with what we've called the Tracs over the last forty years, but this is different. This wasn't one ship—it was a small fleet, and the design of these ships was different as well." As he spoke he brought up a grainy image on the holo screen.

"We're getting more gun-camera footage downloaded right now, but I tell you these ships are different than what we dealt with before. They're warships."

Justin leaned forward to look at the screen. Though the image was blurry he could see weapons pylons studding the bottom side of the vessel and what looked like gun mounts bristling down the main axis of the ship, topside and underneath.

"Their tactics sucked, though. They came in loosely, no

mutual support. The Colonial forces ripped the shit out of them."

Justin could detect a note of admiration in Mahan's voice.

"Damn lucky they did," Justin said, "I think they would have kicked our asses if all of them had gotten through."

Mahan nodded in agreement as he ran a playback, tracing the trajectories of the Trac ships from where they were first detected all the way in to the attack on Earth.

"The tactical deployment seemed off, though, as if they expected to simply wander in and cut us apart."

"Maybe that's exactly what they expected," Mahan replied, "and they got more than they bargained for. Those Colonials, you've got to hand it to them. They were ready, we weren't."

"They always were, sir." Justin said, knowing he was rubbing salt in the old wound.

Mahan looked up at him coldly but said nothing.

"So why do you want me?" Justin finally ventured to break the silence.

"Listen, Bell. I think you cut and ran when I needed you the most. You didn't like what happened at Bradbury. Neither did I, and remember *I* was the one responsible, not you. But I stayed on and took the heat."

Again there was the flash of memory, the spread of warheads impacting across the Martian plains, a hundred thousand dying in one incandescent holocaust of fire.

"And I still maintain it was a legitimate military target. The Colonials will never admit it, but you saw the Intel report. Then you go and have a fit of conscience and run away. Bell, you've sure done a hell of a lot with yourself since."

"Did you call me here to tell me to straighten up and get my life back in gear, sir?"

"No. I frankly don't give a damn what the hell you do with yourself, but the service needs you."

"There was something called the Code that we learned at the Academy . . . do you remember it, sir?"

"Of course I remember it, Bell, so what?"

"You taught it to me, sir, or have you forgotten that you once taught that course on Ethics and War?"

Mahan shifted uncomfortably and averted his eyes.

"Cut the shit, Bell, and get to the point," Mahan snarled.

"You broke that code, sir, and so did I. You used that old classic line, 'the end justified the means.' You thought taking down their suspected antimatter facility at Bradbury would destroy their ace in the hole and bring them to the negotiating table. You and the Joint Chiefs couldn't wait for better Intel, you said we had to strike now and it would win the war."

Justin paused for a moment and waited for Mahan to finally look at him again. He felt cold, as if he were out there again, the chilled, dry, antiseptic air in the room reminding him of the feel of a ship's bridge. At length Mahan stirred and looked up at him with dark hollow eyes.

"Well, sir, it didn't," Justin sighed. "To this day we don't even know if that facility was there to start with. They sure as hell came up with an antimatter bomb and propulsion system a year afterwards anyhow and beat us to production, thereby winning the war. We still don't have it. I think someone made the wrong call, and a hundred thousand innocent people died and we lost the war. Those people and a lot of close friends dead, sir. Something went wrong there at Bradbury and I've got to live with it the rest of my life. How are you living with it, sir?"

Even as he said the last words he regretted them. There was a flash of pain in Mahan's eyes and he could see that Mahan had handled it just about as well as he had. Sighing, Mahan returned to his desk. He pulled open a drawer, reached inside, and pulled out a bottle and two glasses.

"I think there's something unethical about giving you a shot, but we need it."

He poured out two drinks and handed one to Justin.

"To comrades gone," Justin whispered, offering the traditional toast when Academy grads got together.

They both hesitated as if wanting to say more, then

downed their drinks. Justin sighed, glad for the bracing effect as the whiskey burned into his stomach.

"Why did you call me back?" Justin finally asked.

"Because, Justin, *they'll* be back. The other times these bastards have shown up they had just one ship. For that matter, I half-suspect this might be another group entirely. These were war vessels, heavily armed. We lost over twenty percent of our entire fighter forces taking down just five of theirs."

Justin looked down at his empty glass, stunned. Mahan poured him another shot, which he swallowed in a single gulp. Twenty percent, well over a hundred and fifty fighters. He didn't even want to ask who, afraid to hear yet more names.

"And remember, that was *after* the Colonials had torn them apart. We could wake up tomorrow and see a hundred of them closing in. If so, it is over. Then again, we might have a little time, but I don't think we're going to have years the way we did in the past."

Precious time, Justin wanted to add, that had been wasted away.

"Intel believes that whoever these bastards are, they were engaged in fighting somebody else and that war seems to be winding down."

"How do we know that?"

Mahan hesitated for a moment.

"Have you ever heard of 'Dark Eye'?"

"Rumors . . . supposedly deep-space surveillance."

"It grew out of the SETI program after the first Trac contact forty years ago. We geared the operation back up more than ten years ago."

"Ten years ago! Why?"

"We got worried. First the Tracs show up, we finally bag a ship, then nothing. We have some mirror systems located on the Moon with arrays of nearly a kilometer in diameter. Dark Eye actually got some visuals of what looked like nuclear strikes on a system seventy light-years out. We also got some radio fragments."

Mahan punched a button on his computer. A warbling tone startled Justin, sounding almost like a ship's alarm, and then there were voices, otherworldly, which sent a shiver down Justin's spine. He looked over at Mahan, astounded; he was hearing voices that held all the mysteries and dreams of humanity's reach to the stars.

Mahan let the recording play for several minutes; there were interruptions of static, the voice fading, then reemerging, and then finally drifting away.

"I'm no philologist, but the specialists tell me those guys are in the middle of a fight. Don't ask me how they know, but I kind of believe them. We've got several dozen hours of such recordings."

"Any visuals?"

"None."

"And this last attack?"

"Recorded ship to ship, more than twenty hours' worth. Not the same language, not even the same races; the experts tell me that the physiology of the vocal cords is different between the two. Again no visuals but I'll tell you this . . . by the end of the recordings on the last attack even an idiot can tell they're scared shitless. All of this tells us that someone's fighting out there. Not just here, but out there as well."

"Well, that's certainly comforting to know," Justin said coldly. "And since I never heard anything confirmed about this, even when I had a double-A security clearance, it must mean that the government decided to keep this information classified. There's more to this. Why?"

"We had our own war to fight," Mahan replied, and Justin could detect the exasperation in his old commander's voice, "and the Colonials had in their possession the parts of the one Trac ship that was destroyed in our system. The government decided we shouldn't let them know what it might be capable of."

"There's no logic to that. We're facing a common threat."

"You don't have to tell me," Mahan replied coldly.

"Whoever they are, we figure they're expansionist and

it looks like we might be next on the list. Why they didn't throw everything at us at once, I don't know. Maybe they thought, based upon their recon raids of forty years back, that what they were sending was enough. Hell, it might even be that two different powers have given us a call and the one didn't know about the other. We've made a lot of advances since then, learned in the Civil War, that gave us at least a bit of an edge."

"A great way to learn it," Justin said dryly.

"Look, Bell, I'm sick of your attitude. Your country needed you after Bradbury and you walked. As far as I'm concerned you could rot after that. This recall order didn't come from me, it was a request to us from the Joint Chiefs of the United States, not the USMC."

"Thank you for the confidence, sir."

"Just shut the hell up, Bell."

Justin stood silent. He knew he should almost feel sorry for the man in front of him. Mahan had carried the blame and guilt for Bradbury. Not that there was any blame passed around at the time. After all, it was war, and thought to be a legitimate military target. It was like Dresden from the Second World War, a targeting decision that Mahan had cited in his classroom lectures. Only afterwards did some start to doubt the rightness of what had been done. He knew Mahan well enough to know that beneath the exterior the inner man was tormented by the holo images that the Colonials had broadcast across the solar system showing the thousands of dead, the women and children burned beyond hope, lying in rows inside a bunker, waiting to be euthanized. They looked almost grateful as weeping medics knelt by their sides and administered the doses.

"I'm sorry, sir."

"For what?"

Justin hesitated.

"Just sorry."

"All pilots demobilized since the war were recalled yesterday and that included you. You were not, however, recalled under the General Order, and we don't want you to fight . . . at least not yet."

Caught off guard, Justin looked quizzically at Mahan.

"That's right, Bell. You're being sent on a little diplomatic mission."

"To where?"

"Mars."

Justin sat down, stunned, not even bothering to ask permission as he poured another drink. The last place he ever wanted to see in the universe was Mars, not after everything that had happened.

"Working for who—the United States, the USMC, or the United Nations government?"

"We're still the space-based defense forces of the United Nations," Mahan said evenly.

Justin could not control the sarcastic smile that crossed his features.

"Those bastards, after what they've been saying about the service. You'd think that the United States government, or at least the Russian government, would have the guts to tell them to go to hell."

"And back it with what?" Mahan replied sadly. "The Earth Defense Forces of the United Nations received control of all orbital-based nuclear weapons this morning."

"What?" Justin looked at Mahan in dazed disbelief.

Mahan nodded sadly. Without offering a refill to Justin, he poured himself another drink and downed it.

"The UN declared a State of Emergency and Council General Zhu had his people aboard our orbital stations within an hour, claiming the weapons were needed for point defense and it was no longer USMC-controlled property."

Justin was silent, trying to figure it all out. The EDF had been a creation of the United Nations in the last year of the war, supposedly to unite ground forces of all the Earth's military for defensive purposes if the Colonials should ever try a direct strike. At first many in the Corps saw it as a simple boondoggle by an increasingly erratic

UN to try to extend its control. The militaries of the United States, Russia, and the European Council had not gone along with it, but there were plenty of other countries willing to join in on the deal. Ever since the coup in the UN government at the end of the war the real game plan was becoming obvious.

"What the hell did the U.S. and Russian governments do about it?"

"You know what our own president is like . . . a throwback to a couple of our former great leaders who caused the Second Revolution. The war's over, so let's cut the military to the bone, let the UN handle things. The same with the Russians and the Brits. In the confusion of the onset of the Trac attack they made their move."

"You should have resisted," Justin said quietly.

"With what? We weren't mobilized for a defense against the Tracs and it was pulled off before we even knew clearly what was happening. Now that they've got the hardware the governments of the United States and Russia are rolling over and playing possum, hoping the threat will simply go away. As it is, the UN is blaming us for the breakthrough, and smoke-screening the seizure as an act of strategic necessity in order to have a unified command."

"Then they have everyone in the barrel now except defenses beyond geosynch orbit," Justin said coldly. "So who am I working for?"

"Us. This is a USMC mission even though your participation was requested by the United States."

"And what if I refuse?" he blurted out. "This whole thing is looking more screwed by the minute."

"That shit won't float a second time, Bell," Mahan snapped. "I'll have you up on court-martial charges and by heavens you'll sit in the darkest hole I can find for the rest of your damn life."

Mahan walked around from behind his desk and sat down in the chair opposite Justin.

"Not that I think such a threat really matters to you anymore," Mahan finally continued softening his tone.

"Look, son, it's a tricky job, and though it might sound off-the-wall I think the Joint Chiefs were right to suggest you for it. This war is different, Bell. It's not old comrades fighting old comrades like the last time. What happened this morning was unprovoked murder by an enemy we don't even know, that we've never even seen. There was no chance to talk, to try and reason. Either they simply want to cripple us, to keep us out of space, or it might be expansion to annihilate or enslave us as a colony. They definitely got more than they bargained for, thanks mostly to the Colonials, but I think it's a foregone conclusion they'll be back, and this time will come armed to the teeth. Now it is kill or be killed, and I don't think you are the type of man who can turn his back on such a fight.

"Or," he added quietly, "that any graduate of the Academy could turn from such a fight. Justin, it's a call to a duty we once pledged our lives to."

Justin finally nodded in agreement and then reached towards the bottle that still rested on Mahan's desk. Mahan moved quickly and pulled the bottle away.

"You're cut off from now on, Justin."

"Don't give me that father-act shit," Justin replied angrily.

"I need you straight and sober. First off, you're flying within the hour."

"To where?"

"Like I said, Mars."

Justin felt a cold rush of emotions. Mars . . . it was back to space then. It was also back to Mars, to Bradbury.

"This is strictly USMC business for right now. I want someone I can trust going there."

Justin laughed softly.

"So you picked me?"

"I know I can trust you to keep your word."

A bit surprised, Justin looked up at Mahan.

"You just reminded me that I once taught Ethics at the Academy, Justin. I remembered all too often these last three years that you were my best student. On one level I hated you for walking out on me after Bradbury. But there was another part that admired your guts for taking the stand. We're getting caught in a game within a game . . . the Tracs, relations with the Colonials we now desperately need, and the UN with God knows what they're planning next. I need a contact person with the Colonials and you're it."

"They'll tear me apart the moment I land," Justin said quietly.

"I doubt it. They were once comrades at the Academy, nothing can break that bond. The Colonials have the one means of blocking the Tracs or whoever it is that's attacking us if they show up again. They have the remains of the Trac ship. I'm giving you the job of trying to persuade the head of the project to share the technology with us before it's too late."

"Who is it?"

"Your old roommate," Mahan said quietly, "Matt Everett."

Justin realized that his hands had just started to tremble. Was it the need for the drink, or was it the memories?

"No," he whispered, "not again, not again."

✧ Chapter II ✧

Justin hesitated before replying to the inquiry from Mars' space-to-ground control. He had survived more than one raid into this sector, and the sight of the surface below triggered all the old emotions.

"This is USMC ship Frederick George One Niner Three, requesting landing clearance at Bell Station."

The radio was silent for a moment.

Justin banked his fighter slightly to starboard and looked down. It was all so ironic. Down below he could see the Martian City named for his own grandfather, who had been a crewmember on the first mission to Mars back in 2025. Perhaps the Colonial government had insisted upon his landing here as a means of rubbing a little salt into his wounds. After all, his grandfather was now buried down there. Just before open hostilities broke out, the old man had gone back "to die on ground I'm proud of," as he put it when they had said a final farewell. At least he had not lived long enough to see what had become of his only grandson. The old man never voiced it, but Justin knew that he was ashamed that one of his blood had sided with the government of Earth against the Colonies.

I feel so damn old, Justin thought sadly, again wishing for a drink. He leaned back in the cockpit chair and stretched. There was a time when he could stand the confinement of a *Glenn*-class fighter for weeks. The five-day ride out from Earth was now about all that he could handle. It wasn't just the confinement, with barely enough room for cockpit, bunk, and head; it was the loneliness of the long watches, the silence.

Funny, in North Carolina it's what I sought. It was different here, though. He had missed space with the aching passion of an old man remembering the first love of youth, yet now that he had it back all the other memories returned: the terror of contact, the deadly explosions rippling in silence across the starry night, the screams of the dying as their ships burned or burst asunder, tossing their crews into vacuum. And the memory as well of the voices, more than one of them from Academy days, more than one of them in ships he had locked into his gunnery computer.

"USMC ship FG 193, you are cleared for Landing Approach Beta. Lock your auto-land to 1185."

"Activating 1185."

Justin leaned over and switched the auto-land system on. Seconds later he felt the kick of his thrusters as the ship pivoted into retro position, engines firing up, pressing him back into his chair.

He rode the trail of fire down across the Martian sky, with Bell Station looming up in his rear projection screen. Crossing into the thin atmosphere the ship pivoted again, presenting itself at a high angle, the ablative shield underneath heating up. Wings deployed, locking into place, and the ship went through a series of S-turns, bleeding off speed, spiraling downward. As he swung into the final approach pattern he saw the old impact points from area bombardments stitched across the far hills north of the city, bombardments he had helped to deliver in the third year of the war. That was still in the early days of the conflict, the target a series of command and control centers defended by heavy particle beams and SAM sites. They had never knocked the place out, giving up after losing an entire squadron of ships and a battalion of space-to-surface marine assault troops in the last attack.

His ship turned onto final approach and he felt a tightening in his gut. Instinct still told him that coming in straight and high without evasive maneuvers was an invitation to get fried over *this* place. He settled back and let the autopilot handle the landing, hands poised lightly on throttle and stick in case of a malfunction. Thin-atmosphere landings were a bit tricky with the Glenn fighter and even a glitch of several milliseconds with the computer could trigger an irretrievable stall.

The fighter's nose rose up as it shot past the outer beacon, crabbing to starboard for a crosswind landing. Green lights snapped on, indicating wheel-lock, and the ship touched down.

"FG-193, take Ramp Three on your starboard side and follow the lights into Docking Bay Forty."

Justin lightly touched the controls, following the winking lights embedded in the runway, which led him to the ramp and down a slope into a hardened bunker beneath the surface. Double plastisteel doors slid open at his approach and slammed shut behind him as he taxied into the bunker. He shut down his fighter and waited for the green light on the bunker wall in front of him to come on, indicating that the room was pressurized. The light snapped on and Justin popped the canopy open. As he stood up he felt wobbly for a brief moment after the five days of weightlessness. The Glenn fighters were far too small for the expense and luxury of one of the new artificial gravity and inertial dampening units.

Climbing out on the wing, he looked around for a ladder and ground crew. The room was empty. He tried not to smile at what he suspected was an intended insult. He walked gingerly down the side of the wing and leaped off, lightly dropping the ten feet to the ground, and headed for the access door that opened at his approach.

The sight of a light blue Colonial uniform unnerved him slightly.

"Captain Justin Bell?"

Justin wasn't quite sure what protocol to follow at the sight of an obviously very junior lieutenant. Something in the back of his mind told him that visiting officers were to be met by an officer of equal rank according to the rules of protocol, and it was obvious that this recently minted fuzzy-cheeked officer was the only one present to greet him.

He decided to let it pass.

"You have him," Justin said quietly.

"Follow me, please."

"Lieutenant?"

The boy turned and looked back at him.

"Remember, the war's over, son, and where I come from we still salute superior rank, even if he was an enemy."

The boy looked at him disdainfully for a moment, and then, barely coming to attention, he saluted. Justin returned the salute.

"Now that the formalities are over with, let's go wherever it is you're taking me."

The boy turned around and started off. Justin made it a point not to match his rapid pace as they stepped out into the main corridor of the base. The kid was just trying to run him a bit and he would be damned if he'd let a wet-behind-the-ears lieutenant set the pace.

The hallway was packed. Many of them were civilians rushing to catch flights, but a fair percentage were military personnel. With the mobilization for war fourteen years before, the distinction between military and civilian transport blurred . . . which was part of the problem that led to more than one mistake.

Justin could sense the hostility as he walked down the corridor, eyes straight ahead, his white USMC uniform shining like a beacon in the crowd.

The lieutenant kept ahead of him, as if trying to distance himself.

"You bastard!"

The blow caught Justin across the back of the neck,

staggering him. He whirled around and crouched low, ready to take the next strike. An elderly woman stood before him, bag raised.

"I know you," she shrieked, "you're Bell. I lost my husband at Bradbury, you son of a bitch."

She started for him and he backed up, frantically looking for his escort to intervene. The lieutenant was now lost in the crowd, moving away, obviously ignoring the fact that his charge was about to get mugged by an enraged gray-haired widow.

Justin raised his hands up to ward off the next swing. A crowd started to form, most of them watching with either amusement or, worse yet, open hatred, as if they were about to join in the fun. He remembered the old family story about a distant ancestor who had been forced to run the gauntlet while he was a reluctant guest of the Shawnee. Several members of the crowd started to urge the woman on, one of them moving to get behind Justin.

"What the hell are you people doing?"

A dark-haired woman in a green uniform pushed her way through the mob, stepping in front of the widow as she started to bring her bag up for another strike.

Justin felt a quick flood of emotion at the sight of the woman in the green uniform, even as she motioned for him to turn around and get moving. He pivoted and saw a man nearly his own age leaning back to sucker punch him from behind. Justin ducked beneath the blow and with a catlike ease put him down on the ground, hitting him hard, but not enough to break his neck—which he could have so easily done.

Justin backed away from the man, not saying a word, hoping that he would give up. Several hands reached out from the crowd and pulled his gasping assailant away.

He felt a body behind him, covering his back, and again there was that chilly tingling feeling.

"This man is a guest of your government," his savior shouted. "This is a hell of a statement as to who you are. He's here because of the Tracs, here to help you, and this is how you greet him."

"Help us?" someone taunted. "Let the Tracs fry Earth."

The crowd started to edge closer.

"Break it up! Come on, people."

At the edge of the crowd Justin saw several military police moving in and he breathed a sigh of relief, glad for the first time in his life to see MPs.

The crowd drifted away, except for the old woman who came around in front of Justin, tears streaming down her face.

"I hope you rot in torment, the way I do," she gasped.

Justin looked into her eyes.

"I do," he whispered softly.

She looked at him, ignoring the MPs that now flanked her. A sob shuddered through her, and she turned and fled.

Justin watched her go, wanting to say more and knowing it was useless.

He turned to look back at his rescuer.

"Tanya Leonov."

Just saying the name brought back a flood of emotion, some of it wonderful, most of it bittersweet and painful. She looked up at him with her bright oval eyes, a smile crinkling her features. Funny—she looked older, not how he remembered her at all, with flowing black hair, high Slavic cheekbones and pale complexion, and her bewitching green eyes. But that was nearly fourteen years ago, he realized. Of course she would look older. Thin lines now creased the edge of her mouth and the corners of her eyes, the nick of an old scar tracing under her jaw, a few wisps of gray tracing through her raven-black hair. Yet still, in his eyes and in his heart she would be forever eighteen.

"Bell, you look like shit! What the hell've you been trying to do, kill yourself with drink?"

The same old Tanya, he thought with a smile.

"Every time I see you again you always have such a friendly greeting," Justin said softly.

"Well, that's because you're usually screwing up somehow."

"This from the woman whose life I saved how many times?"

"I paid you back double for that and as far as I'm concerned you still look like shit."

"You haven't changed a bit, my dear."

The beginning of a smile started to form and then she looked past him.

"Lieutenant Haverlock, you certainly know how to do your job."

Justin looked over his shoulder at his escort standing behind the MPs.

"Thanks for the help, Lieutenant," Justin added, wishing the young man were in USMC service rather than Colonial. He'd be standing double watch for one hell of a long time to come.

"If you're finished visiting, Captain, I suggest we continue," Haverlock announced coldly.

Justin looked back at Tanya.

"Care to come along?"

"That's what I'm here for. I wanted to get to your landing bay ahead of your one-man reception committee." She looked over with a sneer at the lieutenant, "But you touched down a bit early."

"You weren't invited," the lieutenant announced testily.

"Young man, you recognize this uniform?" Tanya snapped, and Justin stepped aside with a smile as she stormed up to the lieutenant, thrusting her face into his so that he was forced to back up.

"It's the uniform of a senior member of the Bilateral Peace Commission, or are you color blind?

"By the agreement signed by both the Colonial and Earth governments," she continued, not letting him even begin a response, "I have full authorization to visit all military and nonmilitary sites without the requirement of prior notification and/or authorization. My responsibilities also include the overseeing of any personnel from rival forces visiting such facilities on official business. Captain Bell is here on official business, and given the piss-poor display of security I've witnessed here I am personally taking an interest in seeing that he is delivered safely to his destination. And by heavens if I hear another word from you I'll file an official complaint to the C-in-C Colonial Forces, and let me add that Admiral Brian Seay is a personal friend and former classmate of mine."

She took a deep breath.

"Now, have I made myself perfectly clear?"

Justin looked at the lieutenant, who started to open his mouth and then just stood there for several seconds looking completely ridiculous. He could almost feel sorry for him.

"Well, let's get a move on then," Tanya snapped, shooing the lieutenant away as if he were a lost duckling.

The boy turned and beat a retreat, looking back quickly to see if he was being followed.

"And you three," she snarled, turning to face the MPs. "I'd like an escort, so look like you're doing something instead of just occupying space."

The senior MP, barely able to hide a smile, saluted and fell in behind Justin and Tanya.

"You haven't changed a bit, Tanya," Justin whispered as they started back down the corridor.

"I guess it helps with this damn job," she sighed. "So tell me, Bell. You just seemed to disappear out of existence. What happened?"

How could he even start to explain? Yet as he looked over at Tanya he knew there was no need to explain, not to her.

"What about you?" Justin finally replied, not wanting to discuss himself with her.

"Since when?"

Since when? Hell, he wasn't even sure where to start; since things had ended between them when she resigned her post to join the Bilateral Commission, since he dropped out after Bradbury? He didn't know. He sneaked a quick glance down at her left hand.

"Never did marry, did you?"

"Didn't have the time," she replied, and he saw that she took a quick glance at his left hand as well.

"Besides, I'm supposed to be part of a neutral commission to keep the war from escalating into wholesale annihilation. Hell, anyone I might have been interested in was in the service on one side or the other. Marry and I lose my job."

She looked up at him and smiled, and again he felt that tug.

They walked on in silence, Justin wondering once more about the "what-ifs." There was no denying that even after all the years of separation he had never quite gotten Tanya out of his system. Since the first day they had met when both were first year scrubs at the Academy she had bedeviled him, usually in an all-too-painful way, but on occasion in a wonderfully delightful way as well.

They reached the end of the corridor and the lieutenant stopped, pointing down a side hallway.

"Your transportation is waiting for you down there, sir."

Justin stopped, expecting that Tanya would take her leave, but she simply brushed past the lieutenant and started down the side hallway.

"Ah . . . ma'am?"

She looked back at him.

"I just invited myself," and she continued on.

Justin looked over at the lieutenant.

"Son, don't even try to argue with her. I gave up on it twenty years ago."

Justin followed Tanya through the airlock, which was connected to a ground car. Climbing into the back seat, he settled in while Tanya went through the routine of showing her credentials to the driver, arguing with him for a moment and leveling the usual threats before the sergeant relented.

Leaving the station, Justin turned in his seat to look back at the hills that rose up beyond the landing strip.

"Your grandfather's buried back there, isn't he?" Tanya asked.

"Nearly sixty years since he first landed here. And all the changes. I wonder what he'd say."

"I think he'd be proud of you."

"I don't know, Tanya. Remember, he came here to die right when the war started and I fought for the other side."

"I don't think that's the point anymore," she replied. "I think that more than anything else what counted for him was whether we did our duty. You chose your path, I chose mine," she hesitated for a moment, "and so did Matt. We did our duty and I think for that he would be proud of you. Remember, that's what Thorsson taught us."

Justin smiled sadly at the mention of Thor Thorsson, his old mentor and founder of the Academy. On the day that war was declared by the United Nations against the Colonies Thorsson had called all the cadets together, giving to those who wished to fight for the Colonies the right to leave. Feelings were running high, former classmates turning on each other in the final days before the declaration, with a number of brawls breaking out between rival sides.

Thorsson had defused them with the simple statement that no man or woman could be condemned for following their call to duty, no matter where it might lie. Pointing to the Academy flag, he noted that it represented all the people of the solar system, and not just one political faction or another. That it was a bond of comradeship that nothing, not even a civil war, could ever divide. He finished his speech with the request that every cadet present, no matter which side they were on, would renew their oath to the traditions taught at the Academy and swear as well to fight for their side with honor, integrity, and compassion for their opponents who had once been friends. Every single cadet complied.

Coming from nearly anyone else the appeal might have fallen on deaf ears, but Thorsson *was* the Academy and all that it stood for. He had shocked both sides when in closing he announced that he was resigning as well, since he could not bring himself to raise a hand against so many of the cadets who would serve on one side or the other. In leaving he also declared himself a neutral, stating that he would fight for neither side.

After leaving the Academy Thorsson founded the Bilateral Peace Commission, and by sheer weight of his authority forced both sides to recognize it as a moderator. Across the fourteen years of conflict the Commission served to enforce the "Rules of Engagement," as they became known, thereby preventing the war from slipping into a conflict of annihilation.

Justin looked over at Tanya. She had followed Thorsson into the Commission, an act that he realized took far more courage than going to fight. The Commission had succeeded in its work and, as with any moderator in a conflict, it had come to be both hated and admired by both sides.

"Did Thorsson have something to do with your 'just so happening' to be here when I landed?"

Tanya smiled.

"I'm not supposed to give away trade secrets," and she furtively reached over and quickly squeezed his hand, then let go. The mere touch of her hand sent an electric shock through his system. He wanted to hang on, but she withdrew and settled back in her chair.

Turning into a narrow valley, the hover car wove its way down into the canyon to the north of Bell Station. Impact points from numerous air strikes marked the side of the canyon; wreckage of military equipment, hover cars, battery emplacements, and parts of several crashed fighters and landing craft were strewn across the valley floor.

"This was one hell of a tough nut to crack," Justin said, looking at the missed strikes and the ruins of several SAM sites.

"You ever visit here, sir?" the driver asked, looking into his rear view mirror.

"Most certainly did," Justin replied quietly. "I was with the 23rd Space-to-Ground Attack Group for a couple of years."

"Then I guess you could say we've met before," the sergeant announced. "I was a gunner with the First of the Third Ground Defense. Spent most of the war right here."

Justin looked at his face in the mirror. There was no sign of hostility.

Justin tentatively extended his hand.

"You did a good job, sergeant, we never did knock this out."

"Thank you, sir. Though you don't know how close you came a couple of times," and the sergeant took his hand.

"Look, sergeant, if I got time later, how about a drink? I think we both owe it to each other."

"Will do, captain. I was always curious to hear what you Feds thought of this place."

"It scared the shit out of us."

The sergeant grinned at the compliment.

"Here we are, sir, the place you wanted to get."

Part of the hill directly in front of them started to roll back, boulders shifting to one side to reveal a heavy set of blast doors concealed behind the camouflage. Justin took a quick look around the narrow valley, trying to remember the attack runs he had made. The opposite side of the hill was scarred black from impact points. They'd been hitting the wrong side of the mountain!

The sergeant looked back in his mirror and grinned.

"That's right, commander, we laughed our asses off."

"Well, I'll be damned!"

"I guess if the show starts up again we'll have to dig a new access. Either that, or I guess we'll just have to keep you here forever," the sergeant said with a laugh.

"Captain Bell has sworn an oath of silence regarding any military facilities he might see here," Tanya interjected sharply. "I'll vouch for his honesty."

"Sorry, sir, though if it was me I'd have a hard time keeping it secret. We took down a lot of your people while they were hitting nothing but rock."

The car passed through four sets of blast doors and came to a stop in a long, cavernous corridor. A lone figure stood in the shadows.

Justin climbed out of the car, Tanya by his side. Coming to attention, Justin saluted and then extended his hand,

genuinely glad to see his old squad leader from his first
year at the Academy.

"Admiral Brian Seay! Damn, it's good to see you, sir."

"Two old scrubs of mine, almost like the old days," Brian
replied with a smile, motioning for them to follow.

Turning down a side corridor, they stepped through
another blast door into a simple office, furnished with
nothing more than a cot, a battered standard-issue desk
and a bank of holo screens on one wall.

For the C-in-C Colonial Forces, Justin somehow
expected more.

Brian motioned for Justin to be seated, and then looked
at Tanya.

"You know you weren't invited to this."

Tanya simply grinned and took a chair beside Justin.

"You damn Bilateral people! If the war had kept up much
longer I swear you folks would have been running the
whole show."

"It's what we wanted," Tanya said easily.

Brian smiled and shook his head, looking back at Justin.

"I guess you've heard it already, Bell, but you look like
hell."

Justin merely nodded his head ruefully in reply and then
went through the formality of presenting his authorization
papers from Mahan along with a briefing holo from Brian's
counterpart on Earth.

Brian looked the papers over carefully for several minutes
and then dropped them on his desk.

"I notice this is not authorized by your government—
it's strictly a USMC affair."

Justin nodded.

"Bell, this is really out of order. This approach should
be through government channels, not one military to
another."

"I realize that, sir. But would your government accept
a liaison visit from the coupists, especially over this matter?"

Brian sighed and shook his head.

"I could have told all of you fourteen years ago that

things would finally head in this direction with the UN. A centralized power like that, sooner or later it will try to take more. It's Parkinson's Law, and it's why we fought. All the signs were there."

"I guess some of us just weren't ready to read them yet, sir, and besides, some of us still believed in our oaths, not only to the UN but to our respective governments and the USMC as well."

"Maybe we should skip the politics for right now," Tanya interjected quietly, knowing that Justin was leading into the classic argument by Academy personnel who had stayed with the federal government, "and stay focused on the Corps request to the Colonial Fleet."

Brian looked over at her and then back to Justin.

"So you want our help, is that it?"

"Something like that, sir."

"It's still Brian. We go back a long way together, Justin, in spite of everything else that's happened.

"I hate to ask this, but I want a few things perfectly clear before I continue. Do I have your oath that all information you receive or observe, if listed as classified, will be kept secret by you unless I personally clear you to release it?"

"I give my oath on that," Justin said quietly.

"Secondly, that whatever information I authorize released to you will be conveyed only to the USMC and to no other individuals, organizations, or governments?"

"I give my oath on that as well."

Brian looked over at Tanya.

"So the old man wanted you in on this too, is that it?"

"Thor asked for Justin, he asked for me as well."

"Then your Bilateral Commission oath still stands?"

"Of course it does, Brian, so let's get on with it."

Brian paused for a moment and then turned and activated a holo screen behind his desk. The image of a ship from the last attack came up on the screen.

"That's what hit us," Brian announced. "There are three variations of models. We think one was a flagship; the others are roughly equivalent to your Earth corvette designs, several hundred tons of mass, and there were four that were approximately frigate size, with an estimated mass of around seven hundred tons. If you ask me, that's awfully light craft to be sending in here like they did. Their damn flagship was in the lead and we intercepted a lot of high-frequency transmissions from it. It's all gibberish, though, apparently highly encoded, and without a language base to work from our computers can't crack it.

"It was one of the first ships we took down," Brian continued, "even before they cleared through Jupiter orbit. After that their attack was uncoordinated, and it was essentially a mop up."

"Did you get any parts, any wreckage?"

"They're out there scouring a couple of hundred billion cubic miles of space right now. Just fragments. It seems that when we finally pop them off, the tendency is for their matter-antimatter fuel pods to rupture. It's the same problem with our ships—when that stuff cooks off there isn't much left afterwards."

"We've yet to experience the problem," Justin said dryly. The fact that the Colonials had managed to crack the antimatter drive first had given them the decisive lead that ended the war.

"So what do your people with the Corps think about this?"

"Mahan said that the analysis of the Trac attack indicates that it is probably the beginning of a general offensive. They sent twenty-seven ships and look at what they did. If it hadn't been for our improved military, both yours and ours due to the war, they would have crippled us. We took a hell of a pounding on Earth. I'm authorized to tell you that if we face another strike of forty or more similar ships, our probability projections indicate that we'll be overwhelmed."

"Is that supposed to be a concern of ours?" Brian asked smoothly.

"That's a pretty stupid question," Tanya replied hotly.

"Look, Tanya, the war's still on in spite of what people are saying about peace being signed. Remember, we signed that peace with the old government, and then they were out and those new lunatics are running the UN and rattling the saber. They've yet to officially acknowledge the legitimacy of the treaty.

"Earth is the past. The old historical trends that we once studied under Thorsson are coming to pass, the gravity-bound empire being replaced by the new. The Colonies are the future. We showed that in winning the war. It's a replay of the shifting of the center of power on Earth in the 19th century from the old world to the new.

"Remember too—of the twenty-seven ships that attacked four got through to Earth, but only one made it to Mars. We nailed over three-quarters of them ourselves. Our ships were the only ones capable of scrambling fast enough to get into position."

"I think whoever is out there is tending to see us as being in the barrel together," Tanya replied, "and if they come back it'll be for all of us."

"Don't try any of that racial harmony crap on me or anyone else out here," Seay snapped back angrily. "My parents wiped the dirt of Earth off their boots and said good riddance to it. The bureaucracy and the incompetent—or outright sinister—government intervention and waste back there were stifling. The Americans fought their second revolution over that and managed to briefly turn it back, but then it came on even stronger afterwards.

"Both of my parents died settling Mars. I lost an uncle on Titan and lord knows how many other relatives settling the asteroids, exploring the outback, or fighting in the war. As far as I'm concerned Earth is nothing but a sinkhole, giving precious little in return. I hear your damn Luddite Movement back there are even calling for an end to involvement with space outside of Earth orbit. Well, let them."

"The Tracs might change that."

Brian laughed softly. "Oh, they most certainly will."

"What the hell do you think was part of the purpose of the Bilateral Commission?" Tanya interrupted. "Thorsson always said that our Civil War was part of a historical process, but it was not the main show. That's why he fought so damn hard to keep the destruction under control. He knew that the real threat would come from outside our system, and if we busted each other up too much we'd be easy pickings for whatever was out there. He knew that we would both need each other again, that's why he set the Commission up."

"The Commission had an agreement with us and the old government on Earth," Seay retorted. "That's part of the reason Earth's government fell after the peace—Lin Zhu, that psychotic underling of his, Hassan, and the others claiming that the Corps fought with one hand tied behind its back and that the Corps was glad to let you do the tying."

"I guess you heard about the EDF coup?" Justin asked. Brian nodded grimly.

"We got the information. That puts your headquarters on Earth directly under their guns and your fleet without the ability to enforce the law anymore. I'm willing to bet that within the month the Bilateral Commission will get kicked out or arrested and then we'll be fighting again."

"The real threat isn't each other anymore," Tanya said sharply. "It's out there," and she pointed towards the image of the Trac ship.

"Hey, Leonov, Bell knows that and I know that, but there're a lot of other people who don't. If the coupists take over the fleet we'll be at war again, and this time it'll be no holds barred. And frankly, if Earth's willing to fight us with nukes, sooner or later they'll win. Free-floating Colonial systems simply wouldn't stand a chance against that. We have the technical edge with our antimatter fighters but we can't protect both innocent civilian and military targets all the time . . . there are simply too many of them. Unfortunately, in spite of the Tracs, I still have to keep Earth as my major concern. Remember, we lost one of our Skyhook towers in that Trac strike and the other was damaged. Getting resources off this surface will be a lot tougher now."

"And while we're squabbling the Tracs will come back and pick up the pieces."

"We're caught between a rock and a hard place," Brian replied sadly. "Lord knows I wish we could get a united front together."

"That is what I'm here for, in part," Justin interjected. "The attack last week was only the beginning."

"Oh, really? We know your deep-space surveillance is better than ours—I wonder just how much you really do know."

"All right, I got the full briefing before I left and I'm authorized to share it with you."

"But not unless you have to, is that it, Bell?"

Justin smiled. "You cleaned me out in too many games of poker to show my hand from the start."

"Go on, then."

"I studied the briefing in that holo cube I gave you on the way out here. Intel USMC's been monitoring transsystem activities ever since our first contact with the Tracs forty years ago. They geared up a major operation ten years back called 'Dark Eye.' "

Brian leaned forward, his interest obviously stirred.

"You know, that's one thing we were never able to crack. Oh, we could see the arrays—it was what you were finding out that had us crazy with curiosity."

"We've been using visual with up to four kilometer baseline systems on the Moon, along with some deep-placed radio arrays out beyond Pluto's orbit that you folks never knew about. We think we know at least four systems that are inhabited, the closest one being Procyon only twelve light-years away. The problem is, of course, that whatever data we've been picking up is years, sometimes decades old. We have detected, however, several confirmed incidents of high-yield bursts, both atomic and matter-antimatter, on half a dozen different fronts."

"So they're fighting wars elsewhere?"

"It looks that way. It looks like a pretty chaotic universe out there, with evidence of a number of conflicts. Several years back we picked up two planets in one system suffering massive nuclear and antimatter bombardments, all on the same day. The event actually happened sixty-eight years ago, but it is evidence of one hell of a killing war going on out there.

"What we can say for certain is that while we've been having our little squabble back here, there've been some damn big wars going on out there.

"Intel believes that the earlier raids here were not part of a coordinated effort. The other encounters were maybe just raiders, freebooting pirates that wandered in, and one of them got his clock cleaned before he could get out."

"You're not telling me anything new, Bell. Our own people surmised that years ago. Remember, we've got the wreckage of the one ship, and if that ship's their military standard then God help them."

Justin smiled at the little tidbit Brian had just given him. When the war started the Colonials had seized the research facility on Europa where the wreckage of the one Trac ship that had been recovered was stored, and moved it back to Mars. So they had been busy with it, as Mahan figured they would be.

"This last one, however, was different," Justin continued. "Either it was part of a freebooter fleet looking to move in and take over, or worse, a reconnaissance in force serving as a prequel to a full-scale attack."

"And Earth Intel believes it's a recon in force that met more than they bargained for?" Tanya asked.

"Something like that. Anyhow, about the only good thing to come out of this war is that it stimulated a quantum jump in space-based combat systems. The Tracs apparently came in with outdated information regarding our capability and paid the price. This indicates that they were working off some old reports."

Brian nodded thoughtfully.

"We thought about that as well, so you aren't telling me anything new."

"But do you have the deep-space surveillance capability that we have? If so, I'm requested to ask for a briefing on what you've found out."

Brian hesitated for a second.

"No. We were too busy fighting you to budget for that. It most likely cost you billions to build the array on the Moon, and billions more for the system out past Pluto. We just haven't had the resources. So what do you think they have?"

"Our guess is a fleet with ships numbering in the thousands, based on the scale of the conflict we've detected. Like I said, whoever is fighting out there has the capability of annihilating entire systems in a single day."

"That strike, the one that did in those two planets— did you get any evidence of any defense against it? After all, it could have been a low-tech system that got wiped."

"Hard to tell," Justin replied. "We picked up a number of bursts off-planet, some of them at the outer edge of the system under attack, which indicates there was combat off-planet. Brian, there were over ten thousand nuclear or antimatter bursts recorded in one twenty-four-hour period."

"Merciful God," Brian whispered.

"My guess is, whoever hit us came in cocky based on old data and figured we'd follow a normal growth curve, not one accelerated by the war. They figured they'd achieve orbit, take out our defenses and then simply hold the high ground of space until they did whatever it was they decided to do. Well, we wiped them."

Brian nodded again.

"That's sort of what I figured."

"So what are you going to do?"

"Forward defense," Brian said. "Try and keep them as far back from Mars and the other Colonies as possible."

"And for Earth? You're the people with antimatter drive, not us. Mahan authorized me to tell you that testing has been completed on our own antimatter drive, though you didn't hear that from me."

Brian nodded thoughtfully. "We thought you might be on the edge."

"But it'll be weeks, maybe months before they integrate the system into our fighters, so that still leaves us with our butts up in the air waiting to get kicked."

Brian looked over at Tanya. "Earth can kiss my ass as far as I'm concerned. Your damn government should be here with official representatives, not a remobilized captain without any credentials other than a personal endorsement from the Corps' Commander. Just what the hell do you think this is?"

Justin looked at Brian angrily and the Admiral's features softened.

"Sorry, Justin. It's nothing personal, but I was told to tell you that by my government. But what the hell can you do, what can Mahan do?"

"Mahan sent me here as a representative of the old Corps. He wants you to know that we still know what our mission is and will do it, if needs be, in spite of what our government says and that includes coordinating our defenses."

Brian looked over at Justin with open surprise.

"Is he crazy?"

"No, he's maybe the only sane one left. Mahan and the fleet know where their duty lies and it's my job to get that across to you. If we can coordinate our response it might help both sides. They emerged into our sector coming inward towards you first, then shifted towards Earth, I guess when they picked up the higher volume of signal traffic. If it should be from another direction next time we'll scramble to meet it, and if needs be, will protect Colonial property and lives."

"He'll get hanged if he orders that."

"EDF and the UN might control near-Earth space, but that's as far as it goes. We've talked a lot about oaths, Brian, and we took an oath twenty years ago to defend the innocent. That still stands, no matter whose side they're on. Mahan wants to know if you'll do the same."

Brian sighed and looked up at the ceiling for a moment.

"If by defending the Colonies that means we help to defend Earth as well, we'll do it."

"And it just so happens that getting to Earth necessitates going through Colonial space first," Tanya interjected.

"Unless they come in at a right angle to the orbital plane," Brian replied, "but hell, since every other time they've come in on a direct track back in towards the inner galaxy, I guess it'll be the same again."

"Thank you, Brian," Justin said feeling a warm flood of emotion for his old squad leader, who had made his first summer at the Academy a living hell so long ago, and in the process had begun to shape him into a man.

"The problem is, Bell, I'm going to lose a lot of well-trained kids and some damn precious equipment doing this. Your Intel's most likely figured out by now that we took a bit of damage in the last attack. Think about it— we'd be sacrificing what edge we have over you in this fight. It might give Zhu even more reason to push for a renewal of hostilities if we take losses again like we did last week."

"That'd be madness," Tanya interjected. "It's time both sides realized our war, at least for the moment, has to be buried if any of us are going to survive."

"He's right, though, Tanya," Justin said sadly. "Mahan asked me to assure you that the Corps, at least, sees where the real threat is now."

Justin hesitated for a moment.

"I am authorized to tell you that if the UN orders the USMC to attack Colonial property and personnel, civilian and or military, it will refuse the order."

Tanya looked over at Justin with open-mouthed amazement.

"That's mutiny," she whispered.

"No, it's survival," Justin replied coldly.

"But what about the EDF?" Brian asked.

"We'll cross that bridge when we have to. I don't think it'll come to that, though. The coupists might be fanatical, but they're not insane. They know the real threat as well as we do, and until it's resolved I think they'll keep that saber sheathed as far as you're concerned."

Brian snorted disdainfully.

"We'll see, but we both know that as long as those bastards are in power there's going to be another showdown some day."

"Let's hope not. I think once around was enough for all of us."

"So what's the rest of the message today?" Brian asked, changing the topic.

"I have two requests from Mahan."

"Go on then."

"First, that you share with us the secret of your antimatter ship drive and explosives."

"You've got to be shitting me," Brian replied with a cold laugh. "Hell, Justin, the fact that we beat you to production is the only thing that turned the war around in our favor. Give that up and we'll be at your mercy again. You just said you've got your own system online."

"The containment field is rather shaky. Yeah, we can put kids in a seat in front of the engine, but we might lose quite a few."

"Well, we did too," Brian snapped. "We had a seven percent failure rate, per mission, for the first two months until we got it right."

"We know that . . . I think we're crossing through the same problem. Your input would save a lot of lives, Brian, because we have to go to antimatter now if there's any chance of fielding a response in the next month or two."

"It's a valid point," Tanya interjected.

"Just whose side are you on in this?" Brian retorted. "I thought you bastards were supposed to be neutral."

"I'm on both sides," Tanya replied. "In the three years since you achieved containable antimatter reaction, just how many ships have you fitted out? A hundred and fifty, maybe one seventy-five."

Brian looked over at her coldly and said nothing.

"Our intelligence is as good as what both of you have. You lost at least thirty, more like forty percent of those ships last week. The Federal forces have the industrial capability to make those losses good in a fortnight, but it'll most likely take you the better part of a year. Earth and near-Earth orbital industry still can out-produce the Colonies by ten to one. Antimatter drive ships outfitted with inertial dampening systems are the only craft with any hope of intercepting incoming strikes. Without Earth's production capability we don't stand a chance. Don't let your side commit suicide over this, Brian."

"It'll be suicide if we give it away."

"The Commission would oversee the transfer of technology. My suggestion would be that only Colonial engineering officers be allowed to operate the systems in-flight. That way, if any hostile act was directed towards Colonial interest they could shut the system down. We'll also oversee production of such ships on Earth, make sure there's no secret run, registering the vessels and keeping track of them. We'll even install failsafe systems that will shut them down if need be."

"Are you authorized to make such an offer?" Brian asked.

Tanya merely smiled in reply.

"I'm not sure how some of our people would react to Colonial officers aboard Federal ships," Justin said quietly. "Academy traditions or no Academy traditions, there are a lot of reservist officers with some pretty hard feelings about it even now."

"You stupid shits, you're supposed to be on the same side now! Isn't that what you were sent here for, Bell?"

"I can't authorize such a transfer," Brian interjected.

"But you could support it," Tanya replied. "And you don't have months to screw around with this proposal. We might have no time, in reality. With luck it could be weeks, maybe longer. This is a crash program that has to get online immediately, so if you support the idea get it moving. You've got to match your knowledge with Earth's ability to produce the weapons we'll need. The hell with the new government, it'll be USMC people flying the machines, and they'll respect the agreement."

"And if the Tracs don't come back?"

"Do you really believe that?" Tanya asked.

Brian finally shook his head.

"I can't authorize it," he said softly, "but I'll pass the recommendation along. Now what else?" Brian asked.

"Access to the Trac ship. Our Intel suspects that your people are on the edge of getting a replica of it operational. We want to look at it."

Brian went behind his desk and sat down, looking over at Justin and saying nothing.

"Well?"

"Just where the hell did you get that data?"

"I wasn't told. My guess is we have some people deep-covered in your research facility. I know revealing that might put them in jeopardy, but we had to bring this out into the open."

"I'm not authorized to discuss that with you," Brian finally said.

"God damn it, Seay," Tanya snapped, "get real. It's a whole new game now."

Brian leaned over and touched a button on his computer console. Seconds later the door into the room opened to reveal two burly MPs.

"Gentlemen, would you escort the lady out of here? She said she needs to take a walk."

"You can't do this, it's in violation of the rules . . ."

"To hell with your rules, you've been breaking some yourself this morning," Brian snapped. "Now get her out of here."

The MPs stepped in front of Tanya. Justin watched, fascinated, wondering if she was actually going to start a brawl. To his surprise she stood up and stalked out of the room without saying a word, slamming the door shut behind them.

"You know she'll file a protest," Justin said.

"She always was a pain . . . sometimes I wish you hadn't

saved her life back in your first summer with the Academy."

"The thought's crossed my mind more than once," Justin said with a grin.

"How about a drink? You look like you could use it."

Justin did not object when Brian pulled a bottle of vodka out from the bottom drawer of his desk, and poured two tumblers full, handing one to Justin.

"To the Academy," Brian announced solemnly, and downed his drink. Justin followed suit.

"All right, what gives with the Trac ship?" Justin ventured, nodding his thanks when Brian refilled his drink. "And if you want, it's strictly between the two of us—I won't even carry it back to Mahan."

"Oh, hell, Mahan and I already talked about it on a secured channel yesterday."

Surprised, Justin could only chuckle.

"Along with everything else we just discussed."

"I had a general idea but I needed to hear it from someone I could trust . . . like you, face to face. But for the moment, this is strictly between the two of us. OK?"

"Sure, you got my word on that."

"All right then. Regarding the Trac ship, we've built a replica, finished it three months ago." He hesitated for a second. "What Tanya told us about your production of antimatter we suspected was coming, though we didn't know it'd be this quick. This Trac ship was the ace up our sleeve. There's only one problem, though."

"What's that?"

"We don't know how the damn thing works."

"You're kidding me."

"No, honestly. We don't. The moment we snatched it we gave it our highest priority, just below cracking the antimatter question. In fact, some of the stuff we learned reassembling that ship gave us the clues to get the containment fields and thrust systems built. Shit, even without figuring out how they do translight, the project was still worth it for that alone. We covered thousands of trillions of cubic miles of space tracking down fragments the size of a pinhead in our effort to reassemble it and then built a model that worked.

"A lot of the technology is the same as ours. Holo memory computers, the inertial dampening systems, even the lousy toilet, though it seems they do function a bit differently than us. But the damnedest-looking thing of all is what we figure to be the translight device. We just don't understand it."

"Have you tried it out?"

Brian shook his head.

"It's the only one we got, and even reassembled it's still a torn-up piece of junk glued back together again. We've built one replica and have started a second, but the decision was made to hold off testing until we have several replicas online."

"There's no time for that now."

"I know. If your Intel reports are valid, that might be an argument for it."

"So why the secrecy with Tanya?"

"Those Bilateral pains in the ass don't know a damn thing about this project other than what we want them to know. I'm telling you because I trust you, even if you are, or *were*, the enemy. With this attack last week I demanded that we test fly our single replica, but no dice. The head of test-flying for the project, in fact the only person who even has half a grasp of how it might work, simply won't let it go. He claims it isn't ready yet, and he's also worried that by testing it we might reveal to the UN what we've got. If that happens he's afraid your side might launch a raid to seize the ship. My government's left the decision up to him and he won't budge on it. Now, I could order him to do it, but that headstrong bastard might just tell me to go to hell and quit, and if he did it'd really set us back. That's why Mahan sent you, because we both agree you might be able to shake things loose. You're about the only person from the other side I think he might trust."

"And who is it?"

"Matt Everett."

Justin looked at Brian, unable to reply for a moment.

Brian slowly grinned.

"He requested a non-combat assignment just about the same time you quit. Hell, he was our best pilot, and he suddenly refuses to fly. For awhile there we didn't know what to do with him until somebody thought to assign him as chief test-pilot to the project. Well, the son of a bitch is now running the show and he has final say on everything. He claims we're at least a year away from a test flight in spite of the emergency, and he also made it clear that this is a Colonial project. So that's where you come in. I'll tell you right now I'm not ready to share this project with the UN no matter what. We'll concede antimatter as long as we have this new ace up our sleeves, Tracs or no Tracs. Mahan's agreed to that as well and is willing to assure non-interference from the USMC regarding this, but our head honcho at this project needs to hear it. Mahan did ask that we at least allow a USMC observer to get a look-see at the project to see how it might fit in on a defensive strategy. I finally agreed, and thus you got picked.

"I also figure you might be able to shake him loose on things and get that bird out and flying. Hell, when I asked Matt to fly regardless he simply laughed at me. That bastard knows he can't be fired, he simply is too important."

Justin laughed softly.

"Sounds like Matt."

"Don't you get it, Bell? Just why the hell do you think your C-in-C sent you out here to me?"

"They said they thought I could do the job."

"Listen, stupid, it's because I asked for you."

"You?"

"Sure. I sent the request into Mahan hours before the strike even hit. We had it figured out the same as you did, though your Intel confirms it. I want you to go see Everett, get his ass off-center. If your Intel is correct we've got to get Trac-comparable ships operational as soon as possible. Holding the high ground is the oldest maxim of war. Sargon the First most likely figured it out five thousand years ago. The high ground today is defense outside our system—otherwise we'll get fried. If we can get enough of these ships going we could even try forward projection of power, fight them on their home turf rather than with our backs to the wall.

"You were Matt's roommate for six years and know him better than anyone in this system. I've arranged transport to where Matt is right now . . . there's a jump-jet waiting outside for you."

"So why did you cut Tanya out of the loop just now? She did make some valid points, and let's face it, we're going to need the Bilateral Commission to help broker a deal with my government and your government as well."

"Oh, she can go with you, the three of you were one hell of a team back at the Academy. It's just that I wanted to rattle her cage a bit. You always did let that girl get the better of you."

"Yeah, I guess she's sort of a weakness of mine."

"Then heaven help you, Bell, heaven help you!"

◈ Chapter II ◈

Exhausted, Justin settled back in his seat to try to grab at least a few minutes of sleep. It was hard to believe that only a week ago he was out on his porch, drunk, watching the sunset. Everything had been turned upside down since then. He spared a quick look over at Tanya, who was strapped in beside him, fast asleep.

The jump-jet banked sharply. There was no sense in trying to figure out where they were going. The windows in the cramped cabin were sealed shut, a curtain was drawn behind the pilot's seat, and there was an MP sitting across from him, just to make sure that he didn't attempt to peek outside. They might be willing to let him know where one of nearly a score of command and control bunkers was located, but there was only one R&D site where the Trac ship was hidden.

He looked over at the MP and smiled. The return gaze could, even with the best intentions, only be described as frigid. There was no sense in even trying to talk with him.

The jet banked again. It felt like it was in the opposite direction. Without instruments, and especially in the light gravity of Mars his inner ear couldn't be trusted. Undoubtedly the pilot was jinking about a bit just to throw his sense of direction and distance off even further. For all he knew they might just be flying a big circle, coming back to land in the same canyon.

The whine of the engines changed and he sat back up, listening. The nose of the plane pitched up, there was a mild bounce, and then another.

"Here already?" Tanya whispered, sitting up.

"Guess so."

She looked at her watch.

"Only an hour and ten minutes. That means it could be a kilometer away or a thousand. Are you going to report that back to Mahan?"

Justin looked over at the MP, who was staring straight at him.

"Remember, the war's supposed to be over," Justin replied, while staring straight back.

He felt the bump of a ladder against the side of the plane and the hatch opened. They were inside a pressurized bunker. Justin looked out and there was no one there.

The pilot stuck his head back through the curtain.

"This is where you get off, folks."

"Thanks for the hop."

Justin hoisted his flight bag and looked back at the MP.

"Hope you have a good day," and then he ducked out through the hatchway, not bothering to wait for a response.

In the dimly lit hangar he recognized Matt at once, the tall gangly frame, slightly hunched shoulders that the Academy could never seem to straighten, the unruly shock of red hair that no comb could ever give a semblance of neatness to. Justin felt a lump in his throat as he went down the ladder and started towards him, hand extended.

"Matt! Good lord, Matt."

Matt Everett stood silent, watching him approach. Tanya shoved her way past Justin, and ran up and threw her arms around him. Justin felt a twinge of jealousy. Hell, she never gave him a hug and he fleetingly wondered if something might have happened between the two of them in the years since the start of the war. After all, she was on Mars for a fair part of it, while he himself had been busy bombing the planet.

"How you doing, Leonov?" Matt asked, but his eyes were still on Justin.

"Hey, at least give me a kiss, will ya? It isn't everybody I hug like this."

Matt stepped back slightly from her.

"I think your visit here is a waste of time," Matt said, his voice even, "so I suggest that the two of you just simply get back aboard that jump-jet and head for home."

He turned without another word and started to walk away.

"Damn you, Matt, wait a minute!" Justin snapped, pushing past Tanya to grab hold of Matt's sleeve.

Matt turned and looked back at him.

"Justin, let's just call it quits, and don't lay that Academy comrade shit on me. The others might balm their conscience with it, I gave up on that a long time ago. Now just leave."

"Bullshit, Everett," and he tightened his grip.

Matt started to jerk his arm away but Justin hung on.

"Look, Bell, I could beat the shit out of you twenty years ago and from the looks of you I still can, so let go."

Tanya moved up in front of Matt.

"I can't believe this crap, Everett. I don't care what happened in the war, he's still your friend."

"Yeah, right."

"You remember my uncle?" Matt asked, looking back savagely at Justin. "The one who saved me when my parents were killed back when I was a kid?"

Justin suddenly knew and loosened his grip.

"He died at Bradbury, along with a lot of others that you helped kill, including a girl I was . . ." His voice trailed off.

"Jesus, Matt, I'm sorry."

"I bet you are."

"If you only knew," Justin whispered.

Justin let his grip on Matt's arm slip away. He turned and started to walk back towards the plane. Well, so much for the plans of Mahan and Seay. The nearly uncontrollable urge to get drunk tore into him as it had for every night for the last three years. Now it would be worse. Now there were more faces to put on the dead, faces belonging to the family of his closest friend.

"Bell, don't you move a damn inch."

Justin looked back over his shoulder at Tanya.

"Both of you, you want to start rattling off the names of the class of '76 that we all killed? Everett, you most likely helped to kill more than one of them. You were at Gilgamesh, Second Titan, Ceres, Mercury Station Ten, and, Bell, you were in several of those campaigns as well. You both have blood on your hands."

"I don't need the speech or the memories," Matt said coldly.

"Well, hiding in a bottle, Bell, or burying yourself out here, Everett, isn't going to change it. I'm not going to make any apologies for what Bell did other than to say that you might not know this, but he resigned his commission immediately after the strike and has been drinking himself quietly to death ever since."

Tanya looked up at him and he refused to return her gaze.

"So cut the crap and at the very least let's go have a drink."

Matt hesitated for a long moment and then almost imperceptibly nodded his head. Tanya looked back at Justin.

"Maybe some things are better off buried and forgotten," Justin said quietly.

"We don't have the luxury of that now," Tanya retorted. "And Matt, you've had a briefing on what the Tracs did. That's what Bell is here for."

Matt looked back at Justin, then lowered his head.

"Come on."

Matt led them through an airlock and down a narrow corridor into what Justin assumed was his private quarters. A couple of old holos hung on the wall, one he immediately recognized as a photo of Matt's parents taken only days before the accident that killed them. That photo had rested on Matt's desk back at the Academy so long ago. There was another one of a young oriental woman with long black hair, dressed in a Colonial uniform. He knew it was better not to ask.

"I don't have anything to offer other than tea," Matt said.

"That's fine, and besides, Bell went back on the wagon today."

"You look like you could use a drying out," Matt said looking over appraisingly at Justin.

"I don't need the two of you nursing me along," Justin replied testily.

"Well, we sure as hell did it often enough at the Academy," Tanya said with a smile.

"Don't talk about the Academy," Matt snapped bitterly, his back turned while putting three mugs into a microwave. Seconds later he pulled them out and passed two over to Tanya and Justin. Just the smell brought back memories to Justin—Lapsang Soochong tea. Matt always had a cup late at night while studying. It was an old sailor's brew from a long-ago Earth, redolent with the scent of tar— an appropriate drink for the sailors of the solar wind, which Matt had once been.

Matt finally turned around and looked at Justin.

"It isn't ready to fly and won't be for another year, maybe two or three. So, that being said, your trip out here is a waste."

"Suppose Seay orders you to fly it?"

Matt laughed.

"I'm the only one who even half-understands it. Let him fire me. Whoever else they bring in will take a year just to figure it out. Hell, I'll just hoist some sails and cruise off in the opposite direction of where these Tracs are coming from."

"And leave everyone to fry, is that it?" Tanya asked coldly.

"Look, Leonov, I was born to solitude. My mistake was to get involved, to believe in something, and then lose everything to it. A little solitude would do me some good right now. As long as they got the bastards who started the war it'd be fine with me."

"I can't believe I'm hearing you say this," Justin interjected.

"You obviously found your answer to the madness," Matt snapped back, "though it's kind of hard picturing old straight-arrow Bell a typical post-war drunk."

"That really sucks," Tanya shouted, slamming her mug down, spilling most of her tea across the table.

"It's the truth, though," Justin whispered.

Matt seemed to soften a bit.

"So what was it, Justin, Bradbury?"

Justin nodded his head.

"We were lied to. We were told that there was confirmation that your antimatter facility was located in the heart of the city, concealed there in violation of the nonmilitary siting protocol. It was therefore a legitimate target."

"So why not surgical strike it?" Matt asked coldly. "Shit, you guys were getting good at that—work a target over, suppress ground fire, then send in the marines."

"That's what I suggested. Mahan overruled it, though. Said we'd only have one chance to take it out, that if a surgical strike failed your people could pack it up and move it somewhere else in a matter of hours while we were trying to pull our people back before a second strike could be called in." He hesitated for a moment. "And besides, they wanted to get not just the site but your research personnel as well. We had a list of names and it was believed that most of your team was there. The only answer was nuke penetrator rounds to dig the city out and smash it."

"That was murder," Tanya snapped.

"No. If they were engaged in military R&D, they were part of the military," Matt interjected, to Justin's surprise.

"But their families?"

Justin nodded his head.

"The argument was that there was only one chance at it, and the decision was made to use a nuke strike. They said that if we didn't, your side would win the race and get antimatter first. So we went in and I helped. They told us guys who were delivering the strike that Bradbury had been evacuated of all personnel not related to the project and was therefore purely military."

Justin looked away for a moment.

"And Matt, I knew your unit was based there as well."

"It was war, buddy, couldn't be helped."

"And then I saw the news footage the Bilateral people released," Justin continued in a flat voice. "The dead, the kids in the hospital, the euthanasia rooms for those who were going to die from radiation poisoning and didn't want to wait around for the final act in the show."

Matt visibly flinched, and Justin suddenly knew that someone, either the girl or his uncle, had finished up in one of those rooms.

"So I quit, and you can fill in the next three years yourself."

"You know, you almost got it," Matt said.

"What do you mean?" Tanya asked cautiously.

"Just that—you almost got the R&D site and the team."

"Your side claimed after the armistice that it was hidden near Goddard."

Matt shook his head.

"It was right at Bradbury, but they moved it to Goddard, along with key personnel, ten days before you hit."

Justin leaned back in his chair, hoping that his paranoid assumption wasn't true.

Matt nodded slowly.

"Don't you get it? Someone in our government let it leak to your side that it was there, then quickly pulled the personnel out. I was there, already assigned to test-fly the first antimatter ship we were working on. They moved me, but they didn't move a lot of other people. I didn't know at the time why we pulled up stakes so quickly and got the hell out of town. It took awhile to figure it all out."

He hesitated for a moment, looking away.

"You hit it, we let you assume you took it out and then had a propaganda coup as well—even you Bilateral people were pulled into it. The whole thing was planned that way."

Matt sat down across from Justin.

"We both got the shitty end of the stick. Typical—governments start wars, tangle the military in, and then blame them for everything that goes wrong while they wash their hands of it."

Justin nodded, unable to reply.

"Who did it?" Tanya asked quietly.

"It doesn't matter now," Matt replied.

"Why not?"

"Because when some of us found out, we killed the son of a bitch."

"You mean you murdered him?" Tanya asked.

"Not personally, but I flew in the team that paid a visit to his hideout. We made it look like some freebooters did it.

"I'll still maintain that the Colonial government is a damn sight better than Earth's. But by its very nature government can draw some real scum into its ranks. So some of us in the military took matters into our own hands when we found out the truth. There'll be a couple of more reckonings over this. We didn't fight a war of independence just to get another corrupt government that hides behind liberal platitudes while screwing everyone blind. Call it frontier justice, but I'd rather have justice coming from men and women who've laid their asses on the line for freedom than coming from the hands of some stinking politician who hid safely behind the lines while other folks died."

"And Seay buried you out here till things cooled off."

"You mean Seay was in on this killing too?" Tanya asked.

Matt merely smiled in reply.

"After it was all over I wanted out as well, and Brian posted me to this project. Besides, I spent a couple of summers here back before the war, and I guess I could say I was the best pilot they had. I test-flew the prototype antimatter engines and so I got the project."

"What's it like?" Justin asked, trying not to show any curiosity.

"It's sweet—generations ahead of what we have, but I tell you it isn't ready to fly."

"We don't have time for that now," Tanya said.

"And I say we do. Look, I got the report on the Trac

attack. You people claim it's the start of an offensive. Well, maybe I'm paranoid, but I don't buy it. I saw just how effectively a couple of scum in my own government could lie to me, and I know damn well, Bell, that you know yours does too, and now they're a hundred times worse with this new regime taking over. For the life of me I still can't understand why you fought for it."

"I'd taken the oath, I couldn't break it. Also, I never dreamed the war would last as long as it did. I figured we'd have a couple skirmishes, then wiser counsel would prevail and the old service would keep on going. I loved the service, I wanted to stay with it."

"If they'd let us professionals solve it, the war never would have gotten started. But they fooled all of us, didn't they, and we paid the price."

"I guess so."

The two fell into a long silence, staring into their mugs of tea.

"Can we look at it?" Tanya asked, unable to contain her curiosity any longer.

Matt looked over at her and shook his head.

"No."

"Seay ordered you to cooperate."

Matt leaned back and laughed softly.

"For all I know this whole thing might just be a scam to get me to fly the thing. Then they take it over and have a real doomsday machine. Make fifty or a hundred of them and whichever side gets it first wins the war in a single day."

Justin looked at Matt closely. Yet another casualty, even though he was still whole. The man was half-crazy with paranoia. He had lost everything else—now there was nothing, except maybe for the project.

"You saw the evidence of the last attack."

"Could have been doctored, recycled footage from the war."

"Do you really believe that?" Tanya asked quietly.

Matt hesitated.

"I don't know what to believe anymore."

"I saw the strike come in on Earth. Atlanta, Jacksonville, half the power grid, I saw them go down, Matt, it was for real," Justin replied quietly.

"Are you sure? It could be just an elaborate scam. I mean, did you go up to a wrecked Trac ship and poke the body inside with your own hands?"

"Come on, Matt, that's crazy and you know it. Not even my government would blow up its own cities and kill millions just to get a hand on your precious ship. This is for real."

"You only saw the strikes in America. Hell, it might have been EDF getting even with your old country."

"Matt, as long as the Corps is around that will never happen and you know it."

Matt got up slowly.

"You can stay the night, both of you look beat. I'll get somebody to haul you back to headquarters tomorrow. There're bunks in the next room. Nice try, guys."

Matt walked out of the room, the door sliding shut behind him.

Tanya exhaled noisily.

"I think he's nuts."

"Who isn't?"

"No, I'm serious, Bell."

"No crazier than I am. Hell, Leonov, when we joined the Academy you couldn't have found more idealistic kids anywhere in the system. Thorsson made sure of that. He taught us to dream a higher dream. Then the goddamn politicians screw it up and start a war. And when you think about it, just what the hell was the war about? It was over which government got to control space. Thorsson and most of us saw space as freedom for everyone, but the politicians couldn't see it that way. They just couldn't handle the idea of anyone just wiping their hands and saying 'so long, suckers.' So *they* started it and *we* did the dying."

"At least what Thorsson taught us kept it from turning into a blood bath that would have sent us back to the Dark Ages."

"Yeah, but it finished off a lot of young lives awful quickly, and most times rather nastily."

"Don't forget, I fought in it as well for the first year."

"I know," Justin said, still surprised that in the opening action Tanya had led a Colonial militia unit.

Justin finished his tea.

"Let's turn in."

She nodded in agreement and went into the next room. Suddenly he felt nervous, wondering what he should do next. Should he just follow her into the room? Was she in the head, undressing, or what?

A couple of minutes later he heard a soft voice.

"OK, Bell, come on in here."

He walked to the door and it slid open. She was curled up in the lower bunk, her clothes folded neatly on top of the dresser.

She looked up at him and smiled.

"Sorry, but it's top bunk, Bell."

He turned off the light, not wanting her to see his disappointment.

A rattling noise out in the next room awoke him. Stifling a groan, Justin looked at his watch—0900. Which time, Greenwich standard or Mars standard? He couldn't remember if he had changed it or not.

He rolled over and looked down at the bunk below. Tanya was fast asleep, the covers kicked back. Part of him wished she didn't like to sleep naked . . . it was almost too much to bear. It was such a wonderful view, and he felt guilty for looking, let alone enjoying it. Again a rattle. Someone was in the next room using the microwave.

Moving down to the end of his bunk he lightly rolled off and landed on the balls of his feet, barely making a sound in the one-third gravity. He pulled on his trousers and shirt and went to the door, paused and then leaned over Tanya's bunk, pulling the blanket back up around her shoulders. She murmured slightly and rolled over. Again that chilly feeling hit, remembering the brief time when they had shared a bunk together. He forced the thought aside and opened the door out to the kitchen and living room.

Matt looked up at him, a bit blurry-eyed.

"Sorry, did I wake you?"

Justin shook his head. Matt had always been waking him up to study at four in the morning, and he had always lied so his friend wouldn't feel bad.

"Couldn't sleep, guess I never lost the habit of getting up early," Justin said. "Make a cup for me while you're at it."

"Already have. I heard you stirring in there," and he handed a steaming cup of tea over to Justin.

The two stood in awkward silence for a moment. How many watches had they stood together, talking the night through. He looked back over at his friend.

"I'm sorry," Justin finally whispered.

"About what?"

"Bradbury . . . *everything*! It's torn at me ever since. Damn it, Matt, I knew you were down there. That by itself drove me crazy, but I didn't know that, worse yet, people you loved were there. I hung on the casualty lists for days afterwards until I saw that you were safe. After that, after the news footage and the thought that I might have to face you again, I just couldn't take it any more."

"Same here," Matt said quietly.

"Kind of drove me crazy after awhile. I guess it did for most of us. The volunteers and reservists never understood that about us, how the Academy bound us together stronger than any war could pull us apart."

"Got kind of morbid though, drinking the old toast to comrades gone even while we tried to kill each other."

"Weird as it sounds, I guess Thorsson wanted it that way," Justin replied. "He is a cagey old coot. Sometimes I think he had all this figured out. That our real enemy would be what was out there and this little war of ours was a training ground, to get us ready for the big show. I remember him talking about the two sides of war, that it was a natural process that tragically killed people, yet if controlled it was also a process of advancing, changing society and technology at an accelerated rate. He always said the real enemy some day would not be ourselves, but the process of survival in the universe."

"Yeah, I thought that too. Tell me, have you seen him?"

"Thorsson?"

"Yeah. Lord, he must be well over a hundred now."

"No, not since the day it all started and he resigned. Nobody sees him now. He stays holed up at his home in Norway, refuses to see anyone from the Academy except those on the Commission."

Justin hesitated for a moment.

"You know what he would want you to do," he finally ventured.

Matt looked up from his drink.

"That's not fair."

"It's the truth."

Matt finally nodded.

"I guess I knew all along how this would come out. There was part of me hoping the damn thing would never fly so we couldn't use it on each other. But there were always the Tracs, the lousy bastards were always in the background. My only fear is, if they don't show up again, that some bastard, either one of our damn civilians or yours, will get these things produced and use them to really finish the war up good and proper. Hell, Justin, this thing will supposedly go translight, and that will be the ultimate edge. We were barely able to control the war last time! I think blood is up so high now, especially with your coupist government claiming that they should have won, that it'd be impossible to control next time. Those crazy bastards will start launching nuke attacks and that will force us to nuke back in reply."

"You know the Corps would refuse to do that."

Matt shook his head.

"Then they'll get rid of the Corps and send in those EDF storm troopers. That's the problem with people who haven't really fought—they can screw things up real easy-like, then step back and let others do the dying for their mistakes."

"Look, Matt, I'm here not for the UN, but for the Corps. Listen to me, this whole thing isn't bullshit, it's deadly and it's real. The big concern now isn't the coupist government rattling the saber, it's the Tracs or whoever it is out there. They damn near swamped both your forces and ours last time. Mahan and Seay agree that after the defeat we handed them this time, they'll come in next time loaded for bear. We need something to counter them and we need it now. And frankly, I think that whether you want to or not your ship is going to fly. It's simply too important and if you don't go with the flow, someone else will."

"If they drop me it'll set things back months."

"I guess that's why they sent Tanya and me. Damn it, Matt, you know you can still trust the two of us, and we're both telling you it has to fly now."

"And suppose the Tracs don't come back, then what?"

Justin wanted to give him a line but knew he couldn't. "We'll have to cross that bridge when we come to it. I'd like to think that if your government has some of these ships it'll put you generations ahead of the UN."

"There's always a leak at some point—no technology can ever really be kept secret for long."

"Then there's a balance, but it'd be years before Earth could even get something online. In the interim I can promise you that we both have enough friends back with the old Corps serving Earth to block any wrong moves. The EDF might control the military environment out to Geosynch, but after that, out to lunar orbit it's still Corps territory. We still hold the high ground. But that's years away, Matt, and we've got to look at right now."

Justin paused for a moment.

"We were best friends once, and in all those years you know I never lied to you. Everett, you're still my best friend in spite of everything that they made us do, and I'm telling you it has to fly and you're the one who can do it, who has to do it."

Matt sat in silence for several minutes and then finally put his tea down.

"Come on, I'll show you."

Justin hesitated.

"Should we get Leonov?"

Matt smiled conspiratorially. "Nah, let her sleep. It'll drive her nuts that she didn't get to see it first."

Justin put down his mug and followed Matt out of the room and down a series of corridors. The final set of plastisteel doors were blocked by Colonial marine commandos and not just the usual MPs. They eyed Justin with open hostility, but apparently had already received orders to let him pass. They stepped aside and the doors slid open.

Justin hesitated for a moment by the door, feeling like a kid on Christmas morning just before storming into the living room. He realized that for the first time in years he was truly excited about something. The two stepped out into a dark room that Justin could sense was expansive by the echo of their footsteps.

"Lights, one-half, rear quarter," Matt said.

The glare forced Justin to close his eyes for a moment. Excited, he opened them back up and squinted.

Somehow he expected more. He was standing about a dozen meters away at just about amidships, and quickly guessed that the ship was roughly thirty meters in length. It was obviously the original, the sides blackened, riven by thousands of fracture lines. He stepped back for a moment to look at it. It was streamlined, unlike the ungainly looking ships designed for flight outside a planetary atmosphere. It reminded him vaguely of the old drawings of space craft from the 1940s and '50s—fins aft, sleek wings that were nearly razor thin. nose tapering to a needle-sharp point. He looked at it in awe. Before the war they'd reassembled barely a tenth of it, the one time he had been allowed a look at the ship. It was simply tens of thousands of pieces spread out on a hangar floor like some madman's fantasy of a jigsaw puzzle.

He drew closer started to extend his hand, and then looked back at Matt.

"It's all right," Matt said with a knowing smile.

With a near reverent wonder Justin touched the side of the ship.

So this was the great mystery, the dream of a thousand generations—to reach out and touch the stars.

"I wonder if it's locked inside our genes somehow," Matt remarked.

Justin looked back at him questioning.

"This, the legend of Prometheus," Matt whispered. "He gave us fire, but the gods kept him from giving us the true secret, the secret of where we came from, of who we truly are. I think at times that I finally helped to unbind Prometheus from his aerie of torment, and this is the gift we were truly meant to have."

Justin reverently walked around the machine, pausing for a moment to study some writing on the side of the wing next to the fuselage.

"Near as we can figure, it simply says, 'no step,' " Matt said. "Funny, quite a few of the things written on the outside appear to match up with our own warnings."

Justin walked to the aft end. Five exhaust nozzles protruded from the back of the ship, each of them big enough that Justin was tempted to crawl inside for a better look, but he figured it was best not to.

"I don't get it," Justin said quietly, stepping back from the ship. "They look like antimatter pods."

"They are."

"Hell, and that's the secret of translight?"

"There's a lot more inside, that's the mystery. We figure the engines are for low-velocity maneuvering. Low velocity with acceleration up to .2 light, I should add, with two thousand gees of acceleration."

"You're kidding!" Justin whispered. "We've only clocked your new fighters going .1 at three hundred gees."

Matt simply grinned, then motioned for him to come around to the starboard side of the ship. Part of the hull was wide open for nearly a third of the ship's length.

"We're still looking for that part. Chances are it was

vaporized. Near as we can figure they had an antimatter destruct mechanism onboard . . . we found part of it. Fortunately for us the damn thing failed to detonate completely, so they only had a partial reaction. We're guessing that it was secured to where this part of the hull was located. It got vaporized, but the rest of the ship was simply blown apart."

Matt stepped through the destroyed section and Justin followed. Most of the inside of the ship was bare, support beams fully exposed, and he felt a wave of disappointment.

"Most of the inside is in the lab; different teams working on the various components. We assembled the outside to get an idea of the dimensions. I'd take you in to the labs and show you, but there really isn't all that much to look at, because everything's disassembled for analysis. I don't think you should know this, but what the hell—I heard that close to ten percent of our entire defense budget was going just for this one project. We had it so well covered that there were even some research firms on Earth working on it, figuring they were doing defense work for the Feds."

Matt stepped back out of the ship and walked off into the darkness, and Justin followed him.

"Light Section B, full power."

Another section of the cavernous hangar burst into light and Justin stopped, awestruck.

"This is *Prometheus,*" Matt announced, the pride in his voice evident.

The ship was jet-black; it looked sinister and yet elegant. It was an exact replica of the first, but without the thousands of cracks and fissures it was one seamless streamlined hull. Justin walked up to it, running his hand along the side.

"It's a single body," he said quietly.

"Unbelievable, I know. That really threw us. First off, you're looking at a molecularly engineered alloy of titanium manufactured in vacuum and zero gravity. Spun plastititanium wire is built up around a mold into a single body, then the mold is melted out. That was one bitch of an operation; it took nearly four years and a hundred tries before we got that right. It was even tougher since there were hundreds of access channels grooved into the frame for various components, fiberoptical bundles and controls.

"Just figuring out how to make the metal drove us crazy until we offered an R&D team back on Earth a cool billion to come over to our side. They were reported missing in an attack; actually, they simply boarded one of our ships and then we blew theirs up. Hell, they're living like kings now."

"This is generations ahead of anything we've been able to do up till now."

Matt nodded and smiled as he walked up to the side of the ship and put his hand against it just aft of the wing.

A door silently opened, the seam where it was located so well-crafted that Justin had not even been able to see it.

"Why all this streamlining? I mean, hell, the damn thing's supposed to fly in space."

"That had me and everyone else confused as well to start with. It was even tougher because the wings fold in and inside the wings there are weapons pylons which can be extended down," Matt said, as he stepped into the ship and motioned for Justin to follow.

Justin bent low and then realized that the hatch had a high clearance. As he stepped into the ship he looked up and realized that there was a good seven feet of clearance in the narrow corridor running fore and aft. Matt looked back at him.

"Yeah, I kind of like it myself, being taller than you."

"The theory is they've been evolving on a planet with a lower gravity than Earth's, and they're taller as a result."

Matt turned and led Justin forward down the corridor. There were no side doors or access hatches.

"What's behind these bulkheads?" Justin finally asked.

"The gizmo."

"The what?"

Matt looked back and shrugged his shoulders.

"We call it 'the gizmo.'"

"Oh, great."

"No, I'm serious. Farther aft are antimatter containment fields for the engines, but there's a hell of a lot of other gear as well. It's all what they used to call black-box units. No moving parts, nothing to burn out, you can access it all through a hatch back by what's a pretty standard matter-antimatter reactor core. By the way, that helped give us some clues in building our own unit."

They reached the end of the corridor and a door slid open into what Justin guessed were living quarters. They were Spartan, three bunks, on one wall, what looked like a galley and a tiny compartment for a head and shower.

"Yeah, it's pretty sparse arrangements. The sociological people went nuts over this; those types always do when given a couple of fragments of information to build a report on. Hell, a couple of those folks have built up case studies on the entire society of these Tracs based on the toilet and food prep area. Amazing what professor types can cook up with a little grant money to justify their existence."

Justin looked in at the toilet, it was remarkably similar to the old standard ship's head.

"Well, I guess they have input and output the same way we do."

"Basic diet has the same elements as well. A couple of food fragments were found frozen to the remains of a storage container and some waste matter was found inside a section of pipe. Primarily meat, that's the analysis. Some speculation is kicking around that there's ritual tied to it, aggressive carnivores and all that. But then again, they could claim ritual around how we throw cocktail parties or cadet beer-bashes."

Justin looked around the room.

"Is this an exact replica?"

"That was debated out some years ago when the decision was made to build this ship. It was finally decided to make it exact in every way possible, otherwise we might unknowingly change something that might be crucial to the ship's function."

"Where's the control room?" Justin asked, unable to hide his eagerness.

"This way."

Matt walked towards the forward door, which opened at his approach, and stepped into the cramped forward cabin. There were three oversized chairs arranged side by side. Justin found himself a bit disappointed at first; he had expected some sort of bizarre science fiction type of instrumentation and equipment. The display panel in front of what he assumed was the pilot's seat seemed almost familiar. There was a row of CRTs and holo field displays banked in a semi-circle around the seat, and to his amazement there was even a joystick, studded with half a dozen buttons on top.

Matt motioned for Justin to slip into the center seat, and then leaned over and punched a button.

The screens in front of Justin lit up, and directly ahead part of the hull pulled back to provide an outside view forward.

"The glass for the windshield is something entirely new, and a bitch to cast! Incredible stuff—it can take a near-miss from a nuke, instantly blocking out the light and damn near all the radiation within a millionth of a second after the first ions impact. It variably adjusts to even low-level solar radiation. The glass actually contains a magnetic coil that blocks the radiation, but only inches away it has no affect whatsoever on the instrumentation.

"We figure the seats are for the pilot in the middle, the co on the left and navigation and weapons officer on the right," and Matt sat down to the right of Justin.

A holo field mounted in front of Matt's chair showed a projection of the solar system, starting with a broad view at right angles to the orbital plain and then focusing down on Mars, zipping through a projection of the planet and then zooming in on the surface, pinpointing in to where the ship was located. Watching the display, Justin realized that they were located less than a hundred kilometers from Bell Station, buried under the Titov Mountains.

Matt pursed his lips and looked at Justin.

"I'm going to have to ask you to forget what you just saw on that screen," Matt said.

Justin looked up at Matt and smiled.

"Sure, buddy, you know you can trust me to keep quiet if that's what you want."

Matt sighed. "It's been too long, Justin."

"So many times I wished we were back twenty years, still kids at the Academy, and that it could have stayed that way forever."

Matt smiled.

"Happens to everyone. It's just that you never quite believe it's going to happen to you, and then suddenly one day you turn around and you're getting older. Lifelong friends are no longer friends and you realize that time is somehow speeding up and pushing you along with it."

"You had me worried sick," Matt said. "I kept an eye on the casualty reports same as you did. Funny, when I knew your unit was in an assault I actually was hoping it'd win just so you'd be OK."

"Same here." Justin said. "Even with Bradbury, I thought you were down there and . . ." His voice trailed away, and he struggled for a moment to hold back the tears.

"I'm sorry," he whispered. Funny, he had not cried in years and now suddenly it was impossible to hold it any longer. He lowered his head and the two friends sat in silence.

Justin finally looked back up. Matt, forcing a smile, fished a crumpled tissue out of his pocket and handed to Justin, who wiped his face.

"What was her name?" Justin asked.

"Mariko. Her parents were sailors like mine until the war started and their ship was confiscated by the Feds. She had a degree in magnetic containment field studies and was part of the R&D team for the antimatter system. When they moved us out she stayed behind since her dad was sick. Of course, no one tipped us off as to what was coming, so I left, figuring I'd see her a week or two later when she caught back up with us. She died three days after the strike."

"I'm sorry."

"You didn't know," Matt said wearily. "I guess there are quite a few people I should be saying I'm sorry to. Remember Madison Smith?"

Justin grinned.

"Sure. I heard she was still doing archaeology work on that Martian site."

"She lost a brother at Gilgamesh fighting for the Feds. I was there, I might have been the one who did it."

Justin nodded his head for a moment, the memory coming back.

"Yeah, I remember hearing about that."

"You know something?" Matt said. "I think we're all guilty and we're all innocent. Sometimes I wish we of the old service had simply told our governments to go to hell! If they're so eager for war, let them do the fighting."

Justin smiled at the thought.

"There's another side to it, though," Justin finally said.

"What's that?"

"This ship. If it had not been for the war research on this ship would have continued at a lower priority. Given the progress that was being made it'd still only be half-finished, and that's after nearly twenty-five years. The pressure of the war goaded your side into a crash program, pegging the survival of the Colonial government on figuring out how this thing worked. You just told me your break-throughs on antimatter containment came out of this, a good three years ahead of what my government's been able to do. That's the other side of the coin. That's the only solace I can find out of the madness. Perhaps it might give us the chance for survival against what's coming."

"Do you think it's for real, then?" Matt asked cautiously.

"I told you I was there. My government's done some amazingly stupid things, especially the coupists with their collective prosperity platform and claims that the wealth of the solar system has to be shared equally. But believe me, not even *they* would be so insane as to blow up the largest city in America."

Matt nodded thoughtfully.

"America. Sometimes I think we, the Colonies, are the real America. My uncle always used to say that America was not a place—it was an ideal that we carried inside ourselves. That it wasn't a government, it was a dream of what should be, and that the Colonists were the true carriers of that dream."

Justin smiled, remembering his grandfather had often said the same thing.

"So tell me about the rest of this ship," Justin finally said, feeling relaxed for the first time since seeing Matt. He almost felt as if they were again back in their dorm room at the Academy, talking about dreams and schemes and all that they would do and see with the service. But now they were sitting inside a machine that might hold the promise of the stars.

"You know what scares me about this ship?"

"What?"

"No one yet has figured out how it really works. Let me put it to you this way. Suppose you could take an old-style internal combustion engine fighter plane, say a P-51, back to 16th century Italy and find a place to land it. A fair number of folks would most likely consider you a warlock and want to burn you at the stake. Something as innocent to us as a little nose art, say of a devil throwing a lightening bolt painted on the side, would send them into a frenzy, and they'd rip you and that plane apart. But let's say that out of the crowd gathered around your plane comes a guy named Leonardo. He manages to get hold of the plane before the mob tears it apart, but you've already attended your own barbecue so there's no one for Leonardo to talk to.

"I dare say that if given enough time fooling around with it, he most likely could get the damn thing to run. He might even get it off the ground after a little experimenting and maybe even get it back down again in one piece. But even a guy like that . . . if you asked him how it really worked he would scratch his head. He could come up with some theories, but most of it, especially the electrical equipment, would be a complete mystery to the poor guy. For that matter the electrical stuff wouldn't be working right anyhow since there wouldn't be any radio stations and nav beacons sending the signals in to tip him off. Beyond that, getting the gas, hydraulic fluid and oil to run it would be beyond him as well.

"That's the situation we're in. I heard some of the team leaders on this project say that a lot of the hardware strains the credibility of even our most far-out theoreticians."

"It still amazes me you got it back together again."

"We got lucky. The guts of the ship were pretty well intact, it's just that we don't know where it was until after the war started. A fair part of the midsection of the ship that contains all the goodies was picked up intact by a solar sailor who simply hauled it in as scrap and then hung onto it when he realized what it was. About six months after the war started he turned it in, claiming he just didn't want the wrong guys to get it."

Justin shook his head and grinned, remembering how even his own father had been involved in the early search for parts of the ship after he and Thorsson had helped to destroy it out in the asteroid belt. After all the hundreds of thousands of man hours of searching, it turned out that some of the key equipment was already in someone else's hands.

"Anyhow, they got all the internal stuff reassembled nearly five years ago. But then two big questions came up—first off, just what the hell is it? Second and far more basic, just how the hell do you turn it on?"

"What about computer hardware and software?"

"Ah, that became the holy grail in the search. We figured if we could reassemble the ship's computers and somehow retrieve its memory we'd be onto something, since after all, unless these people are really strange, the software when broken down had to be binary code. Then again, imagine some tech-head from the 1970s or '80s attempting to plug in our holo core memory fields and accessing into a couple million gigs of that data that go into the running of some of the latest orbital stations.

"About four years ago they finally managed to get a model of the ship's computer up and running, and Justin, we're talking about molecular-level hardware. Some of their stuff was holo, like ours, but other stuff involved the manipulation of individual electrons into memory fields contained within magnetic fields. Now here came the real problem. We figured that part of the autodestruct system involved wiping the memory field."

Justin nodded; it was to be expected. It was part of the mechanism built into any fighter or combat ship, frying the core memory if the ship crashed or was autodestructed.

"So we lost everything then?"

Matt grinned.

"Not completely. Yeah, some stuff we would have loved to get, especially their nav memory would have been great. It could have pinpointed exactly where this ship came from and how to get there. However, some of the basic operational software for the ship survived—with a lot of gaps in it, to be sure. So for the last four years we've had several thousand people and half a dozen of our latest 9000-series computers working on trying to fill in the gaps and program this ship."

"So the big question now is, just how does the damn thing work?"

Matt shrugged his shoulders.

"Beats the hell out of me and everyone else. One theory involves magnetic waves for maneuvering, another is that somehow they're able to maneuver using gravitational fields. It seems like there are elements of both in here."

"What about interstellar flight?"

"Again, it beats the hell out of me. For awhile we thought they just simply got this thing up to relativistic speeds, up past .99, and simply took the long trip, but the argument against that was real simple."

"And that is?"

"Their galley only holds enough food for a couple of months and the same with air supply and liquids."

"Could it be that this is not a translight ship?"

"For awhile we thought that too, that maybe it was hauled here aboard a mother ship. If so, we're really screwed. However, I don't think so. For one thing, the whole aft end of this ship is packed with hardware that we don't really understand and it has to be there for a reason. Secondly, this seems like some sort of cargo hauler as well . . . there's a lot of space underneath and amidships that was empty. I can't see hauling something like this in a mother ship just to come swinging in on a half-assed raid. They must have smaller, more maneuverable fighters for that. I think this baby was made for the long haul."

"Have you taken her out yet?"

Matt shook his head.

"We've tried to build reality simulators first, plugging every bit of data we have in, then running the simulation to see what happens. All I've done is flown the first-level sims using the antimatter engines, but this, the real thing, has never been out of the hangar."

"Well, I think it's about time it was flown."

"And like I said, buddy, it just ain't ready yet. I don't care what Seay or anyone else says, we can't risk losing this one just to speed up the schedule. This is the only prototype we have; there just wasn't enough money to build a second one.

"If you let my side in on it, we could have mass production running inside of months, Matt. There's been a lot of progress made on robotic replication machines, just feed the data and raw material in and out comes what you need."

"Great, and the damn coupists have a fleet and we don't."

"Matt?"

"Yeah."

"After all these years, after all that's happened between us, do you still trust me?"

Matt smiled, pushing back an unruly wisp of red hair off his forehead.

"Of course! I never lost trust in you in the first place."

"Then let me ask this. Take her up. You pilot, Tanya and I will fill the other two seats. Just sort of take her around the block, nothing fancy. I know you well enough to know that you are more seat of the pants than cautious engineer and you want to see this bird fly as much as anyone. Do that and I promise you this: If the threat does not come back, I'll lie my ass off to everyone. I'll tell them the damn thing is a deathtrap and you guys have wasted one hell of a lot of money on nothing."

He looked closely at Matt, not breaking eye contact.

"Come on, buddy. It'll be even better than when we hijacked the assistant commander's ship for that little binge down at Copernicus Station and then talked our way out of it later. And you know Leonov, she'll play along, if only for the chance to fly it too. Otherwise you and the rest of those tech-heads playing around with this thing will still be thinking up excuses not to fly ten years from now. That's always been the problem—you guys are afraid of breaking your toy. The damn thing gets so expensive and so precious no one has the balls to finally say go."

Matt looked at him, the beginning of a grin tracing the corners of his mouth.

"Think about it, Matt, we'll be the first to fly a machine that must be worth a couple of trillion bucks. You got to do it sooner or later, and you even admitted that after all these years you're still not sure how it works. Well, there's only one way to find out. Take the keys, be Leonardo, climb into the cockpit and turn the ignition switch on. And besides, there won't be another chance for me to be flying it with you."

Justin looked at him hopefully. For a moment all the burden of what he was really here for had slipped away. It was like the old days again, one of them trying to talk the other into some hare-brained caper.

A mischievous smile brightened Matt's features.

✧ Chapter IV ✧

As the primary thrust shut off Justin felt his stomach rising up into his throat and then settle back down. They had achieved escape velocity from Mars, riding up inside *Prometheus*, tucked into the belly of a *Nagara*-class transport.

Justin was still surprised with the rapidity with which the Colonial government could function. Returning to Matt's quarters and ignoring the angry protests of Tanya at being left out of the visit to the ship, Matt had placed one phone call and then settled back. Within minutes Justin could hear the hum of activity escalate out in the corridor. Soon there was a steady flow of technicians streaming into Matt's quarters, all of them first eyeing Justin with suspicion and then launching into a barrage of questions. Most of them were obviously excited about the decision to go, but more than one came to argue for more time.

But once Matt made a decision Justin knew that it would stick. Less than twelve hours later a specially converted Nagara transport with extended cargo bay to handle the thirty-meter ship was wheeled in through the airlock. *Prometheus* was rolled underneath it and then hoisted up.

There was little preflighting—Matt pointed out that the ship had been kept at a near-ready standby, with antimatter tanks fully loaded, for nearly a year. There was always the fear that the Federal government might discover its whereabouts and, peace or no peace, go for a commando raid to take the ship.

The only real argument had come when Matt announced that Justin would be in the co-pilot's seat and that Tanya would handle the navigation and weapons chair. The two who had been training for the slots came in and raised a holy stink. The nav officer, Chelsey Webster, tore off her shoulder strips and hurled them at Matt, then stormed out of the room.

"I never liked her anyhow," Matt announced quietly as the door slide shut behind her, blocking out her steady stream of curses. Justin said nothing, sensing that at least from Chelsey's viewpoint it involved a lot more than simply getting bumped from the flight.

As soon as the transport had lifted off Matt visibly relaxed; if a callback signal came through, he had already passed the word to the pilot of the transport to ignore it.

"*Prometheus*, you are cleared for undocking. Good luck, and Godspeed."

Matt looked over at Justin and back at Tanya with a grin.

"*Prometheus*, go for undocking at ten, nine, eight . . ."

Justin cinched in his shoulder harass and seconds later felt a slight nudge as small thrusters attached to the top of the ship fired. The view of the cargo bay's bulkhead shifted and then, seconds later, the brilliance and darkness of space filled the forward window.

"Thrusters disconnected," Matt announced quietly.

Leaning forward and looking up, Justin watched as the transport turned and moved away. He could well imagine the excitement of the observation team aboard the ship, but knew it could barely match what he was now feeling. He looked back at Tanya and grinned.

"You might be getting a kick out of all of this, Bell, but I sure didn't sign on for a test flight when I met you yesterday."

"Hell, Leonov, you're the logical choice. You're the

neutral on the team. It was the only way Justin or I would agree to work it," Matt said with a sardonic grin.

"It's been years since I naved. I don't even know what the hell these instruments mean!"

"Well, you're just about on par with the woman who had the job before you. Just try and figure it out, and while you're at it, trace out a plot that doesn't drill us into Mars. We rigged a standard keyboard into the bulkhead to your right. The holo field directly in front of you should show our present position and orientation in relation to Mars. That holo monitor strapped beside your seat is a standard Polaris nav system as a backup."

"Think I've got it," Tanya announced after several minutes of quiet cursing.

"When you've finished your calculation, simply punch the old enter button and that supposedly will feed it into my thruster control."

"Here it comes."

Justin felt a slight jolt as attitude thrusters pivoted the ship on its Z-axis.

"Supposedly, we should be able to feed in where we want to go, set the time we want for flight duration, and it will do the rest, but let's just see what the old-fashioned stick and throttle will do. Everyone ready?"

Justin felt a knot in his throat, suddenly wondering just how rash he had been to con Matt into doing this. Everything up until this point had been theory. Well, if the theory was wrong they most likely would either look like damn fools, at best, or, at worst, not even comprehend what had gone wrong before being vaporized.

Before Justin could even say anything Matt tapped the throttle forward. Justin felt a brief pressure easing him back into his seat and then nothing. He looked over at Matt, curious.

"What happened?"

"I'm not sure."

Matt gazed down intently at the holo display in front of him and then shook his head.

"I'm not even sure if this is the right screen."

"I think we're moving," Tanya announced. "Our relative position on my screen is changing in relation to the transport. It is now four point three klicks behind, now five seven, now six four. Hell, we're up over a klick a second!"

"I barely felt it," Justin said quietly. "Our own inertial dampening is only ninety-five percent effective on our ships. At this rate of acceleration we should be swallowing our eyeballs. The Tracs have a hell of a system here."

"Here goes!" Matt announced, and he pushed the throttle up higher.

Again there was a surge, this one harder, lasting several seconds, Justin guessing that they had pulled at least three gees and then dropped back to normal.

"Two hundred klicks out, three hundred, four hundred. Shit, we're flying!" Tanya shouted.

"All right, let's put her in reverse," and Matt pulled the throttle back past the center line. Out the side window Justin saw twin streams of incandescence from the matter-antimatter reaction flaring out from reverse scoops, which he assumed had deployed at the aft end of the ship to redirect the blast.

He swore briefly as he was slammed forward in his seat, and then the surge died off. "Damn near to a relative stop. Now starting to back up, picking up speed, transport now two hundred klicks out, one hundred and fifty, one hundred, fifty. Hey, we're going to slam ass-first into Mars if you keep this up!"

Matt eased the throttle forward again.

"Reverse velocity nominal, relative forward again at two point three klicks a second."

"We could yo-yo like this for hours," Matt said shaking his head. "We're going to have to figure out how to punch in a nav coordinate and let the ship's computer do the rest."

Even as he spoke he jockeyed the throttle up and back several times and *Prometheus* surged forward. Justin, his right hand on top of Matt's left, felt the gentle nudges on the stick and was amazed at how responsive it was.

"Designed for fighting," Justin said. "They seem to believe in having the pilot still control the ship in combat. There's something to be said for the bastards on that score."

Matt settled back and with a childlike grin looked at Justin.

"Give me a ship and a star to steer her by."

"My God!" Tanya whispered. "We've actually done it!"

Justin realized he was grinning from ear to ear. He hadn't felt such a thrill of excitement since he had first soloed. He looked at his two companions. It was as if all the years had peeled away. They were kids again, plebes at the Academy, and the universe awaited.

"Mind if I run her for a bit?" he asked, unable to suppress the excitement in his voice.

Matt grinned. "Sure, buddy, have at it!"

"Hey, me next!" Tanya cried, but Justin could see the sparkle in her eyes. Her delight at seeing two old friends reunited, flying together again, transcended any wish to interfere.

Justin let his hand slip down onto the throttle as Matt withdrew his grip. Matt gave him a good-natured punch on the shoulder.

"Let 'er rip!"

Justin tapped the throttle forward. Again a momentary surge, not more than a quick couple of gees, and then the dampening system cut off the sense of acceleration.

"Accelerating three point seven klicks a second relative to our departure point," Tanya announced. "Damn, what a kick!"

Justin eased back on the stick and the starfield shifted. Startled, he looked over at Matt.

"Hey, look out the side window. I'm going to ease down on our Z-axis—tell me if you can see any thrusters."

Justin pushed the joystick forward. The starfield in the forward viewport slowly shifted, Orion rising out of view, until he was centered on Sirius.

Matt shrugged his shoulders.

"Weird. Nothing. How does it do that?"

Matt tried a roll on their X-axis. It felt smooth, but again nothing was visible.

Boyish enthusiasm overwhelmed him. "Hang on!"

Before Matt could voice a protest Justin jammed the throttle forward. His stomach slammed back against the seat, the thrust startling him. After several long seconds of what he guessed was at least five to six gees he eased back slightly, and then the dampening system took hold.

"Two hundred fifty klicks a second," Tanya chortled. "What a rush!"

"Better throttle back," Matt announced, and Justin could tell his little prank had made him nervous. "This is getting a bit over the edge for a first flight."

"Ah, relax, buddy!" Justin replied, using the same tone of voice Matt had so often used when leading his friend into trouble.

"Come on, ease it back. We're six thousand klicks out from our observer ship."

Laughing, Justin let his hand off the throttle. Matt tapped it off, then gently eased the joystick back. Nothing happened, and Justin felt a momentary surge of anxiety. Had he broken something?

Matt tapped the throttle forward again, then eased the stick back a second time. Orion shifted across their forward view, starfields shifting until the north pole of Mars appeared at the top of the window. Matt gently pushed the stick forward.

He looked over at Justin and grinned.

"There must be some thrust directional. Had you worried, didn't it?"

Justin smiled and said nothing.

"You know, we're the first to do this," Tanya said.

"What do you mean?" Matt asked.

"Just that. We're the first humans to ever pilot an alien ship. My great-grandfather was the first human to walk in space, but I never, ever thought I'd get my name in a history book as well."

"Come on, heroes," Matt said. "Let's head back to the barn. The tech-heads must be having strokes with us buzzing around like this."

"*Prometheus, Prometheus*, this is Control One."

"See what I mean?" Matt laughed, flipping on the comm channel. "*Prometheus* here."

"Have just received word you are to clear the area at once at best possible speed."

Surprised, Matt looked over at his companions.

"What gives, Control?"

"Have been advised that we have an unidentified reported inbound. Combat control just acquired lock on its antimatter trail."

"How fast is it coming in?" Justin asked, and Matt repeated the question.

There was a pause for several seconds.

"Last reported velocity was .32 light-speed, faster than anything we've got, coming in on a head heading of 231 degrees solar standard, two degrees declination up. It'll be here in less than thirty minutes, so clear the area."

Matt looked over at Justin in surprise.

"It's them."

"Think it's because of us?" Tanya asked.

"They might have been loitering around out there, monitoring, picked us up and decided to try and run in for a closer look. Something must have stirred them up."

"Tanya, give me a right-angle trajectory to that incoming, but keep us in the orbital plane."

"Locking it in . . . now!"

After several anxious minutes Justin felt the ship nudge. He watched the starfields in front of him shifting, as *Prometheus* pointed down towards the center of the solar system.

"Just a minute, patch us back through to the observer team," Justin asked.

Matt hit the comm link button and nodded.

"This is Captain Bell. I want an encoded top-priority message sent to Mahan, USMC. Alert him to what we are doing. Also request a full upload to us on all recon data related to surveillance of this incoming from Dark Eye."

As he spoke he looked over at Matt, who nodded.

"Sir, we have no authorization to contact the USMC regarding this matter," came the reply from the observer ship.

"This is Everett. Put Captain Bell's message through to Admiral Seay with my endorsement."

"Right, sir."

"If they're coming back," Tanya said, "we're really all in one boat now."

Justin looked down at his wrist watch.

"It'll be a couple of hours before they can cycle that around. Let's hope Mahan can keep a track on us. Tanya, change our direction—aim us in for a close loop around the sun."

Matt looked over at Justin and nodded.

"Locked in."

"You folks ready?"

Justin leaned back in his seat, bracing himself.

Matt slammed the throttle forward.

Justin gulped hard, grunting for breath, his vision blurring to the pointing of graying out.

"Holy shit!"

He tried to turn his head but couldn't. Even shifting his eyes felt like he was trying to move two heavy lead weights that were sinking into his skull.

"Four hundred klicks a second, four fifty, five hundred . . ." Tanya's voice came out in short explosive gasps.

The inertial dampening system started to catch up, the g-force lightening, but Tanya continued her chant ". . . one thousand fifty, eleven hundred, eleven fifty . . ."

"Just how fast will this thing go?" Justin gasped.

"Damned if I know, but it's goin'!"

They had already gone beyond anything Justin had ever thought possible. Finally, Tanya's chant started to slow down, "Twenty-eight thousand fifty, twenty-nine thousand eight hundred, thirty-one thousand. We seem to be plateauing at thirty-one thousand one hundred . . . we're leveling off at .11 light."

"Elapsed time?"

"Five minutes forty-five seconds."

Incredulous, Justin looked over at Tanya, who returned his stare angrily, as if he were accusing her of lying.

"It's the truth," she said almost defensively.

"Just how does their inertial dampening work?" Justin asked. "It's way beyond anything we have."

"Like I said, damned if I know, but if it should ever wink off, even for a millisecond, we'll be homogenized protoplasm. Tanya, you sure on that velocity figure?"

"That's what the instruments say. Wait a second. I think I'm getting the hang of it on this computer. Ask the transport to give me a burst signal."

Tanya remained hunched over the computer screen and waited for the signal to come back, then punched in a calculation.

"It's dopplered to .118 light—we're on the mark with those figures."

Matt shook his head.

"What's wrong?"

"Actually, I'm a bit disappointed."

"What the hell do you mean?" Justin asked. "The damn thing just did the fastest takeoff anyone has ever ridden. Your Colonial ships could barely do one-*tenth* that rate of acceleration. What the hell's wrong with that?"

"It only went up to .1. Hell, that means it's still just over thirty-five years to the nearest star in this jalopy. Sure, it accelerates quicker, but it doesn't have the max speed we already got with our fighters. Something isn't right here. What's our velocity now?"

"Wait a minute . . . we've dropped slightly, down to thirty thousand six hundred, now down to thirty and five."

Surprised, Justin looked down at his own plot board. After several minutes of nervous experimentation he got the same screen as Tanya's. The velocity was definitely dropping off.

"I don't think it could be drag . . . not enough stray atoms kicking around out here for that. Solar wind?"

"Our silhouette is too thin. Must be something else."

"What, then?" Justin asked.

Matt scanned his instruments and Justin wanted to laugh, realizing his friend was just as confused as he was.

"Tanya, can you get a lock on that incoming?"

"Let me hook back to our transport, ask them to patch the signal up to us. I think it's best we don't point any radar in their direction."

Justin unbuckled himself and tentatively stood up.

"The artificial grav feels fine, and I think your people were right about the lower gravity of their planet. This feels like it's set at around .6, maybe .7 standard."

"Feels like hell to me," Matt said quietly. "Remember, I've been on Mars for a long time."

"I'm getting that signal back from the transport," Tanya announced.

Justin went to stand behind her chair, leaning over her to look at the screen. For a moment he found her presence to be a distraction again—she was wearing the same perfume she had favored at the Academy. It was ever so faint, but it brought back a hell of a lot of memories again.

"There it is," Tanya said. "Funny, he's decelerating as well, dropping through .1 light, now down to .098. Something else as well—point of origin on the original Trac ships and also their attack force was a bit different than this one. Could it be someone else besides the Tracs?"

Justin watched the screen intently.

"He's starting to shift, turning . . ." He paused, running a quick mental calculation. "Shit, he's lining up on us. Matt!"

"Yeah?"

"Can you start throwing in some lateral moves? Nothing fancy, just a couple hundred meters a second back and forth . . . make it random."

"I think I can, wait a minute."

"Range is just under ten million klicks, closing now at six hundred and forty kilometers per second."

"He's definitely after us," Justin said, surprised that his voice was pitching up slightly. It'd been too long, he realized, and the professional edge had blurred a bit.

"Think I've got it," Matt announced and Justin felt a slight lurch. Inertial dampening didn't seem to work so well on lateral maneuvering verses acceleration and deceleration on the long axis of the ship.

"What the hell was that?" Matt shouted.

Justin looked up but saw nothing, and then there was another flash.

"Laser fire," Tanya announced. "Hell of a shot at ten million klicks, must have seen us moving on a straight trajectory. Matt, I'd suggest increasing those random maneuvers."

The ship lurched again. Justin watched Matt as he leaned over the main control screen, studying it intently, and then punched data into the keyboard interface. It seemed primitive compared to the verbal control systems that were common on most ships, with the older system simply there as backup. Without a knowledge of the language, the engineers had apparently decided to play it safe and go for the old hardwired method of control.

Another burst of laser fire streaked past, several hundred meters to port.

"Recharge time for long range firing?" Justin asked. "How long between shots?"

"Two minutes thirteen seconds," Tanya announced.

"Now that we're jinking they'll most likely cut it out."

Justin watched the ship's chronometer ticking off time, and after five minutes he finally started to relax.

"They'll let the range get closer . . . how far now?"

"Still closing, though speed differential is down to five hundred and twenty a second and dropping off fast."

Curious, why would they be bleeding off speed? At the corner of Tanya's screen the velocity indicator was spinning downward as well. They were now below twenty-eight thousand klicks a second.

As if reading Justin's thoughts, Matt hit the throttle again.

Their speed nudged up slightly, several hundred klicks a second, then leveled off, and even with throttle open started to drop off.

"Shit, it simply shouldn't be doing that," Matt said quietly.

"Well, it is," Justin replied. "Could be a lot of things causing the drag."

"Like what?" Tanya asked.

"Gravitation fields, magnetic fields, Matt, you said no one was sure how this damn thing runs. Well, now we're going to find out," and he turned and started aft.

"Where you headin'?"

"To get a drink," he paused, "of coffee."

He was surprised that he had actually managed to doze off and a bit embarrassed that it was Tanya waking him up. The dream was something he definitely couldn't discuss with her.

"That signal just came in from Mahan. It was burst-concentrated and encoded. Hell, we didn't have the code aboard until I realized that he had enclosed the code break at the start of the message. We've loaded it into our computer.

"How far to the sun?"

"Under thirty minutes."

"And our company?"

"Matching speed now, seven hundred and eighty thousand klicks behind us."

"Matching?"

"Yeah, it's like we've both hit a wall. We're at ten thousand klicks a second. Damn, if we had Colonial fighters anywhere close they'd be able to overtake the bastard."

Justin rubbed the sleep from his eyes, then swung out of the bunk and went back forward. Matt was right where they'd left him, his eyes red-rimmed.

"Sorry, I just dozed off."

"You needed it. Now tell me why you chose this direction."

"Tanya, have you fed the supposed location of the Trac systems into the computer?"

"Locked in."

Justin looked over her shoulder and the realization suddenly hit.

"You know, this one appeared right on a lineup with Procyon."

"I was just thinking that myself," Tanya replied. "Curious."

"All right. I want you to set up a course . . . we're going to loop the sun and I want us to slingshot around, then come out pointed back towards where this ship came through. Then we're going to punch the throttle to the wall. With luck he won't figure it out and will sling out at a different angle. By the time he recovers we'll be on our way."

"Sort of what I was thinking," Matt said with a grin.

Justin settled into his chair, turning to watch while Tanya plotted the course in. Working a laser stylus, she picked out Procyon in the holo field and cursed softly for several minutes, then tried it again. A line appeared on the screen tracing back towards the sun, an orange light flashed at the bottom of the screen.

"I think that's it," she announced triumphantly. "Look, I think I've figured out how to work this . . . it seems to parallel our own nav systems in a lot of ways, with point-and-trace while the computer figures it out."

Justin looked forward. The sun filled most of the forward view, the window darkened down to cut the glare. They were hitting the edge of a standard ship's tolerances. Outside temperatures were most likely above three thousand. Apparently the ship had some means of deflecting the heat since the cabin was still holding at a comfortable, though slightly cooler than normal, temperature.

The ship suddenly lurched, and Matt looked over at Tanya in surprise.

"I guess you locked it in somehow—it's running on auto."

The ship's nose rose slightly, thrusters firing. Seconds later it leveled out, thrusters firing again. The bulk of the sun started to shift downward out of the forward view. A surge of deceleration hit, slamming Justin forward in his harness and then the starfields began to shift. He looked over at the nav screen, watching as the line tracing their course started to bend.

"We're slingshotting," Tanya announced. "Other ship is still holding course; they're disappearing from view, still turning, still turning." Justin was slammed back in his seat. "Main engines firing on auto, coming around, lining up, we're on the mark!"

"Got a side glimpse of the other ship," Tanya suddenly announced. "It's going in, engines retrofiring."

Justin held his breath, waiting.

"They've dumped something!" Tanya hissed. "It's coming across the forward edge of the sun, accelerating—some sort of missile, radar-guided!"

"Have you figured out the weapons board yet?" Matt asked.

"Hell, you didn't give me any time!" Tanya replied.

Justin looked down at his screen, swearing, and pushed what he guessed was a reset button. Different images flashed into view, showing what he assumed were fuel stores, systems checks, and then a screen appeared filled with icons, some of them looking like missiles.

"What do we have aboard?" he asked.

"Just our own ordnance," Matt shot back. "Standard lightning-strike antimatter-tipped warheads, and Hornet defensive anti-missiles."

"Got one."

"Feed a lock in from Tanya's track, then let it go."

Justin followed Matt's orders, hoping he was getting it right. The system seemed to work like what the standard fighters of both Colonial and federation forces used—pick a missile, toggle in the lock, then hit the release.

He felt a lurch run through the ship.

"It's away," Justin announced, watching on his screen as the Hornet turned around, accelerated and then activated its independent tracking system. It bore straight in on an intercept with the incoming round. The kill was easy, no decoys or counter-bolt submunition rounds deploying.

"They still haven't calibrated to our frequencies," Matt said, leaning over to watch Justin's board. "Either that or they're awful stupid and don't have any counter-defense measures."

"How's our scramble coming from Earth?"

"Several dozen fighters, light frigates, and destroyers moving towards our projected outbound vector," Tanya announced. "He's reemerging behind us and breaking off on a different track . . . either he didn't anticipate our maneuver or picked up the reception committee. Heading outbound on solar plane 311 degrees negative four degrees to orbital plane."

Justin breathed a sigh of relief.

"I just got a query from Earth orbital defenses," Tanya announced, looking over at Justin.

"What is it?"

"It was a direct inquiry for you. They're requesting that we rendezvous in lunar orbit."

Tanya looked at Justin.

"It's not from Mahan, it's from EDF command."

Justin leaned back in his chair and sighed.

"Shit, they must have tracked us somehow."

"What do you want to do?"

"I think you know the answer to that," Matt said coolly.

Justin turned to look at Tanya. She hesitated for a moment, then shook her head.

"He's starting to come about," Tanya said, looking back at her screen. "Damn, full retro firing, he's turning, definitely lining up for another pursuit."

"How much of a lead do we have on him?" Matt asked, momentarily diverted from Justin.

"Just over three million klicks."

"Tanya, how far off our outbound trajectory would diverting towards Earth take us?"

"Eleven degrees."

"We have the fuel for a turn?"

"I don't even know how much we burned," she said.

"Give me a couple of minutes," Matt interjected. He

got out of his chair and went over to Tanya's board, where he punched in commands until the figures came up on the screen."

"Weird, not much more than four percent. Hell, we did a full-thrust burn for over fifteen minutes and a lot of other maneuvering. That can't be right."

Matt, shaking his head, went back to his own seat and strapped in.

"Either our instruments are way the hell off or something's working here I don't understand."

He looked back at Justin.

"Now explain why you want to divert towards Earth, and it better be damn good."

Justin noticed that Matt's left hand had slipped down by the side of his seat, and he heard the snick of a case opening.

"What are you doing?" Justin asked.

"I can't let you take this ship," Matt replied.

"What do you have?"

Matt raised his hand, a Glock automatic resting lightly in it.

"Come on, Matt, just put the damn gun away," Justin snapped peevishly.

"Not until you do some explaining."

Justin looked over at Tanya.

"Come on, will you tell this idiot to calm down?"

"Start talking, Bell."

"Look, the only way to run from the guy was to go nearly in the opposite direction, which was towards the sun. If we'd headed off at a right angle he'd have caught up. As soon as I realized that I figured we should slingshot and then line up on the direction we've been picking up this inbound traffic from. The fact that it was within eleven degrees of Earth was a coincidence. Besides, by the time we went down and came back up, it'd give some of my people a chance to scramble and set up an intercept."

"On who—him or us?"

"Him, of course. What the hell do you think this is?"

"I'm not really sure at the moment."

"Damn it, Matt, stop being paranoid."

"I think I have every reason to be paranoid."

"So why head towards where they're coming from?" Tanya interrupted.

"This is a test flight, isn't it?"

"Yeah."

"So let's go all the way. With what this ship's got we can make it out to Neptune in a couple of days, versus a couple of weeks with the top fighters you have, and hell, they don't even have *that* range without a carrier transport. Let's go check it out, and maybe go beyond."

Matt looked over cautiously at Justin.

"Is that what you really wanted?"

"Didn't I give you my word on that?"

Matt nodded slowly and then put the pistol back into his flight bag.

"So what about this request?"

"Tell them we'll comply with the request to go into lunar orbit and divert towards them, trying to keep ahead of our company astern. Then just simply blow right through. They'll have one of two choices. Either fire on us, or let us run. We'll bullshit them by saying we don't know how to slow it down. I can guarantee you, though, that they'll fire on whatever is behind us, and maybe scrape him off our backs."

Matt finally started to smile.

"I'm sorry. I hope you understand."

Justin tried to hide his sadness. Since first laying eyes on *Prometheus* all the pain had disappeared. Things had, for that wonderful span of time, been as they once were. The flash of distrust in his old friend had rekindled all the memories.

The run-through of the near-Earth approach had been surprisingly easy, Justin thought as he finally settled into his bunk. The fact that they were accelerating up to .1 light certainly helped. He had taken the comm link from

Matt and announced that the throttle was jammed and they had no idea how to slow down, and besides, unfriendlies were less than a million klicks behind them. It reminded him of some kids driving by a police station late at night and throwing a couple of beer bottles and taunts at the station as they sped by. No one fired and they just simply kept going. Whoever it was on the line from Earth Defense Forces shouted himself hoarse, demanding that they shut down and come into orbit. The alien ship, however, had decided not to risk it and diverted while still a good four million klicks out. By the time it had circled around the defensive zone, their lead was up past ten million klicks and the pursuit was as good as lost.

The anomaly of their speed was still a puzzle, though. Acceleration had slowly picked up when it should have in fact slowed down as they climbed out of the gravity well of the sun. Tanya had run a crosscheck on their flight in and found that at any given distance it nearly matched their velocity on their inbound run. Something was at work which he simply did not understand.

Given their accelerating ascent towards Neptune they would cross beyond its orbit within two days. There were only two things he truly wanted until then—a good stiff drink and uninterrupted sleep, neither of which he had experienced since the war started. If he couldn't have the first, he soon found that the second was still available and Justin quietly drifted off, not even disturbed by the presence of Tanya, sleeping in her usual state, sprawled out in the bunk below him.

Admiral Mahan settled back behind his desk and looked up silently at the intruder in his office.

"Well, that really screwed it," Ibn Hassan snarled.

Mahan looked up at the Head of Defense of the UN government.

"Think he was lying about the throttle?" Hassan asked.

"It's possible."

"If we ever get that son of a bitch back here I want his ass in the clink till hell freezes over."

Mahan sighed. "Remember, it *is* a Colonial ship."

"I don't give a good goddamn," Hassan roared, slamming his fist on Mahan's desk. Mahan leaned forward.

"Sir, in this office we behave in a civil manner."

Mahan was as shocked at his own response as the key man behind the coupist government was.

"You white suits answer to me now, just remember that."

"Due to the decisions of the United States, Russian, Japanese and old NATO block, sir, I and my command have been withdrawn from the aegis of direct United Nations control. The USMC now answers to the Joint Chiefs of NATO. If you have a problem, you can take it up with them."

Hassan smiled coldly. "But of course. I'm so glad that you reminded me."

Hassan did not back off, but continued to lean over the desk, looking down at Mahan.

"I've received a report that this reactivated Captain Bell went to Mars on your personal orders. Why was this not cleared with me?"

"Because, sir, it was a strictly military matter, not a civilian one."

Mahan struggled to keep control. Near-chaos had reigned when the decision was issued by what was now being referred to as Northern Bloc nations. The old dream of a United Nations effort in space, which had been dealt a savage blow by the Civil War, was now disintegrating on Earth as well because of the change in command of the USMC and the split with the rival EDF.

It was all so damn frustrating. Seay had already made clear indications that if the Tracs did attack again he'd be willing to coordinate defensive efforts. There had even been a glimmer of hope that somehow, in light of this new threat, some sort of joint command could be set up— a reunification of the USMC with their old comrades in the Colonial Free Forces. Zhu and Hassan had destroyed that with their demand that the EDF be the supreme command. The Northern Bloc's decision to fully withdraw what was left of the USMC from Zhu and Hassan's control was the result. *So now we're three rival forces,* Mahan realized sadly, *at a time when we should be one.*

"The military better learn to start answering to civilian authority in all matters, Mr. Mahan, do I make myself clear?"

"You've always made yourself clear. But I must remind you again, I no longer answer directly to you."

He had waited for months to be able to say those words, and it gave him immense satisfaction.

"You played far too intimately with the Colonials in the last war, but it will not happen again. I'm requesting a full report on this Bell, his mission, and what we know about this ship that the Colonials built. For all I know you've been helping them. If we are to be prepared for these people you call the Tracs, we need those ships."

"That's easy enough. Strike a deal with the Colonials."

"We don't negotiate with terrorists and traitors to the rightful government."

"So you're going to turf-fight while the rest of the universe comes crashing in through the front door?"

"What we decide as policy is none of your concern, Mr. Mahan. Your only concern is to follow orders, and believe me, your so-called respective governments will be more than happy to cooperate."

With half a dozen orbital bombardment platforms now controlled by the EDF, Mahan thought, *there was precious little else they could do.*

"Bell was directly ordered by me to bring that ship in and he refused."

"You were asking him to betray his pledge to Admiral Seay and to his closest friend. That was an impossible and an immoral order."

"I've had enough of this shit about the Academy," Hassan snapped testily. "That's all I've been hearing from you military people since this damn war started—self-serving whining about Academy brotherhood and old comrades 'even if they are the enemy.' I wish to hell Thorsson had dropped dead on the day he ever though of starting it up."

Mahan stirred uncomfortably in his chair, barely able to contain his growing rage.

"Don't like to hear it, do you?"

"No."

"Your military was ordered fourteen years ago to destroy the Colonial rebellion, and you failed at that mission. You could have won it in a year if you had wanted to."

"Sure we could have. Simply nuke every rebellious Colony out there. And then what do we have?"

"Space that belongs to us."

"And a hundred years of progress destroyed. That was not our mission; our mission was to preserve and expand what we had created. You don't blow up all that work and tens of trillions of dollars worth of investments just so people out there will shout '*Sieg Heil*' whenever whoever is in charge down here gets on the phone."

"I'll have your stars for that comment, mister," Hassan said coldly.

Mahan looked at him, keeping his silence. For a moment he wondered if indeed he had gone too far.

He watched Hassan closely. Were they really ready for another coup, this time against the Corps? He doubted it, not with the current crisis triggered by the Tracs.

"If we had smashed our infrastructure out there, we'd be open bait now for the Tracs. Like it or not, the Colonials got antimatter drive first, and *they've* launched the first Trac model ship. If the Tracs come back again, we're going to need the Colonies in order to survive."

"Are we really?"

"Just what does that mean?"

Hassan smiled.

"Never mind. But back to Bell. If he ever gets back here I want him turned over immediately for trial."

"He'll stand trial, if he does stand trial, before a military court of the United States government, not a civilian one."

"He can go before an EDF court."

"And be summarily shot? Like hell, sir. He's one of ours and we'll handle him; that is, if it can be proven that he violated any military law, which from the evidence I've seen so far is doubtful. He was sent out there to negotiate with Everett, not to put a gun to his head."

"If and when this Bell returns I want him arrested for failure to obey a direct order, and he is to be turned over to EDF authorities at once for a full debriefing."

"You mean torture, don't you?"

Hassan looked down coldly at Mahan and then smiled.

"I'll make sure you follow those orders," and with a look of superior disdain he turned and stalked out of the room.

Mahan sighed, then reached into his desk and fished out a half-empty bottle of scotch. He poured himself a drink. *No wonder Bell had wound up a drunk*, Mahan thought as he downed the shot.

The threat was obvious . . . sooner or later there would be the showdown. But they knew that a coup against the military would leave them open to a possible noose being drawn in by the Colonies. The EDF was acquiring the hardware but it'd be years before they could go against the Corps, and even more years before they could go toe-to-toe against Colonial forces. If a coup was attempted, chances were a hell of a lot of personnel would simply trade in their white uniforms for blue and join the Colonials.

EDF and the coupists simply weren't ready for that.

He turned back to the report that Intel had forwarded regarding analysis of the ship Bell was on and the ship which had pursued them down to the sun and back out again.

It was a hell of a ship, and the maneuver was typical of what Bell would have cooked up. He still was the finest tactician in the fleet and Mahan raised his glass upwards in a salute.

✧   ✧   ✧

Va Hild of the Gar watched in silence as the ship continued to accelerate away.

"They have the secret."

Va Hild turned to look at his second and he started to laugh as he shook his head.

"We come out here to see what happened to the youngsters in that attack fleet. Then, mystery of mysteries, we find the wreckage of their fleet and these barbarians are using a ship of our design, *and* they know how to fly it."

His second did not reply. Va Hild looked over at him disdainfully. The fool was still shaken by the fact that the barbarians had actually fired back. Coward.

Va lowered his head for a moment to clear his thoughts. It was obvious that ships of the Gar had been destroyed by these barbarians. No other ships of the Imperium or the Hive were in this area. It meant that this place would no longer be an easy one to pick over.

There were many pleasures in war—the thrill of the hunt, the conquest, the lamentations of unbelievers, and for that matter, believers as well, if on that day they were the enemy.

"We thought they were toothless," Va Hild mused. "This will prove to be most amusing, and we might just be able to pick up the pieces. There are advantages to be found in this."

"Poor fools," his second sighed. "The universe is about to come rushing in upon them—little do they even dream that this will become the new battleground of empires."

✧ Chapter V ✧

Justin awoke with a start. Rubbing his eyes, he sat up. *Damn, a drink would be good right now.* The old ship routine had reasserted itself the moment he stood upon a deck again. The only problem was the forced drying out that his body was still rebelling against.

His mouth tasted like a sewer and as he swallowed to clear his dried throat he barely suppressed a gag. Matt, who was sitting at the small galley table across from him nursing some coffee, smiled and then nodded over at Tanya.

Her blanket was half-pulled-back. Even though she had stopped sleeping naked, she was nevertheless a delight to behold in her military-issue skivvies.

"I wish to hell she'd sleep with all her clothes on," Matt whispered.

"Well, you don't have to watch," Justin said, a little bit annoyed at his old friend. Their rivalry for Tanya's affections and her frequent explosive rages at one or the other, or oftentimes both of them, had run through their entire six years at the Academy. At the very end of their Academy days Justin knew that his best friend was more than a bit upset over the fact that he had won.

Justin looked over at her, sleeping so peacefully. Their brief affair right after graduation, in the early days of the war, would always be a bittersweet memory. He glanced at Matt and felt a twinge of jealousy. Had his old buddy had an affair with her as well? He was tempted to ask, but decided not to. Maybe there were some things, even between the best of friends, that were better left unknown.

Matt motioned him over to the table, pointing to a cup of coffee.

"How'd your watch go?" Justin asked, gulping down half a cup. It was jet-black and thick with sugar, the way Matt always prepared it.

"Quiet, though damn confusing."

"Still accelerating?"

"Up to .33 light. Fastest man has ever gone."

"Or woman," Tanya said, opening her eyes and looking over at the two with a sleepy smile.

Noticing that a fair part of her body was exposed, she shook her head at them with mock anger and pulled the blankets up over her shoulders. Reaching under her bunk she pulled her pants and shirt into the bed and dressed under the covers. Matt chuckled at her obvious discomfort.

She slipped out of the bed and sat down by the table, gladly taking the third cup Matt had brewed.

"*Bodja moi*, Everett, your coffee's going to eat your guts right out of you some day."

"I should live so long," Matt replied, giving the standard reply of pilots when cautioned about some future danger to their lives or bodies.

"Any pursuit?"

"Nope. Oh, he's following, but a good fifty million klicks back. There's been some traffic from both the Colonial and Fed militaries, wanting to know what we were up to."

"And what did you tell them?"

Matt smiled.

"Not a damn thing."

Justin could see that this little adventure had sparked something inside of Matt. A lot more of his old friend had emerged over the last day. He was ready for a lark, never able to turn down a bit of adventure, and always willing to thumb his nose at authority.

"You'll have to turn back sometime," Tanya replied, putting down her cup of coffee and motioning for Matt to refill it. "Fuel alone."

"That's the strange thing—we've burned maybe a little more than fifteen percent since setting out. We could reverse-burn, and power back in and still have plenty to spare. It's damn weird."

"Well, there's going to be hell to pay for both of you running off like this."

"Most likely," Justin said with a smile. "But figure it out, Tanya, you're on the Commission. We go back now and the Colonials have a ship generations ahead of Earth's. The damn thing maneuvers, but we don't understand why, and it has ten times the acceleration of the latest Colonial fighters. Do you really think my government back home is going to calmly sit back? This thing upsets the balance of power far too much. EDF must have tracked us, and they're going to scream for a piece of the action."

"We could negotiate something," Tanya replied. "Maybe turn the ship over to the Bilateral Commission."

"I thought of that. You've got to remember though, like it or not, the Bilateral Commission survived and did its job because both governments saw the wisdom of it and were willing to generally abide by the rules. I doubt if the current UN would agree to that arrangement. They're looking for a *causa belli*, and this could be it."

"So are you two proposing to just keep on going until we run out of fuel and die?"

"We're going to take it all the way," Matt replied. "Now, if the Tracs show up again, hell, then we'll *all* be scrambling and there won't be much time for a war between the Colonies and Feds."

"At least I hope so," Justin interjected.

"But if we can actually boost this thing out of here and get to another system and come back! First of all, it'll show them it can be done. Second, it will give us the chance for a forward defense, and finally, even if the Tracs don't show up again it'll give the Feds and my own government something else to think about and somewhere else to go. Our backyard squabble will be moot when there's the entire universe to go chasing after."

Justin nodded an agreement and inwardly breathed a sigh of relief. He had to defer to Matt as being in command of the ship, and even four hours ago when he left Matt on the bridge after hours of arguing with him he still wasn't sure what he would do.

"So we're going all the way then?" Justin asked.

"What the hell else can we do? Yeah, I know the techs are going to go crazy with me over this. Hell, our testing plan called for at least two years of runs and evaluation before we actually tried to see if this thing could go translight. But like you said when we first met, there isn't time. There isn't time for a whole hell of a lot of reasons."

"So how do you think it works then?" Tanya asked.

"Damned if I know," Matt said with a grin, "but I guess that the answer, if there is one, will be coming up soon enough."

He motioned for them to head into the cockpit and the two followed him forward.

"We're out beyond Neptune's orbit," Matt announced, easing into his chair and pointing over at the nav screen, "and up to .362 light."

"So?" Tanya asked, as if he were in to some secret and keeping it back.

"The data we have on all incursions, be they Trac or unidentified, first establish contact roughly in this zone. If the last one followed a straight line without adjustments for gravitational effects we're damn near on the same line that he took."

Matt looked over at Justin for confirmation.

"The Dark Eye project established a number of concealed watch posts in a line along Neptune's orbital path. Something we kept hidden from the Colonials was an automated base on one of Neptune's moons as well.

That was the trip wire that set off the alarm for the Trac incursion last week. We picked up all twenty-seven ships suddenly appearing out of nothing, their first act being to take out the station. They just simply appeared."

"What do you mean, 'appeared'?" Tanya asked.

"Just that. One second they weren't there, the next second they were. By luck they almost smacked into a passive array which activated when they punched out a radar sweep. The array powered up its cameras and caught a visual of them before they knocked it out. One second nothing, the next something."

"Jump-point theory?" Tanya asked.

"Doubt it, but then again, who the hell knows?" Matt replied, lazily looking down his instrument array and then back up again for the forward view. "Could be that, space-folding, wormhole, tachyon faster-than-light drive. Hell, they've been writing about it for more than a hundred years."

"I'm betting on something to do with gravity waves," Justin interjected.

"Why?"

"Well, there sure is one hell of a strange drive on this ship. Every rule of logic says that when you are climbing out of a gravity well you expend energy, and unless you expend enough to counteract the force of gravity you decelerate, then fall back in. We've been doing the opposite and it's weird. The farther from the sun we get, the faster we accelerate, but we haven't burned our engines since the climb out from the slingshot when we were racing those guys chasing us."

"We're getting a spike," Matt announced. He motioned to the nav screen, cutting Justin off.

Justin looked down at the screen. The acceleration curve had jumped up three-hundredths of a percent, then leveled back down, then curved up again several seconds later.

He had already become used to the inertial dampening of the ship, realizing that in anything manmade such an acceleration would have ripped the vessel apart.

"We've got another, and another one," Tanya announced, and this time there was slight buffeting.

"Strap in," Matt cried. All three scrambled into the cockpit chairs and cinched down their safety straps.

Justin leaned back in his chair and suddenly felt as if his stomach were dropping out and then rising up into his throat as the ship went into zero gravity.

"Accelerating up," Matt shouted. "Holy shit—.3, .4."

"What are you doing?" Tanya shouted, struggling to strap herself into her chair.

"Still accelerating."

Justin looked up at the forward view. The color of the stars was changing, shifting towards the ultraviolet spectrum as they accelerated into the light. Peripheral view started to shift as well, the starfields ahead concentrating into a cone of light directly forward.

Justin punched up a stern view on his holo system. A cone of red light was behind him, growing darker by the second.

"Accelerating through .6, .7 . . ." Matt's voice seemed to fade away, and then there was nothing but the sensation of falling. He wanted to get sick, feeling the coffee rise up in his throat, and then everything just seemed to freeze into darkness.

Prata Bel Varna sat back in his chair and smiled. Even though what he was hearing spelled disaster, there was still a perverse pleasure in seeing those Prata who had been so willing to sell out to either the demands of the Golden Hive or the Council of the House of Zollern sit in their chairs and squirm now. But this was not the time to gloat, and Bel set his features in a serious demeanor, not letting the pleasure at Norru's loss of face become too evident. He realized that there were times that although one might be proven right it was nevertheless a disaster, especially when one was a prophet of doom.

His longtime rival, Prata Norru Garin, stepped up to the podium and nervously cleared his throat.

"We have heard the requests of Ambassador Jof of the Golden Hive, and although they are not in accordance with the treaty reached two hundred years past, I still believe an accommodation can be reached."

Bel Varna looked over at the representative of the Golden Hive and felt a shudder of fear: Insectoid, this one, bred as a leader. The distinctive blue stripe across the back of its carapace revealed its status; it stood silent, its multifaceted eyes unreadable.

There were dozens of different sub-breeds within a Hive, everything from the lowest menial laborer through the various rankings within their relentless military, to intellects of unfathomable capability. What each became was decided long before birth by what was fed to the pupa.

It was frightening and yet so dispassionately efficient. All was planned. If war was expected, and for the Hives war was the purpose of existence, warriors were bred by the hundreds of thousands, their numbers calculated years before they would be needed. In the days of the Great Leap, before the upper limits of machine- and computer-based technology was reached, the Hives bred intellect. Yet it was intellect for one purpose. There was no art, no joy in the art of thinking or creating, no concept of the individual or even of a soul—only making life for what the Hive needed and demanded.

There was only one limit to their aspirations—the material available on their worlds was finite, so they needed access to gateways between stars—that was why the Golden Hive was here.

Efficient! How cold and lifeless that word seemed to him, but as the leaders of the Hive were fond of saying "the universe belonged to the efficient."

How many Hives were there, he wondered. No one really knew . . . dozens perhaps, all of them rivals, all of them implacable, and all of them moving this way, fleeing from their defeat hundreds of light-years away inward towards the galactic core, though none of them would ever admit they had been defeated.

There might be some small satisfaction in that, at least. Too bad the bastards—if such a thing was possible with the Hive—weren't wiped out. Now they were coming, and in his heart he knew there was precious little that could be done to stop them. His small world of Cor was now the bargaining chip between empires.

Holzan di Zollern, representative of the Council of the Zollern Dynasty, sat in the back of the assembly room. He was dispassionate, as if this meeting were a bore to be endured. Though humanoid in appearance, their reptilian ancestry created almost as cold an effect as the representative of the Hive. It was the Zollern Dynasty and the allegedly representative Diet that had been the dominant power in this sector, at least until the coming of the Hive. And Cor, being on the border, was about to be bartered away to the Hive.

The damn Zollern, Bel thought angrily, didn't they realize this was simply the beginning of the nightmare to come? Though the Zollern Dynasty and all that they ruled were a different race, why could they not understand that ceding even one point, even if it was a free autonomous state within their system, was only the first step to annihilation.

The Hive ambassador stood patient, waiting for the turmoil in the room to settle down. That was another factor of who they were that was so disquieting—they had infinite patience. There was an old saying to never try and negotiate with a representative of the Hive, for they would sit with you until you fainted from fatigue and still be waiting when you awoke, not budging in their relentless demands.

"The treaty that you speak of, Prata Norru, was of a different time," Jof replied. "We are speaking of now."

"In other words," Bel interrupted, "you don't honor your treaties."

Jof swiveled its head.

"All things are relative to the moment," Jof replied, its words coming emotionlessly from the softly whispering translating computer clipped to Bel's collar. "At the moment the treaty was signed it was, in that time and place, valid, fulfilling both of our needs. The situation has changed, as all things in the universe change and there is need for revision."

"We at least believe that some things are permanent," Bel interjected angrily, "and have not fallen prey to the belief of *some* that all things are relative. There *are* absolutes in this universe, and a word given in treaty is a bond that is absolute."

"A foolish belief," Jof hissed. "Everything is relative to the moment, and this moment demands a new concept in our relations. To believe otherwise is the thinking of an immature being."

Jof's statement sent a ripple of coughs flowing through the assembly hall—an action displaying anger and shock.

Jof looked around disdainfully at the outbreak of coughing.

"It seems as if the Pratas have suddenly become infected with the illness of rude behavior to the Royal House of the Golden Hive which I represent. I am well aware of your customs; remember, we have studied you."

Even the translating computer caught the inflection of the words, "we have studied you." Bel could sense the cold detachment, as if humanoids were nothing more than caged animals in a lab or insects under the magnifying glass. That imagery troubled him. There was no denying the racial fear and hatred both sides bore for each other, and he realized with a sharp clarity that the Hives viewed humanoids with the same distaste as the Prata did the Hives.

"It is not the illness of rude behavior," Bel replied. "Rather, it is shock at such a cavalier attitude towards a sacred treaty, which *we* have honored."

"A cure is definitely in order," Jof said softly.

"Are you threatening war then?" Norru asked, motioning Bel to be silent. Bel was embarrassed by the tremor of fear in Norru's voice.

Jof's mandibles parted and Bel studied Jof, wondering if the gesture was a smile or a threat. Much time had been spent studying the Hives, their customs, beliefs and methods of war. It was always assumed that they would come back, but now that the time was here, the studies had proven to be useless. They were only the musings of cloistered academics puzzling over the few recordings made two hundred years past when the Golden Hive had briefly appeared in their systems, then disappeared inward toward the galactic core. All that was really known was that the universe was in chaos, and that chaos was coming straight at them.

"Our request is simple enough," Jof said, and the computer translated the statement with an inflection of friendliness.

"And it is?"

"Full use of your planet for the duration of the passage of our Hive."

"Full use?" Norru whispered, and the room was silent. For the last two hundred years a Hive ship had arrived every two months to pick up the processed uranium, antimatter and titanium which constituted the tribute. It had been a two-edged sword, depleting the resources of the world yet at the same time stimulating technology. Full use—the implications were frightful.

"But that was not part of the original agreement," Norru continued, his voice shaking.

Bel shook his head sadly. Norru was sounding far too weak. He was becoming an embarrassment for everyone present. Bel saw more than one of the other Pratas looking towards him for some response, even those from the other side of the circle. Sighing, he extended his left hand, and rapped the side of his desk with his family signet ring, the signal that he wished to interrupt. Norru, who normally would have ignored him, put the scepter down.

Bel stood up; his pale green jacket, inlaid with emeralds around his wrists and waist, caught the afternoon light streaming in from the skylights overhead. Even after all these years, stepping forward to speak before the Pratas gave him a thrill. As a boy he remembered standing in the gallery with the common citizens, hearing his grandfather speak. The room was hushed when the great Bel Val of Taris spoke, his charismatic stentorian baritone filling the vaulted room.

Would grandfather be proud of me now? Bel wondered, and the thought made him feel a moment of inner doubt. Grandfather was now legend, and legends cannot be matched by mere mortals. It was his grandfather who had offered successful resistance to the Zollern, wringing from them the status of a free state fifty years ago. At least the Zollern were devils who could be negotiated with. The Hive was a different matter.

Bel placed his hand on the scepter and the low murmuring in the room hushed. He waited. After all, the Chamber of Pratas was also a room of high theater. For a people who loved a good haggle, who thrived on the cutting of a deal, the deal-making of government was entertainment—even when it was also a matter of life and death.

He looked over haughtily at Ambassador Jof.

"Are you threatening war if we refuse?"

"Your words, not mine. Yet you know resist is senseless."

"The Zollern might."

"They might, but they won't."

A stunned gasp swept through the chamber. Shocked speechless, Bel looked over at the representative of the Zollern Dynasty. Holzan simply yawned and leaned back in his chair to stretch.

Holzan finally looked over at Bel while pandemonium reigned in the assembly hall. The look said everything. Bel sensed a flicker of guilt and Holzan finally offered a most uncharacteristic gesture for his race—he shrugged his shoulders. Several Pratas were out of their chairs, moving towards Holzan with obviously hostile intent. Bel looked at the door and gestured with his hand to the heavily armed guards. They seemed reluctant, but the murder of a representative of the Zollern Dynasty in the Chamber Hall of Cor was the last thing the Pratas needed. He gestured more emphatically and the guards finally moved forward to place themselves between Holzan and the enraged Pratas.

Jof remained as still as a statue throughout the entire display, unfathomable gaze locked straight ahead as if the mad confusion around him was as unworthy of his notice as the scurrying of the insects burrowing in the floor below.

Bel remembered the words of his grandfather on the triumphal day when the Zollern granted free-planet status to Cor, "The Zollern have lost only for the moment. Someday they will find a way of either taking us back or destroying us, so do not celebrate too loudly."

Bel could sense Norru looking at him as well. Norru's family had not supported the defiance of Zollern power and the move to free-state status. But if this was the Zollern payback—annihilation by the Hive—why was the Hive even bothering to send an ambassador here? *Why not just come and take us? Was there a game within a game?*

"I find it curious that you come here seeking an agreement," Bel finally ventured, "when it is obvious that you and the Zollern have already struck the deal that seals our fate."

"Why?"

"Because if you do have such overwhelming power as you imply, then why not simply take us? We know the Hives are the devourers of worlds. So why not annihilate us and be done with it, then take what you need?"

There were gasps in the audience at Bel's blunt and impetuous words. He felt a chill in his own heart as he spoke. Was he indeed pushing the ambassador too far? Would he simply leave and then, in a matter of days, a Hive Fleet arrive and bombard them into submission?

"You tempt the change of your destiny," Jof said.

Bel, confused for a moment did not reply . . . then realized that the Hive saw reality as a preordained universe, a gradual descent of things from organization to chaos, from energy to entropy. They believed that all that stood in the path of such a reality was the precise organization of the Hive. Did they therefore perceive that it was the destiny of his people to not yet be destroyed?

"Perhaps it is our destiny to endure and for you to pass us by."

"Your destruction would not fit our purposes of the moment. That is why we offer you life."

"Answer me—if we refuse this offer, does that mean war?"

"I have not been instructed to discuss the ramifications of your refusal," Jof said smoothly, "and I should add that it is you personally, Bel Varna, who is refusing, for there are more than one in this assembly who might see the wisdom of what I present."

Bel looked over at the Accommodators, as they were now called. More than one of them was nodding his head in agreement.

It was time to delay.

"One thing you have demanded is impossible," Bel announced loudly, and Holzan turned to look back at him.

"To make such a decision immediately is impossible."

"There is no time to wait."

"Tomorrow is Tenth Day. It will give us time to meditate upon what you have said and to consider your proposal. Let us adjourn for now."

Jof looked back at Norru, who rose up, tapping his ring on his desk. Bel walked over to him and handed him the scepter.

"There is wisdom in that," Norru replied quickly.

"You promised that at today's meeting of Pratas it would be decided," Jof snapped.

"Do not deem to order us in our own council," Norru replied sharply. "Bel's suggestion is a good one and I call for a vote upon it."

Rings were tapped to signal agreement to vote, and Holzan looked around disdainfully. Bel caught his gaze for a moment and smiled.

Norru held the scepter up with both hands, signaling the vote, and the entire assembly stood up to indicate agreement.

"Debate over the proposal will continue at our next weekly session."

Bel walked over to Norru and motioned for the scepter, and Norru reluctantly handed it to him.

"And the next debate will be held in private session."

Holzan glared angrily at him, and then turned and strode out of the chamber when the vote was again unanimous to bar the public and the ambassadors from the session.

Bel handed the scepter back to Norru and returned to his desk. He swept up the papers scattered upon it and tucked them into his breast pocket, then started for the door, trying to remain above the chaos that now reigned.

As he cleared the door, ignoring the shouts of support or rage from the gallery, he stopped as Holzan Zollern approached. His fetid breath caused Bel to brace himself. Damn Zollern! The Hive triggered an instinctive reaction because of their towering form, but the Zollern were disturbingly different—scaly and squat, with cold, languid eyes that revealed that even to converse with someone not of their royal line was a chore to be avoided unless absolutely necessary.

They had drifted for eons, smug and complacent in their power. Gone was the will to venture, to explore . . . rather, they simply clung to the power they had.

Could not the Zollern see what was coming now? Cor was but a step by the Hive to on the way to ultimate destruction. It was evident, however, that the Zollern, smug in their superiority over the Hive, simply did not see the threat. Granted, within the Council of Dynasties there were certain elements that still had what Bel would call spirit, such as the maddenly erratic House of Gar. Yet the Gar, who were exciting to trade with, were so damned unpredictable . . . open-handed one minute and at your throat the next. But it was the superior disdain of the ruling Zollern that always set his temper on edge.

"I'd urge you to accept," Holzan announced. "There are simply no other alternatives, Bel. The Hive is implacable."

"The way you accepted? Thank you for informing us first."

"Oh, but Cor is a free state. You people were so aggressive in demanding that."

"Because we're not like you," Bel replied sharply, wishing he could somehow convey in his voice the haughty disdain implying the Zollern were beneath him. The fact that he could not made him even angrier.

"Tell me, Holzan. After they've occupied us and looted us clean, then what?"

"Why, the Hive will move on, of course, beyond our frontiers and glad to be rid of them."

"There are dozens of Hives. You only have an agreement with the Golden, don't you?"

Holzan hesitated for the briefest of seconds, but that hesitation was evident enough for Bel that he had a point.

"After their defeat inward to the Core, the Golden assumed a superior position. They now speak for all."

"Somehow I doubt that."

Holzan shook his head, the layer of scales where there should be hair rustling. It gave off the scent of a perfume that was all but overpowering.

"Ah, so this one small world of yours now possesses all the secrets controlled by the Zollern? We have studied the Hive since the first brush with them hundreds of years ago. Our finest minds have evaluated every shred of data. From this data we have crafted our response. Have faith, Bel."

"In what? The Zollern? We gave up on that generations ago. Did your scholars also see that we could actually win free-state status; was that part of your plan?"

Holzan smiled, and Bel was suddenly struck by the terrible thought that perhaps it was indeed part of their plan. Holzan's toothy grin broadened, and he chuckled.

"Ah, so now you see?"

As if physically struck, Bel lowered his eyes.

"We allowed you to win. We could have marshaled a fleet to smash you in a day if we had so desired. But to what purpose? As you so rudely pointed out, you are not even of the blood of the royal line. Thus, when the Hive did return it was not as if we were ceding royal territory, merely a free state. Face is preserved, the Hive has a corridor of passage, and in another generation they will be gone."

"And Cor is looted and no more," Bel whispered.

"Oh, perhaps if you accept your fate we'll rebuild you once it is finished, or we'll seek out a new transit point and go into an unknown system and find you a new world. That might be amusing! It has been a score of centuries or more since we've indulged in the whimsy of having colonists."

The realization that what had once been held as a glorious moment in their history—the breaking away from the Zollern Dynasty in a bloodless coup and the establishment of Cor as a free state—might very well have been a fraud, unnerved Bel. He decided it was best to simply withdraw.

Offering a formal nod to Holzan he turned away.

"There is no other course left to you," Holzan sniffed. He made a show of pulling out a perfumed handkerchief and waved it about, making clear his opinion of the scent of those not of the blood.

"Bel."

Bel hesitated and turned back.

"Accept your fate. It is necessary for stability. If you try to resist, our agreement with the Hive requires that we occupy you until they arrive."

No mention of that had been made on the floor, and Bel stood silent.

"There's no other way, Bel."

"So you knifed us in the back."

"You knifed yourself in the back, Bel. Your race and their stiff-necked pride. 'Lizards,' you called us, but you forget that we were already faring the stars when your race was barely out of the trees. You could have been part of our system, but your damned racial pride demanded independence from us. So now this is the price."

"How long have we known each other, Holzan . . . twenty

years, isn't it, since you came here as ambassador from the Court?"

"Something like that."

"Though there were differences, still I thought I could trust you. I never trusted your Dynasty, but I thought I could trust you personally."

Holzan stiffened.

"I don't think you like this agreement any more than I do, Holzan. I suspect games within games concealed within this agreement, and I tell you now it will come to haunt you. The Hive is merciless, a remorseless machine, and we are but the appetizer to the meal for them."

Holzan nodded in warning and Bel saw Jof emerging from the hall, Norru by his side, undoubtedly trying to make an impression.

"We'll talk later, Bel," Holzan announced, and with arms extended wide in the gesture the Hive took as friendliness Holzan approached Jof.

Simmering, Bel stalked off, barely noticing his brother's son Darel waiting anxiously by the door into the assembly chamber. Darel wanted to say something but Bel waved him on, using the boy to help clear a path through the crowd waiting outside in the main corridor. Mechanically he touched the shoulders of well-wishers, and dodged past the swarm of petitioners, commission seekers, and sycophants. He slipped into his cluttered office and closed the door behind them, blocking out the chaos in the corridor. He slumped, exhausted, into a chair. Opening a hidden panel in the cabinet behind him he pulled out a bottle and took a very long drink. He ignored the exasperated look of his young nephew, who was usually too quick to lecture on the moral failure of those who indulged in drink.

"We just received a message from Marshal Bathan," Darel announced.

"What? Is the Hive moving in already?"

Bathan knew who on the Council should be warned if such an event were already unfolding.

"Just a little more than a tenth ago, an unidentified ship crossed into our system," Darel said.

"So?"

"It was of a Gar privateer design, but it bore no clan markings."

"It could be an unmarked ship of theirs scouting," Bel said wearily, fatigued after the debate and slightly annoyed that one of his staff would bother him with such a detail. If it was a Gar ship and did not behave aggressively, it could dock at the freeport.

"It's not Gar."

"How do you know that? So whose is it then?"

"The report indicates it might very well be piloted by savages coming from the Ima system."

"Ridiculous. That's beyond all our frontiers." Then he paused. They knew that the system was inhabited—he had heard a report from a Gar trader to that effect, and there had been intercepts of garbled transmissions. There were dozens of worlds like that; life was known to be there, but the crucial nexus points for jumps into their systems simply did not exist. Such worlds were as cut off as desert islands in the Great Sea. There was no way to go there except by long and tedious voyage, and once one had arrived, what was the purpose other than to turn about and make the long journey back?

Could it be that whoever lived there had advanced enough for space flight? But how did they get a Gar ship? And if they did get a Gar ship, how did they make it here other than by brute force and a journey of dozens of years? His curiosity was aroused by this mystery.

"Where is it now?"

"Just under a day's travel out. Curious, it appeared near where we tracked that Gar ship five days ago, the one that disappeared. We just got the signal moments ago."

Bel nodded and then slowly started to grin.

"Could it be a that new nexus point is out there in our own damn system and we didn't know about it?"

"It seems that way, uncle," and Darel grinned excitedly.

Amazingly, it had been decades since a nexus point had been found locally. And it was interesting that it occurred at this particular moment, as well. If they were in a Gar ship, that meant the Gar had found the point into this system. If so, did the Zollern know? And if they did, what part did this play in their game with the Hive?

"And you're sure it's not Gar aboard?"

"Yes, uncle. A query was sent to the ship. No reply. One of Bathan's experts punched a signal in and it activated a display field; there was no security lock on it. He got this image."

Darel handed over a small cam unit. Bel held it in the palm of his hand and turned it on. As the image focused he looked at it with stunned disbelief.

"Contact my office. Tell them that I am retiring to my country home for the weekend and under no circumstances whatsoever am I to be disturbed. Contact my home and have them say, if I am asked for, that I have gone up into the mountains alone to spend the night and meditate. Our ship is still docked to the Skyhook?"

Darel nodded and then groaned.

"I was planning to see Varu during Tenth Day."

"She can wait. We're going out to see who these visitors are. Tell Marshal Bathan that the ship is to be tracked but not engaged, no matter what happens. Tell him to let no one else know about this, and that I will make first contact."

"Where the hell are we?" Tanya whispered.

"Well, it sure isn't Indiana," Justin said, trying to keep the trembling out of his voice. They had been drifting for hours, coasting down towards a star, and still there were no answers.

Justin looked over at Matt and saw the look of fear in his friend's eyes as well. He truly assumed that they were dead, that whatever was happening was totally out of their control. The ship would either disintegrate or suffer any one of a number of very weird theoretical finalities.

"I wonder what the time even is?"

"Thirty seconds lapsed on the chronometer during the transition, eleven hours since then," Tanya replied.

"No, I mean back home. We moved up to .95 light, then I think I blacked out. Suppose we hit nine-point-nine out to ten or twelve decimal points for a couple of hours while we were out. Hell, it could be years, even centuries later back home."

"We won't have to worry about the reception on our return then," Matt replied dryly.

"That's if we get back," Tanya retorted. "Damn it, Everett, you'd think that after all these years that some of those clowns working on your project would have figured all this stuff out."

"Hey, you invited yourself!" Matt shot back. "I sure as hell didn't ask you to come along."

"So what happened?" Tanya snapped, not bothering to agree.

"Damned if I know," Matt said, with a characteristic shrug of his shoulders. "I guess we jumped light, or something like that. Maybe it'd help, Miss Leonov, if you took a look at your nav screen."

Tanya looked angrily at Matt and then turned back to her screen.

Pursing her lips, she simply stared at it. The silence in the cockpit became almost oppressive for Justin. He wasn't even sure what he should be doing. He continued to punch through screens, trying to analyze the data, and he finally noticed one disturbing fact.

"We seem to have eaten up nearly sixty percent of our fuel in all of this," Justin announced.

Matt looked at his own screen and nodded.

"Guess it went somewhere, but a standard engine burn wouldn't have swallowed it up that fast."

"It means that wherever we are, we aren't getting home again," Justin whispered. "While we ran around in our system we burned off our reserves of fuel."

"We'll have to worry about that later," Matt said. "I just want the satisfaction of knowing where we are."

"Well, we're definitely not in our own system," Tanya finally announced.

"I kind of guessed that," Matt replied.

"I've got to start somewhere, Everett, so lay off."

Confused, she finally looked back over at the other two.

"Some of the starfields are shifted, though a number of them, especially those opposite our direction, still seem to basically line up."

Justin looked back up at the forward view. A star hovered almost directly ahead. It was impossible to tell how far away they were since there was no way of knowing just how big it was. It looked to be about the same size as the sun would appear from Neptune, its disk barely discernible.

"Run a spectral analysis on that star ahead," Justin said quietly.

"How?" Tanya retorted.

Exasperated, Justin threw up his hands.

"Matt, don't you know how to run anything on this machine?"

"I think it's Procyon," Tanya interrupted.

"How do you know that?" Matt asked. "Hell, we were oriented at least two hours ascension off from there when we accelerated."

"It's a class-F star, the only one out this way for quite a few dozen light-years. I think we simply got pulled in by the closest star along our route of travel, and that happened to be Procyon."

Justin had to admit that it was the most logical answer. Hell, for all they knew they might very well be on the other side of the galaxy. Being next door to home—only twelve light-years away—was comforting somehow.

Tanya focused her attention back on her system and started to scroll through. Her attention was suddenly broken by a shrill, insistent beep.

Startled, she looked over at Matt.

"I think I know what it is now," Tanya announced.

"Go on—what?" Matt replied testily.

"A radio contact," Tanya said calmly. "Since the last one

I've fooled around with the system a bit. I think I can patch it in."

She looked at Justin and Matt, eyes wide.

Justin felt his heart start to race. If it was indeed a contact it had a hell of a lot of historical importance. It was, after all, the first verbal contact with whoever it was out here. It also might mean that they didn't have much longer to live.

"Put it on the speaker," Matt said quietly.

"*Targ haru na kulmat cor. Targ haru na kulmat cor . . .*"

"What the hell is it?" Matt whispered.

"How the hell am I supposed to know?" Tanya replied. "We never studied alien dialects at the Academy."

"*Targ haru na kulmat cor.*"

"I now have contacts as well," Tanya whispered. "Five, no, make that seven contacts. Bearing in three forward, one to starboard amidships, the other to port, one directly above and one behind."

"Reception committee," Matt said, and he instantly hit reverse throttle and pulled the stick over.

"Shit, the damn thing's acting aerodynamically," Matt gasped. "We're banking, changing direction of forward momentum. What the hell is going on?"

"Well, use it!" Justin shouted. "Throttle it up!"

Matt reversed throttle and *Prometheus* continued to turn, inertial dampening taking out most of the gees but enough were still there to press Justin down in his seat. His breath came in short explosive gasps.

"*Targ haru na kulmat cor.*"

"Closest alien ship is now a million klicks. The one that was to starboard, he's now dead ahead, closing!"

Justin looked up and saw nothing, and then a brief flicker of light.

"Passed us, coming about as well. One that was astern now moving parallel, thirty thousand klicks off our port side."

"Why aren't they shooting?" Matt asked.

"*Targ haru na kulmat cor.*"

"Turn that damn thing off," Matt snapped.

"No, wait a minute! It keeps repeating—maybe it's a hail. Shit, if they were hostile that last ship would have dumped something on us."

Matt looked over at Tanya, surprised.

"You spent too much time on that Bilateral Commission, Leonov."

"She might be right," Justin interrupted. "Stop banking, fly straight for a few seconds, and let's see what they do."

"You're both crazy," Matt growled, even as he straightened the ship out.

"Ship off port side is holding parallel amidships, three coming up from out of the system are turning at just under a million klicks, matching speed. Other ships are holding back, matching our course as well."

"Start to throttle down," Justin said, his voice barely a whisper.

"I say let's get the hell out of here."

"You're outvoted two to one, Everett," Tanya said. "And another thing, these ships aren't the same design as this one or the Trac ships that hit us last week. All but one are smaller, almost fighter-sized; one is roughly our size."

"Big shit, the Colonies have dozens of different ships. So does Earth."

"Listen to her," Justin said. "They've yet to fire—maybe they want contact, maybe they're somebody else."

"If we get fried, there goes the only prototype of this ship," Matt snapped. "It'll be years before anyone can build another."

"If we blow a first contact, we might be losing a chance. These guys aren't the same, I tell you."

"How do you know that?"

"Gut instinct," Justin lied, realizing he didn't honestly have a clue as to who they were contending with.

"Throttle it back," Tanya said forcefully, and Matt looked over at her.

"Never could win an argument with you, Leonov, but so help me, if you two are wrong I'll haunt both of you."

Matt slammed the throttle back, and seconds later Tanya announced that their pursuers were matching the maneuver.

"They're starting to edge in closer," Tanya announced, and Justin finally managed to tap into the nav screen to watch.

"One of them has rolled up on its side presenting its underbelly, but it's still flying parallel."

"Might be a signal of nonaggression."

"Either that or it's pointing a weapons array at us." Matt sniffed.

"Always the optimist," Tanya replied.

"Fourteen years of war taught me to be a realist," Matt replied.

"Holy shit," Tanya whispered, and Justin looked over at her.

She had a visual contact on her screen and Justin looked at it in astonishment—whoever it was it was humanoid. He assumed it was a male due to facial hair. The face was thicker, features coarser, eyes deeper set than a human's, and it had a protruding brow. The forehead receded back sharply and was covered with a thick tangle of black curly hair.

He found it interesting that the man was smiling, and had to hope that a smile was a universal sign of at least some friendly intent. The image was from the shoulders up, his collar green with what looked like inlaid emeralds.

"Targ na haru cor et dolman."

Tanya looked over at Justin and Matt.

"We've got a first contact here," Tanya whispered. "What the hell do we do?"

"Talk back," Justin said.

"And say what?"

"I don't know, anything! You're making history, woman."

"Think I saw this guy in a museum once," Matt whispered.

"What do you mean?"

"Looks like a Neanderthal."

"Well, it's a Neanderthal that can fly and outnumbers us," Justin hissed, "so shut up."

Tanya punched the two-way communications control and the man on the other side looked slightly surprised, then smiled.

"We've come in peace for all mankind," Tanya said and shot an angry sidelong glance at Matt when he moaned.

"Damn it, Leonov, can't you think of something more original than that?"

Tanya punched the comm control button off. "Well, what the hell do you want me to say? 'Take me to your leader'?"

"Be original—how about, 'That's one small step for a man,' " Matt snapped.

"Don't argue now," Justin whispered. "Just let her do the talking."

Bel Varna could not help but admire the woman who appeared on the screen before him. Her raven-black hair, tied back with a white ribbon, set off her features in a most attractive way. She was strangely exotic . . . features too thin, frail in fact, but nevertheless there was a certain appeal. He felt slightly guilty for that reaction. She was after all a savage, and morally beneath him.

Her words were unintelligible. It was to be expected, but annoying.

"Do we have any transmission data from where these people might be from?" Bel asked, looking over his shoulder at Darel.

"No visuals, just audio recordings."

"Language analysis?"

"They think they have the vocabulary and syntax worked out. The problem is that there seem to be a number of different dialects."

"Plug it into the translator. See if it can sort out which dialect she's using."

The woman was still looking at him on the screen, saying something else . . . pointing to herself and saying a word slowly. Her name.

"Taya?"

She smiled and nodded. He pointed at himself and said his name.

"Bell," she repeated, then laughed and looked to her left, saying something to what he assumed was a crewmate and he heard a masculine voice laughing in reply.

What was so funny? Bel wondered.

"The translator's online, Sire."

Bel nodded and looked back at the screen.

"I am Bel Varna, magistrate of the Ruling Assembly of the Free State of Cor."

Startled, Tanya looked at the screen again.

"The voice is synthesized," Tanya announced. "They must have a translator."

"What program is it working from?" Matt asked. "How'd they get the language sample?"

"We have copies transmissions, use with translator."

"Well, I'll be damned," Justin said.

Bel looked startled.

"Orthodox?" and Justin could see what he assumed was a cautious look on Bel's face.

"Religion—be careful how you answer," Matt whispered.

"We aren't sure of your beliefs. Perhaps we can discuss them later?" Justin finally replied.

Bel seemed to relax slightly.

"I don't know if you understood what I said earlier," Tanya continued, wondering if the translator Bel was using was correctly handling her comments. "We've come here in peace, to explore and to discover. We'd like to arrange a meeting."

Bel nodded.

"And to find out who attacked us," Matt interjected.

"Attacked, you?"

"Yes, us."

"One moment please," and the screen went dark.

"What the hell?" Matt snapped. "He cut us off."

"Look, he said he's part of an assembly. Our arrival here is certainly as much a surprise to them as it is to us. The guy's most likely got to check with some higher-ups."

After what seemed like an eternity to Justin the screen finally lit up again.

"Follow us to nearest base. We will talk face to face later."

"Wait a minute, why should we?" Matt snapped.

Bel looked confused for a moment.

"Because I ask it."

"Do you mean order?"

Again there was a hesitation, and to Justin's surprise Bel used the gesture of shaking his head.

"No, not order. But for benefit of you and I it would be good to meet."

"Do you know who attacked us?" Tanya interjected, motioning for Matt to shut up.

"Attack?"

"Yes, attack," Matt replied in spite of Tanya's angry look.

"Attack, when?"

"In our system, that is what we came here to find out."

Bel looked away for a moment, talking to someone off the screen in an animated way. Finally he turned back.

"I assure you, it was not us. Please, we must meet. Follow my ship."

The screen again went dark.

"Should we trust him?" Justin asked.

"I think our best bet is to fire up and get the hell out of here now," Matt grumbled. "We got contact, we've jumped out of our system, now let's get home."

"Yeah, and what about fuel?"

"Look, it's worth a try. Maybe the way this weird system works we'll get some sort of boost out. Hell, if they get us into orbit over some base we're sitting ducks to get boarded or simply blown apart."

"It's worth a shot," Justin replied. "We've made contact. If we jump out now they might take it as a hostile act. I'd be more suspicious if these guys had the same kind of ships that hit us. They outnumber us seven to one and can most likely fly a hell of a lot better than us. If they wanted us dead we'd be dead. Let's not blow the chance at getting some information—I think we're going to need it."

"I'm with Justin, so the vote's our way, Everett."

"I never heard of a ship being run like a democracy," Matt grumbled.

"With me aboard it is," Tanya said with a smile, "especially when I'm with the majority."

"Attacked by whom?" Bel asked, looking over at his nephew as soon as the screen went dark.

"I don't know. There aren't any reports."

"Well, how did someone get to their system? There are no known transit points."

"That is obviously mistaken," Darel replied. "They are here, that is proof enough of a transit into our system. Someone else must know about it as well."

"Are they following us?"

"Whoever the pilot is, he sure is new at it. He's weaving all over the place, but yes, they're following."

"Good, I would have hated to kill them," Bel said with a smile. "They just might be useful. I don't think they understand their system . . . see if you can tap into one of their communications channels and force a download. It might be interesting."

✧ Chapter VI ✧

The medical quarantine imposed by Magistrate Bel had come as a relief. It was something that had been nagging at Justin ever since the contact and docking at their orbital base. Bel had explained the situation and Justin was in full agreement. Two personnel had boarded the ship after achieving orbit and hard dock. Both wore full space suits when they came aboard through the docking collar toting bags of medical gear. The forms were definitely humanoid, as were the faces behind the masks. Fascinated, Justin watched them unpack. They pulled out some equipment that looked remarkably familiar, such as tongue depressors and needles, which he had always hated. Other equipment he could not figure out. As the gear was used on all three of them their purposes became apparent. There was a portable X-ray and a sonogram, a thermometer registering body temperature in the ear, and several other probes that all three of them flatly refused to go along with.

Finishing up with blood samples, the two med personnel withdrew, talking unintelligibly nonstop.

When the screen came back on after several hours of a very long wait, Justin called the others forward.

"We have run a biological check on you, which shows no serious complications," Bel announced.

"Your translator seems to be working better," Tanya replied.

"We took the liberty of hooking a download into your computer through one of your communications channels and fed it into ours."

"Hey, did you bother to ask us?" Matt snapped.

"We did not think you would object."

"Well, damn it, we do!"

"I apologize then. I will be aboard shortly. Please meet me by the door."

Matt, cursing under his breath, followed Tanya aft.

"What did you have in the computer?" Justin asked.

"Thank God we were paranoid about that. No library, no data other than nav, software to run the ship, that's it." Then Matt hesitated. "Damn, the communications feeds . . . it stored all of that. He has information on our solar system, some of the defenses, our testing and not knowing what we were doing, the pursuit, all of it. Son of a bitch!"

"Both of you, quiet," Tanya hissed. "He's coming."

Justin looked through the short airlock corridor and suddenly his heart started to race. The anxiety about what Bel might have found out was forgotten for the moment. It was one thing to deal with the characters in the suits, but now they were actually going to meet another species face to face. It had been the speculation of fiction for over a hundred years . . . he had grown up reading stories about it. At the Academy they had even run a "what if you are the one" seminar. Now he *was* the one.

Justin was surprised by the height of the man in front of him. He stood just over five feet tall with a heavy build. His eyes had an Oriental double fold; his skin color, however, was pale except for his florid complexion and bulbous nose. Justin immediately recognized that pattern—this man was a brother of the bottle. That realization alone set him at ease and for an instant he forgot that he was, in fact, establishing first contact with an alien. What was so disarming was that this alien looked human, or at least as if he were a cousin.

Justin could not help but admire his clothing even though it seemed outrageous compared to the utilitarian military standards he was used to. Bel's surcoat and tight fitting trousers were a brilliant, almost iridescent green, the fabric silky in appearance, green stones inlaid around the collar, cuffs, and waist. There was even a subtle hint of lace showing around his cuffs. He seemed to have a commanding presence that for lack of a better word Justin would have called charismatic.

"I am Bel Varna."

The voice came from a small silver box clipped to his lapel. Bel had turned his head slightly to whisper into it.

Tanya edged forward and before Justin or Matt could speak she introduced herself and then the other two.

Bel smiled and then turned slightly and motioned for his companion to come forward. The assistant opened up a small lacquered red box. Inside was what looked like a hand gun.

"The precaution of inoculations against what we analyzed as potentially harmful diseases is in order before we sit to talk," Bel announced.

Rather reluctantly Justin rolled up his sleeve, closing his eyes when the aide came up to his side. It hit with a punch and he grimaced, trying not to react to a bemused chuckle from Bel.

Rolling his sleeve back down, Justin flexed his arm and rubbed his shoulder with his left hand, looking over at Tanya, who took the shot without any sign of discomfort, and then Matt, who cursed softly under his breath.

As they endured the shots Bel slowly walked about the ship. He touched nothing, but his curiosity was evident. He paused for a moment in front of the nav station and then headed aft to linger near the engine compartment. Justin carefully and silently watched him.

"There is so much to talk about and so little time," Bel finally said smoothly, motioning for the three of them to lead the way towards the galley area. His assistant followed, holding a camera up, sweeping it back and forth.

"It's Gar design," Bel announced.

"Gar? Are they what we call the Tracs?" Tanya and Matt asked simultaneously.

"Like I said, so much to talk about, but since you are, we could say, trespassers in our space without warrant of trade from the assembly, may I be so rude as to ask the questions first?"

Justin felt disarmed by the air of politeness, wondering if the tonal inflections of deference in Bel's voice were part of the translator programming or originated with the speaker.

"As commander of this ship I'd like to ask about the unauthorized download of our data," Matt interjected.

Bel held up his hand. "Patience! All in good time, Matthew Everett."

Tanya extended her hand to Matt and then motioned for Bel to sit at the small table in the galley. She went to the microwave and put five cups in, then pulled out steaming mugs of tea and passed them around. Bel tentatively took his drink, sniffed it cautiously and tasted it. A smile of delight crossed his features.

"Is this drink indigenous to your world?"

"It's called tea," Tanya interjected.

"Perhaps, if everything else works out correctly, we can make a trade agreement."

Justin had to chuckle at the offer. Terran empires had been built on the same brew, and he wondered what these folks would think of good Kentucky bourbon.

"You are from what we call the *Ima* system, beyond the frontier, and this is the *Cor* system."

"We call home 'Earth,' and this the 'Procyon' system," Tanya replied.

Justin watched Bel's reaction and saw that apparently a nod was viewed as an affirmative answer here as well. As he watched Bel he realized that it was fortunate that there were no anthropologists on the crew. They would have gummed up the works with their analysis of every subtle gesture that Bel showed. As it was, he did have a monitor camera on. If Bel could do a download without permission, a quiet taping in reply was not out of order. He could well imagine the theories that would be smashed and the dissertations that would be written if they ever got back alive with the information from this encounter.

"How did you get, or make, this ship?"

Tanya, leaving out the details of the Civil War, gave a brief rundown on the Gar raid, the destruction of their ship, and then the building of a replica.

Bel chuckled with amazement listening to her and looked over at Darel who was listening intently to the exchange. He switched his translator off for a moment.

"Which house of the Gar did this?"

"It has to be the Ya—just like them to find a transit and then go for a little raiding before telling anyone. Also, it might be an initiation rite for their youngsters. Well, these barbarians certainly bloodied *their* snouts."

"Excuse me," Tanya said calmly, and Bel looked over at her. "We consider it to be impolite to carry on a conversation in private when others are present. May I ask what you just said to your companion?"

Bel chuckled in a decidedly human way that Justin found reassuring.

"My apologies. I just said that the group that attacked you is known for raids like that."

"So you're not part of their system?"

"Genetically, no. We are an entirely different race. Politically, we are loosely associated. The way the three of you are."

"What do you mean?"

"I notice the three of you are wearing different uniforms. Is there a reason?"

"We represent different sections of our society," Tanya said evenly.

Bel looked at her closely, sensing a slight tension, catching the quick sidelong glances from her two companions. He had not had time to view the downloads carefully but it was obvious there was some division within their system. If so, it could be used to advantage by a variety of factions.

He continued to pose questions, many of them innocent enough, about culture, relations between men and women which he found to be fascinating. He sensed that both of the men had an interest in her but that she was remaining aloof, and that their knowledge of events outside their system was woefully inadequate.

Justin remained silent, watching the interplay. He was intrigued by what was being asked, and more so by what was not asked. Bel attempted to probe about the political divisions that existed and Tanya skillfully sidestepped his questions, revealing nothing of the Civil War, implying that there were a significant number of similar ships already available for use once this first test run was completed.

Even with the difficulties of such vast cultural differences Justin could tell that Bel was skillful at negotiation, and for a moment he wondered if perhaps the being across from him was telepathic or had some other strange power. It was hard to realize when looking at him that he was, in fact, an alien, and that this was a first contact. It all seemed so strange, the five of them sitting around a table, sipping tea and chatting, almost as if they were aboard a passenger ship on a long haul and were trading stories to kill the hours.

"As your guests," Tanya said smoothly after dodging yet another question that might have led into the internal divisions back home, "do you mind if we find out a little about you and your system? After all, a contact like this might be common to you, but we will confess it is the first such experience for us, other than the less than friendly encounters we've had of late."

Bel smiled expansively.

"But of course."

"You said this ship is of Gar design and that your free state is named Cor. We want to know more about who attacked us two weeks ago."

Bel hesitated.

"Two weeks?"

"Two seven-day units."

Bel absorbed the thought. The definition of a day did seem to be similar if one added in the relativity of the jump the Gar fleet had made and the one these barbarians had just accomplished.

"A ten-day for us."

Tanya moved to gather up the empty mugs, and offered to make another round.

Bel smiled, and he reached into his surcoat and pulled out a gem-encrusted flask.

"Since our physiologies appear to be similar, I think this might be of interest to you."

He uncorked the flask and held it forward. Tanya hesitated but Justin reached over and took the flask, and then sniffed it.

Good lord, it smelled like brandy! Smiling, he raised the flask in a salute to Bel and saw out of the corner of his eye the look of distress on Tanya's face. He ignored it and took a sip.

Damn, it was brandy. Well, almost like it, and smooth. He took a gulp, sighed and passed the flask to Matt.

"Good stuff," Justin said with a grin.

Matt sampled it and then took a long pull as well.

"We have a lot in common, Bel Varna," Matt announced with a smile.

"Ah, so you have similar refreshments?"

Justin chuckled.

"And have been missing them sorely. Alcohol is forbidden aboard military ships."

"So this is a military ship then?" Bel asked with a smile.

Tanya started to open her mouth to speak and Justin interrupted.

"Let's not play games, sir. We were attacked without any provocation on our part. It's our job to find out who did it and address the problem."

"Two weeks ago, you say?" Bel asked.

"Twelve days," Matt replied and then hesitated, "unless we had a little experience with time distortion coming here."

The dumb savages don't know what happened getting here, Bel thought, suppressing a chuckle.

"I can assure you it wasn't us. But might I ask, what happened when they attacked?"

"We destroyed them," Justin interjected quietly. "None of them will ever return home."

Bel kept his focus on the woman. She smiled slightly. It was no idle boast; these barbarians had annihilated a Gar raiding force. It was remarkable and yet they had never ventured outside their system until now. Was it stupidity on the part of the Gar commander, going in ill prepared, or simple luck on the part of the barbarians . . . or perhaps even skill?

"Your one small Gar privateer will not address the problem of a major raiding force. The situation you have wandered into is complex," Bel finally said, choosing his words carefully and hoping that the translation program was working correctly.

"Complex?"

Bel looked at the three and saw their confusion, their sidelong glances at each other, and their obvious uneasiness.

Matt offered the flask to Tanya, who shook her head in annoyance, then offered it back to Bel.

"A gift, the flask and the contents," Bel said casually.

Bel watched Matt closely. There was a flash of surprise and then he looked down open-mouthed at the flask. So these savages place value on such things—good! He turned his attention back to the woman.

"You know nothing of what is occurring in the space around you then?"

"We have some understanding," Justin replied casually. "We've had listening arrays aimed in this direction. Though we haven't picked up any direct radio communications we have observed thermonuclear detonations on several worlds, and what we think might have been an action fought in space using thermonuclear and antimatter weapons. We could only assume there was a war being fought."

"And it is coming straight your way."

"You mean our way," Tanya said softly.

Bel stirred and looked over at her, surprised by her comment.

"You're one of the closer stars to our system. If it's coming our way, it's coming your way too, and I suspect you're none too pleased."

Bel smiled softly. She was shrewd for a barbarian.

"We've been answering a lot of questions," Justin interjected. "Do you mind our asking some?"

Bel smiled and extended his hands in what Justin took to be a friendly gesture.

"I suspect you might be between a rock and a hard place," Justin said.

Bel looked at him, confused.

"He means you are in a difficult situation," Tanya said.

"Oh, yes, 'a rock and a hard place,' very good. Go on," Bel replied.

"You're surprised by our arrival aboard what you call a Gar ship. There's a war coming that you're not part of yet, but you will be."

"Why do you think we will be involved?"

Justin smiled. The question answered by a question was answer enough. "You mention a loose association with the Gar, yet you knew nothing of their attacking us?"

"News travels only as swiftly as the fastest ship."

So there is a finite level, Justin thought. Interesting, and it presented a number of tactical points as well.

"Yet you do not deny your surprise, and you did say war is coming this way. From who, and why? Also, you do see some advantage to be gained from our being here— otherwise you would have already seized our ship."

This barbarian was astute, far too astute, Bel thought. Marshal Bathan had screamed for just such an action. Several considerations had dissuaded him from just such a course. The first was the simple one that if this *was* Gar design, chances were it was rigged with an autodestruct. At the first sign of aggressive action the barbarians might destroy the prize. The overriding point, though, was the sheer audacity of what they had done. They had built this ship based on nothing more than the bits and pieces of wreckage retrieved from space; designing the original, a task that had taken more than a generation.

This was no moribund race resigned to a perceived upper limit to technology, they were surging forward, the building of this ship a quantum jump in tech level for them. They observed the universe through the eyes of a child, and such thinking might present a fascinating alternative that could be useful.

"So you want the answers then," Bel finally replied.

"Yes. I should add the following," Justin interjected. "There are more ships like this one. Our new fleet was simply waiting for the completion of this test run. If you attempt to seize it, all I need to do is touch the autodestruct release and we're all gone."

Justin fished in his pocket and pulled out an old style ball point pen and let his finger brush across the top of it.

Bel looked carefully at the device and then smiled.

"All right. A wise precaution . . . would have done the same."

"So the answers then."

Justin could sense Tanya's simmering anger at his usurpation of the role of negotiator. She had played far too long on the Bilateral Commission, cajoling and coaxing the two warring sides. He suspected they could have played the word games for days with Bel and found precious little. It was time to be direct.

"Do you know of the Hives?"

"Hives?" Justin wasn't sure if the translation was correct or not.

"*Eav vu'hag?*" and this time the words were not translated. "Another race?"

"Yes, another race. I regret to tell you this, but in a short period of time they will be here by the millions, the hundreds of millions."

"The Gar?" Tanya asked. "Is that who you are talking about?"

"No, this is different. Very different. You said you detected a war. You measured the distance by the travel time of light?"

"Forty-seven light-years," Justin said.

He could see Bel was trying to do an estimate. *How do I explain the measurement of time and distance*, Justin wondered. Bel finally nodded.

"And the distance from Earth to here?"

"Twelve light-years. One-quarter the distance to the war."

Bel nodded. "Yes, I see now. The Karrin system. That was the Hive you saw."

"And what is this Hive?" Tanya asked.

Bel's assistant picked up the translation and he shook his head, chuckling.

"How will you explain that we're all dead?" the assistant inquired, the translator picking up his comment and converting it to standard English.

Justin tried not to stir, but he felt a tightening in his chest. He suspected that the Tracs, or Gar, or whatever they were called, were not the real threat, that there was something far worse lingering behind the stage.

Bel looked over angrily at his aide; then, composing his features, he looked back at Justin. He started to say something, then fell silent for a moment.

"He's right," Bel finally said calmly, "we're all dead."

"What does that mean?" Tanya interrupted. "I'm missing something here."

"The Hive, at least that's what we call it, lived inward towards the galactic core. I think our years are roughly similar . . . anyway two hundred years ago our time, the Hive started to move in this direction."

"Why?" Justin asked.

"They devour worlds—it's that simple. There are dozens of rival," he hesitated for moment as if thinking about the right word, "nations of the Hive. All of them compete for resources. They move into a system, devour all that they need, then move on. If whoever lives there fully cooperates, labors for them, they are allowed to survive but their world is stripped, polluted, a wreck by the time they are done. The slightest resistance is met with an annihilating attack until the world submits."

Justin looked over at his friends. "Are they the Gar, as you call them?"

"No," Bel laughed and shook his head, "if they were we could deal with them. The Gar are a loose confederation of several dozen worlds, a different race entirely."

"And you are associated with these Gar?"

"This might be difficult to explain," Bel continued. "There is an arc of systems sweeping at nearly a right angle to the galactic core. One end of that arc reaches here. Half a thousand standard years ago the Gar arrived in this system, having found a transit jump."

"Transit jump?"

"The nexus point that enables a leap between stars."

Justin looked over at Matt, who was staring straight at Bel as if the alien were simply discussing the weather.

"You don't understand that, do you?" Bel asked.

"Of course we do," Matt replied in an even voice, and again Bel chuckled.

"Whatever you say. We can talk nexus theory later. The Gar, along with a number of other nations, do have a central House, the Zollern, who dominate all the royal lines and various planet states. In turn the Zollern grant various rights and privileges. Since we are a different race, we were considered a province of the Royal Zollern house until they recognized our free-state status fifty years past."

Justin, listening carefully, was trying to take it all in. It reminded him of a class in Oriental history he had taken at the Academy. The basic facts and incidents of American history were something that he had grown up with, any advanced classes were simply embellishments on the foundation of knowledge. The Oriental history class, in contrast, had been a nightmare. A whole new geography, political philosophy, culture, and worse yet, *names* had to be learned from scratch.

"Why did they not come to us hundreds of years ago as well?" Tanya asked.

"Finding a transit point is tedious. It can take hundreds of years of careful survey. Then go through and there is no telling where one might arrive—maybe jumping several systems away. Apparently no one knew of the access to you until a Gar privateer most likely found it by accident and decided to have a little fun with the locals."

Justin thought of the flash of light over Atlanta. Bel made it sound like a bunch of kids out for a joy ride or the actions of little boy who had decided to play wrathful god with an ant nest.

"I suspect from the design of your ship it was the house of Ya of the Gar clan. They can be amusing in some ways."

"Amusing?" Matt snorted. "Hell, they killed millions on Earth last week and you call that amusing?"

"I'm sorry, a poor choice of words. Immature is more what I was thinking of. I suspect they wanted to come in, take what you had and strip out what they could before the Hive arrived. An unfortunate incident, but to the Gar you were savages to be exploited."

"Savages who kicked their asses," Matt snarled.

"Asses? Oh, I see, amusing," Bel said quietly. "And how many ships have come to you?"

"The first one, over fifty years ago, then two more. The third one we destroyed. Two weeks ago, twenty-seven more."

"And you destroyed all of them."

Justin nodded.

Bel looked over at Darel and again switched off his translator. "Curious. There's been no Gar ship out here, has there?"

"Some years back there was the rumor of one disappearing out here. Maybe they found a transit point right within our system and kept it quiet. Then these barbarians came back through."

"What about the twenty-seven ships?"

"There must be another transit as well, found by the Gar. This is fascinating."

"Like I said," Tanya interjected, "your behavior is rather rude."

Bel did not understand her words with the translator off but her tone was quite readable. He switched his translator back on.

"My apologies."

"This Hive that you mentioned, are you going to fight?" Justin asked.

"The Zollern's first contact with the Hive ambassadors came two hundred years ago. Typical of the Zollern, they negotiated an arrangement and my world was part of that arrangement. Tribute was allowed to be taken from us. At that time we thought they were coming in all their strength, but something diverted them inwards."

"What diverted them?"

"We don't know, though you did see evidence of what happened. Apparently a force closer to the Core attacked them. Rather than move on they turned to fight, a war that lasted generations. It is evident now that the Hive lost and is evacuating, their direction of movement shifting back this way once again. They will come in waves, spread across an area of space a hundred parsecs across. We, your world and mine, are but two small specks in their path."

Justin took the words in, wanting not to believe them, wishing that he could somehow see a deception in Bel's statements. Yet alien that he was, Bel seemed to be decidedly human as well. The translator, which had been improving the longer the conversation lasted, was now clearly picking up tonal inflections. He sensed that Bel's words were genuine. Suddenly the threat of the Gar attack seemed trivial in comparison.

"Can anyone face them?" Matt asked.

"The Gar might put up a fight, but the question is why? What you have is expansion outwards. The Hives tried inward, were defeated and now come back this way again. The Gar will be pushed; they could move, they could fight. The Royal House will negotiate, as it always does."

"Do they, the Zollern, have a military?"

Bel chuckled. "Yes. Ponderous, slow-moving, too many commanders of the royal blood. The one effective force are the Ya. They still have spirit but their numbers . . . ? Nowhere near enough to face the Hives."

"So you don't see much hope then," Justin asked.

Bel smiled but said nothing, and there was a long awkward moment of silence.

"I'm curious about something," Tanya finally interrupted. "The fact that you're like us."

"Did you think you were the only ones then?" Bel asked in disbelief.

"Well, frankly, yeah, we did, at least of our own species," Justin replied a bit defensively, not wanting to add that if he was human he was at best a distant cousin.

Bel looked back at Darel in surprise and then looked back at his guests.

"You had no records, anything of earlier contact?"

"None."

"I wonder if you are the home world," Bel said quietly.

"The what?"

"The home world. How long back, maybe twenty, thirty thousand years ago, we have a belief that something took our ancestors from another world and left them here with the order to labor. You have no such record?"

"None."

"Curious. Perhaps you are where we came from."

"And the others—the Zollern, the Gar, the Hive?"

"Not like us. The Hive—I think the word is insect. The Gar and Zollern the same race, somewhat similar to us. I'll make sure you receive files on them."

Justin said nothing to the last comment. It implied, at least, that Bel would provide additional information and with it perhaps the prospect of release.

Bel looked carefully at the savages. *The damn fools don't have a clue as to what they've done, they simply put the ship back together and then got it running*. This would take some careful consideration, and he found the whole thing to be a very amusing point.

"Time is passing and I have to leave you now," Bel suddenly announced, downing the rest of his tea. "That was good," he said, hoping that the hint would be taken.

Tanya made a show of going to a cabinet, pulling down a container and handing it to him.

"Just put a bag in boiling water. Do you have honey?"

Bel waited while his translating computer paused, whispering what he guessed was a non-related word into his earpiece.

"Are you speaking an endearment to me?"

Tanya laughed.

"No, it is a sweet produced by bees, insects."

His face wrinkled with disdain.

"No, not like the Hive. Smaller, the size of my finger."

Bel shook his head.

She rummaged around the cabinet, knowing that Matt had developed a fondness for the stuff back at the Academy, and war or no war he most likely had a supply. Finding it she passed it over, ignoring Matt's stricken expression.

"Just add a small amount to your drink."

Bel smiled his thanks.

"I'm sorry to have to leave you aboard this ship and not immediately extend to you the courtesy of a visit to our world. First your inoculation has to neutralize any potential diseases you are carrying that might be a threat to us."

"And second, you aren't quite sure what to do with us yet," Justin interjected softly.

Bel looked over at Justin. There was no sense in denying a logical precaution.

"Precisely. I'll be calling on you again soon. If you require anything, call us. I think it best that for now you simply relax, recover from your exciting journey, and stay where you are."

"In other words, if we should try and power up to leave, your response might not be friendly," Justin pressed.

He could see Bel shift uncomfortably.

"Bluntly, yes. We will fire to disable you."

Bowing slightly from the waist, he turned and headed through the airlock, his silent aide following.

As the airlock closed Bel looked over at Darel.

"Your analysis?"

"Kill them."

"I've thought of that."

He looked down at the two containers given to him by Tanya.

"It really is an excellent drink. I'm curious about this honey. Produced from—what did they call them—bees. Most strange."

"Does that mean you are not going to kill them?"

Bel shrugged his shoulder "I think the Hive or the Gar, if they find out they are here, will strike them with or without our permission."

"In our own system?"

"You forget, half a dozen of their heavy attack ships are now hovering in the next system and we don't know what else they've moved in this direction. The Hive will want the world these people came from. The Ya or perhaps even the Zollern might want it as well for a quick looting before the Hive arrives. Beyond that they will be furious for revenge when the discover how these primitives humiliated them. It'd win a point with the Gar if we simply handed them over."

Bel strolled down the corridor and motioned for his nephew to follow him into his private chamber. He stopped for a moment to order the pilot to undock and head back to Cor.

As he settled into an overstuffed chair, he felt the slight bump of contact breaking, followed seconds later by the surge of the engines powering up.

"Make me a cup of this tea," Bel asked.

A bit annoyed at playing the servant, Darel brewed up a mug and poured a thick drop of honey into it, then passed it over to Bel, who inhaled the fragrance.

"Make one for yourself."

Darel made a grimace of disgust.

"It turned my stomach."

Bel laughed.

"You have no sense of the exotic."

"So what are you planning to do?"

"Let me pose this to you. If the Zollern seize their world, which they undoubtedly could do with ease, then a potential ally is lost."

"Ally? Those barbarians?"

"We have to start somewhere. We thought being a free state was such a wonderful move. Now, if what Holzan said is true, it was all a setup, a trade point to the Hive."

"And the Hive, what of them?"

"These barbarians, or should I say 'people,' arrived at a fortuitous moment. Perhaps there is opportunity here."

"For what?"

Bel smiled, saying nothing, and thoughtfully sipped his tea.

✧ Chapter VII ✧

Holzan di Zollern looked up with surprise. For Bel Varna
to come calling at this ghastly hour was indeed curious
and obviously done in the hope of avoiding notice. Holzan
tightened the cincher to his night robe and motioned Bel
over to a chair by the fireplace.

It was one of the things Cor had in common with the
Imperial world, a climate that in winter brought heavy
snows, though for Cor with its smaller orbital inclination
and greater distance from its sun it seemed as if winter
was damn near year round. Though a fireplace was
primitive, it triggered some ancient instinct that was
appealing. He deliberately kept his sleeping quarters chilled
in order to better enjoy the heat radiating from the crackling
flame.

"Cold night?" Holzan asked, trying to sound friendly
to this man whom he knew was his most masterful foe.

"Looks like more snow."

"It's a most unusual time to be calling, Bel," Holzan
said as his visitor settled into a chair by the fire, extending
his hands and rubbing them near the flames.

Strange race, Holzan thought. So animal-looking and
the hair—disgusting! Yet there was a certain appeal to
them in a simple sort of way. Fiercely loyal to their friends,

almost like the Gar in that respect. Intellectually curious as well. Since the Great Leap and the reaching of what was perceived to be a finite understanding of the physical universe, many thought intellectualism was a cold and empty wall that could never be scaled. The pursuit of esthetics, the seeking of finely crafted beauty, was the pursuit of one of royal blood. Bel and his race called that effete. Holzan smiled at the thought, looking at the crackling fire, enjoying the scent of woodsmoke.

Bel was silent for a moment, staring into the fire and Holzan wondered if one of his race could see the beauty as he did.

"We need to talk," Bel finally said.

"It's important enough for the leader of the anti-Dynasty forces to drop in unannounced?"

Bel smiled. "I really don't like that term, you know. I never really saw myself as against your family. Rather, I was attempting to protect the interests of my own world."

Holzan chuckled. "You have the Hive on your doorstep and managed to antagonize the Royal House of Zollern at the same time—not an enviable situation."

"Holzan, from this system there are transit points to ten different worlds in your system, all of them ruled by some rather influential members of the Diet. You can't let Cor fall to the Hive."

Bel smiled. It was also the strength of their world, since all ten of the families found it so convenient to have a free state on their border with whom they could trade under the table without Zollern interference. He did not add that as of today he knew of an eleventh gate as well.

"You won't fall to the Hive, it will only be a temporary inconvenience."

"And suppose they turn in your direction? You've only struck a deal with the Golden Hive, there are dozens more to contend with."

"Ah, but the Golden Hive is the strongest."

"And thus to be feared the most. I'm willing to bet handsomely that there are other members of the Diet who see this concession not as a buyoff to keep the Hive away but rather as punishment for our free-state status. I think you are setting yourselves up for destruction as well."

"I doubt that."

"This is a key strategic point, Holzan. From here the Hive can move in any direction."

"They'll move off into the wilds from here. They're meticulous, machine-like. They will sweep every bit of your system until they find more gates and then they will be gone. Why fight us when there are thousands of uninhabited worlds for the taking farther on, once they find the path to them?"

"Because the territory controlled by the Zollern is mapped, that's why," Bel replied sharply. "No searching for transit points, just a straight-in move. Could you really resist that if you were in their position?"

"There are more ways to resist than by simply fighting."

"Tell me, is the Diet fully aware of this agreement?"

"There was no need. After all, your free-state status was granted directly by the Zollern and not the Diet. It is not their concern."

Bel smiled. The dance of neutrality required that at least one side wanted his world to stay intact. If no one cared, and simply saw it as a payoff to the Hive, then they were doomed. He looked closely at Holzan, trying to gauge how much truth was behind his words, and felt the chill grow.

Holzan smiled, extending his beefy, scaly hands in a friendly gesture.

"I would hate, of course, to see anything unpleasant develop out of this temporary occupation," he said with a chuckle. "I admit that on a very personal level you and your people do vex me with your obsession for independence. It amazes me, Bel, considering that of all the forces in this universe you turned your back on us who are, by far, the most moderate."

"Except when it comes to religious freethinkers."

"A minor squabble. Come now, Bel, we all pay lip service to the Holy Orders, at least we of the ruling classes."

"I wonder if you would say that before the Kaza Zollern."

"He is a zealot."

"When a zealot sits upon a royal throne he is a danger, and those beneath him must dance to his tune."

"The Diet checks his excesses. You must admit that at least your beliefs were tolerated under us."

"And penalized by taxation, tariff restrictions, and constant threats. We've done better on our own."

"Better? Your current situation is one I would not want."

Bel took a deep breath and then made his stab. "There is something hidden behind this agreement, Holzan."

"What, pray tell?"

"Could it be that you actually want the Hives to move into your flank? There is no love lost between your family and others of the Diet. We both know the strategic significance of this planet and its transit points. Suppose the Hive does move towards the Ya, the Morincara. The houses that are your biggest problem in the Diet would thus be caught between a rock and a hard place."

"What? What do rocks have to do with this?"

Bel smiled. "That is why we sought our independence, because we were sick of the maneuverings in the Diet for royal favor."

"I think those days are over, Bel."

Holzan made a dramatic flourish of hesitating for a moment. Bel stilled his breathing. Something was coming.

"Is your visit related to the arrival here of a courier ship for me from the Imperial court?" Holzan asked casually, while examining his manicure.

That was only partially the truth but Bel nodded. The ship from the Zollern court had docked while he had been away examining the barbarians. Of course he was curious about the latest dispatches and what they might contain regarding to the impending crisis.

"Bel, you must realize that you are but one very small gear in a vast machine of diplomacy. There is the Hive, which is of immediate concern to my family. There are the various factions within the Diet, the Loern, Ya, Barthu, and all the others. Beyond that there are the Shun and their cult of self-annihilation threatening our other border. Beyond that border and the Shun there are yet other threats such as the Perjordin. And after the Hive departs, what is behind them? We know the Hive was defeated. That therefore means there is even a larger threat. You and your concerns about Cor, my friend, are of only minor consequence at the moment."

"They are the center of *my* universe, though," Bel snapped back angrily.

"We can make sure that you, your family, and those who are sympathetic to the needs of the House of Zollern will be taken care of."

"In other words, sell out my people and accept the arrival of the Hive."

"Bel, how long have we known each other?"

"Years, twenty at least."

"Would you call me a friend?" Holzan asked, and there was actually a note of concern in his voice.

"On a personal level, yes."

Holzan chuckled. Standing, he went over to an open cabinet and pulled out a bottle of Vacallin brandy. He uncorked it, then poured two glasses and handed one to Bel, who nodded his thanks.

"What I just said was not meant to dishonor you, Bel. We're all caught in this game and I'm afraid your world will come out the loser. If you want I can make arrangements for you and those close to you to find somewhere else to live."

"Thank you, but you know I can't do that."

"Your stiff-necked pride?" Holzan sighed. "Those who wish to survive must learn to abandon pride when necessary."

"Without pride there is no reason for living."

Holzan sighed, "Without life there is no pride."

Bel sipped his brandy. "A fine drink, this," he whispered.

"I'll have one of my servants deliver a case to your home."

"Thank you."

"Bel, do you believe me when I tell you that I tried to find another way for your world?"

Bel looked at him and finally nodded. "Yes, I can believe that, but you are, nevertheless, of the Zollern line, and the wishes of your family and my world are in direct opposition."

"Be reasonable, Bel, there is no longer an alternative."

"There must be!"

"I'm not authorized to tell you this," Holzan finally began with a staged conspiratorial whisper, "but you'll know anyway in a matter of days. Another piece of the game was made clear in today's dispatches."

"And that is?"

"The Kaza signed an alliance agreement with the Shun two ten-days ago. The alliance calls for the immediate opening of hostilities against the Perjordin. Action has already begun with a Shun offensive of well over two thousand assault ships and twenty-five of their ground-attack legions into Perjordin space. The offensive started today on the other side of our realm, at least that was the plan. The offensive is aimed at their capital and is expected to break through."

Bel sat back in his chair and exhaled noisily.

"Madness. Absolute madness. The Hive is on your border—that is who you should be preparing to face, not the damnable Shun!"

"And what of the Perjordin? They did not expect us to attack first, yet they indeed were planning to attack us while we were diverted. It had to be done and that is why there is no consideration, at this point, of resisting the Hive."

Bel looked over at Holzan and sensed that the ambassador was reading his thoughts.

"The alliance will never hold," Bel said quietly. "No alliance with the Shun ever has, their fanaticism prevents it. Strip your front with them and they'll be down your throats when they sense the time is right to trade sides. They've never honored a treaty with those they believe to be infidels and they never will."

"It'll hold long enough for them to divert the Perjordin. Word of the attack will reach the Perjordin capital within twenty standard days after the attack begins. We'll secure the frontier beyond the border, sweeping up a dozen systems up to twenty light-years outward, deny it to them and then move in towards their space as they withdraw. That will give us the buffer, so that if needs be we can later strip that front to meet the Hive if they should decide to betray our agreement."

"So that is what we now are—just a pawn to buy a little time for your grabs elsewhere? I sense, Holzan, that in the end you expect to fight the Hive and my system will be the battleground."

"I don't think it will come to that, Bel Varna."

Bel tried one last bid though he already knew it was futile.

"In spite of what you've said about the reason behind the granting of free-state status, we both know it has created tremendous profit for many in your family. Without your stifling restrictions and ancient laws we have become the bankers of worlds. Untold wealth has poured through our system and into your hands. You yourself, my friend, have been a beneficiary of that largess."

Holzan shifted uncomfortably. Cor, which lacked so many things, had made its wealth on the support of smuggling, the transfer of illegal goods, the washing of soiled money and "making it white" as the business was called. Being the ambassador to Cor had made Holzan fabulously rich; turning a blind eye to demands from the Royal Court to investigate where money was flowing illegally out of the control of the Zollern had proved lucrative for him.

"You will lose that, you know."

"It can not be helped now. I think you should know, my friend, that there will be a freeze on the exporting of assets into systems under our control in the very near future. The very near future."

Bel nodded his thanks for that warning. "Holzan, what if we should choose to resist on our own?" Bel ventured.

"Bel, are you mad? How many ships do you have? Ten capital ships, fifteen? Maybe a hundred smaller craft? You'd be swarmed under in a day. Would you really embark on such suicide?"

"It's being considered by some."

"Then, as a demonstration of good faith to the Hive," Holzan sighed, "you will fight us as well."

"Would you engage in such madness?"

"No need to, Bel, for you see we have assigned a security force to this system to ensure that nothing unpleasant happens until the Hive moves in. If you should offer resistance that force will suppress it and the Hive will never even be aware of your defiance."

"*What?*"

"The Viceroy of Avla will arrive shortly with his personal fleet to insure the proper transfer of power and to make sure nothing unpleasant occurs that might provoke the Hive."

Holzan almost felt pity at the obvious shock this bit of information caused.

"So tell me, Bel Varna, what exactly are you planning to do?"

"Survive."

"Given your approach during these negotiations, I see that as rather unlikely at the moment. The Viceroy has a particular disdain for your family. I would imagine that you and your clan are high on the list of people he wishes to visit once the fighting is over, if you should decide to resist."

"There will be no fighting," Bel said quietly.

"Oh, really? Say that again, please, I don't think I heard you right," and Holzan made a dramatic flourish of cupping his hand to his ear. "You mean the Viceroy will be frightened away by what you call a fleet."

"It was good enough to win our independence and keep you off our backs for the last fifty years."

Holzan stiffened slightly. "If that is why you've come here, to insult me and the Imperium, then I think this interview is at an end. I leave for the Imperial court tomorrow."

Holzan started to stand up and Bel wearily extended his hand for him to stop.

"No, my old friend. No. I've come to offer terms."

"Terms? It is either agreement or war—you are no longer in a position to negotiate."

Bel lowered his head. He could imagine his grandfather standing beside him, sickened that a descendent of his was agreeing to sign away the independence of his people.

Patience, grandfather, war and politics, advance and retreat, one and the same.

"We will agree to your terms and the right of the Hive to occupy our space," Bel whispered. "I've already talked to Norru and he sees no other alternative as well. You can tell the Viceroy there will be no resistance when he arrives."

Holzan smiled expansively. "Such an agreement is to our mutual benefit, my friend."

Holzan raised his glass. "To our understanding, then."

"It is not an understanding," Bel replied. "Let us just call it an arrangement for the moment."

"Always so dour, you Varna are all alike. You know, I'm really quite glad this has been concluded successfully. Beyond our friendship, I saw this as a professional challenge. How to save you from your own stiff-necked pride."

"Why all the bother?" Bel asked. "Given what you just told me, Avla could have taken us within ten days of fighting and then turned what was left over to the Hive."

"It would have turned into a massacre and frankly, that really would not have looked all that good for everyone concerned. Beyond that, we prefer to win through persuasion rather than fighting. Too messy and unpredictable! Dare I quote your grandfather regarding the unpredictability of war? Really, I abhor warfare, such a waste."

Bel, finishing his drink, stood up. "The Pratas will meet this morning at the usual time. Your presence is requested to sign the accord."

"Ah, the official message to attend, that is why you came. Thank you, Prata Bel, I shall attend."

Bel bowed stiffly and turned to leave.

"Oh, by the way, while I have you here, a question."

Bel looked back, half-suspecting what it would be.

"That ship that arrived on the far side of your system yesterday?"

"Yes."

"What was it?"

Bel looked closely at Holzan. Was this a trap?

"Why are you concerned? Must we already answer for every vessel that makes a port call here?"

"It just seemed unusual. I had a report that you went out there yourself and that it was stopped near one of your outer bases."

"Just a Gar ship, that's all."

"So why the interest, that you had to go there?"

"We were concerned that they might have violated quarantine. Their captain refused to be boarded for inspection and I didn't want an incident with the Gar, so I handled it myself. You know the old saying about if you want something done right."

Holzan nodded finally.

"Thank you. I didn't mean to intrude."

"No bother," and Bel left the room.

They didn't yet know, he thought, keeping his features fixed in a frown for the surveillance holo cams which he knew would be evaluated later for possible clues as to what he was thinking when he left.

The course he must now set had at last become clear, and he suspected that even his grandfather would approve.

"Mind if I join you?"

Tanya looked up from her chair behind the navigation board and nodded for Justin to sit next to her.

"What've you been up to?"

"Just fooling around with the system, trying to figure it out," she replied, rubbing her eyes.

Justin was a bit annoyed at her for letting him sleep through what should have been his watch.

"You two looked beat. I thought I'd give you a break."

"Well, you're just as tired, so don't try the mothering routine on me."

She gave him a quick smile.

"Me, mothering? Don't be absurd."

He smiled and shook his head. Through the years he had often wondered why she had never married, had a family. On the occasions when she was in a holo news feature, involved with some bilateral negotiation, he had always tried to look closely, to see if there was finally a ring on her hand.

"How come you never married, Tanya?" he blurted out, astonished that the words had slipped out of him.

She looked at him, a bit surprised, and he felt a stab of pleasure at having obviously caught her off-guard for a moment.

"No time," she replied a bit too quickly. "Have you forgotten there was a war on?"

"Hell, war doesn't put a stop to that, usually the number of marriages goes up."

"Dumb fools, they meet somebody on a three-day pass, lose their heads, get married. Survival of one's genes, that's all it is, have a baby before you get killed. And if they survive, when it's over they find themselves staring at a stranger. Not me."

"Never quite heard it put so clinically," Justin said quietly.

"Why the interest, Justin?"

"Oh, just curious."

There was a moment of awkward silence.

"What about you, Bell?"

"Too busy, I guess. Several of the cruises I was on lasted a couple of years each with no port calls, and I guess I just got used to being alone."

"Weren't there women aboard the ships who might have been interesting?"

He shrugged his shoulders "I was in command on the last two cruises, and you know the rules."

She shook her head. "Rules never stopped that kind of thing," she said.

Again there was the silence and Justin regretted having even started the conversation.

"Wasn't there anyone?"

There was, but as he looked at her he found that he didn't want to talk about it. Lisa was dead and that had finished his desire ever to become involved with someone in the service again. As he looked over at Tanya he found her presence disturbing, even after all these years. She was, after all, the first. It had been far too brief and through the years the memory of it had become wrapped up in a golden haze of first love, youth, and fantasies of what might have been. All of the rougher side of Tanya, the domineering personality, the aggressiveness, the intolerance for anyone not as capable as she, had disappeared in his memory. The fact that they had once had an affair should have seemed absurd to him—instead it was a warm memory he still clung to and now she was sitting beside him again. As he looked at her he had a flash memory of how she looked in the morning, curled up and asleep by his side, her features relaxed into childlike innocence.

He wanted to reach out and touch her and drop all the years away. He looked at her and she quickly turned away.

"I've been fooling around with this nav system," she said, her words coming too fast. "I think I've managed to figure some things out."

"Tanya?"

She looked back at him and then lowered her eyes.

"Let's not talk about it, Justin. It happened a long time ago and far too much has happened since. We can't go back to that."

Nerving himself, he reached out and touched her on the shoulder and she looked up at him, startled.

"Don't," and her voice came out in a whisper.

"Why not?"

"Because if we get out of this, we'll go our separate ways

again. It hurt too much last time. I don't want it to happen again. I don't need it and I don't want it."

He let his hand drop.

She forced a quick smile.

"I'm sorry."

"Don't apologize, Justin, you know I can't stand that."

He tried to smile. She was playing her role again, the role she had maintained since the first day he met her, ordering everyone else around, and he had to laugh softly.

"Don't you ever get tired of your act?"

"It usually works, doesn't it?"

"Yeah, but lord, can it get tiresome."

"It keeps me safe."

"You two having fun?"

Justin looked over his shoulder, startled, as Matt came into the forward cockpit carrying a tray and three cups of tea. He could see the curious look in his friend's eyes and wondered yet again if something had happened between Tanya and him. A bit flustered, Tanya got out of her chair and took the tray.

"I was just telling Bell here that I think I got some answers on the nav system."

"Oh, really?"

She ignored the tone in his voice. She set the tray down, then took a mug and sipped at it while climbing back in her chair. Matt looked over at Justin with a raised eyebrow and Justin angrily shook his head while taking his cup. As he tasted it he once again found the craving for a good drink washing over him. Drying out was getting a bit tedious and he felt that he was at the point where an occasional drink wouldn't be all that dangerous anymore. What really annoyed him was that Matt had made a point of keeping the flask given to him by Bel and refused to divulge its hiding place. It was really rather embarrassing that an old friend had to treat him like a reforming alcoholic and stash the bottles away.

"Also, I managed to hook into what I think is a commercial holo channel from Cor," and Tanya motioned to a holo display mounted on the bulkhead to her right. "I can't understand a word they're saying, but you sure can guess something important is up."

Justin looked up at the screen, noticing it for the first time. The scene was of a plaza, the buildings lining it looking almost baroque. The plaza was packed to overflowing, with someone addressing the crowd from a balcony. Nearly everyone was dressed alike, heavy black coats and hats pulled down over ears and foreheads to ward off the cold. The clothing was somber, the only ornamentation an occasional show of lace at the sleeves or thin traces of silver thread embroidery around the shoulders and collars.

"I think it's a newscast that someone is voicing over. I saw Bel for a moment—at least I think it was him. Hell, it's hard to tell them apart in those heavy coats."

"Anything about us?" Matt asked.

"My, we certainly have an ego."

"No, seriously. I mean if someone had arrived in our system like we did, it'd be on the news," Justin replied, defending his friend's question.

"Yeah, I thought about that," Tanya finally replied. "Nothing as far as I could see, though maybe I missed it. It's kind of hard to keep your attention focused hour after hour when you don't understand what the hell they're saying."

"Are you recording this? A good linguist program should be able to crack their language pretty damn quick."

"Been saving everything."

"Wish Madison Smith was aboard, she'd go nuts over this," Matt said quietly.

Justin nodded. Madison was one of the few cadets from their class who had truly managed not to get involved in the war, resigning her commission to work at the Mars archaeological site, specializing in translating the fragments of written records found there which dated back more than a million years.

"What do you think's happening?" Matt asked, leaning over to watch the screen.

"Something's gone wrong. You can see it. The crowd isn't happy. By the way, crying seems universal as well. There was more than one shot of people in tears."

"The war that Bel talked about."

"I think so. There were some cutaways to other news. Some of the most bizarre-looking planets, people, one of them a double star system with two suns low on the horizon and obviously hotter than hell. I'll tell you, a couple of the shots scared the shit out of me."

She looked back at the screen.

"Look, there's one of them again."

Justin leaned forward to watch and felt a cold chill. In the far background of the shot what he assumed was a cityscape filled the horizon. It looked dark, foreboding. The scale was difficult to grasp, the buildings rising up like dark beehive domes that seemed to tower thousands of feet into the gray sky. He suddenly realized that the foreground was filled with insectoid forms, hundreds of thousands, perhaps millions, all of them standing rigid in perfectly straight lines.

"What the shit is that?" Matt whispered.

"Yeah, it's chilling. They don't move . . . listen to that!"

Behind the narration there was an eerie chant, a long drawn-out tone that quavered, rose and then fell and it sent a chill corkscrewing down his back. The camera pulled back and, moving into the foreground, a high dais appeared, again filled with more gray forms. However, now there were splashes of scarlet and other forms writhing.

"They're burning people alive," Tanya whispered.

The image faded to be replaced by the blackness of space, though Justin could not force the nightmare image out of his mind. What was it? An execution, a ritual?

"Bastards!"

Justin looked over at Matt and saw the rage in his friend's eyes. For a second he felt that rage was directed at him as well, the memory of Bradbury coming back.

Justin wanted to say something but knew it was useless. Matt's features finally softened.

"Hell, I thought they'd be at least a bit ahead of us out here," Matt whispered sadly.

Justin looked back at the screen as the camera turned, the Milky Way drifting across the screen, and then he suddenly realized that it was not the Milky Way he was looking at. It was ships, thousands upon thousands of ships. The camera closed in, the narration growing more excited.

Justin looked at the image, wide-eyed. Though he had nothing to judge them against, they were obviously made for war, weapons pods bristling, the hulls of the ships studded with turrets. In the center of the swarm he guessed that he was looking at a type of carrier, smaller ships emerging from launch ramps.

He sat back, chin resting on clenched hands, awed by the sight. The service had just started to experiment with carriers in the last few years of the war, with vessels capable of hauling, servicing and launching a dozen *Bormann-* or *Grecko*-class fighters, but from the scale of it, it looked like these ships were capable of carrying hundreds.

The image faded replaced again by what he figured were man-in-the-street type interviews. All the faces were somber, careworn. If there was a war on, at least these folks seemed to have the right approach, he thought. They looked like they were going to a funeral rather the usual crap of cheering mobs and parades.

A comm channel on Tanya's board came to life, an image appearing on the screen. Justin looked at the screen. It was Bel Varna.

"I'm coming in to dock. May I have permission to come aboard your ship?"

"Permission granted," Matt replied quickly and the image faded.

Matt looked over at his friends.

"He certainly is jumping back and forth. What do you think it's about?"

"Obviously we're tied into this war. One of a couple of things—either he'll hand us over to someone else or let us go."

"Well, that doesn't seem very logical," Justin replied softly. "His best bet is to keep us here."

"If he was going to do that, he wouldn't be coming aboard," Tanya replied.

"Hell, they might just have him send the signal to us to make us think he's on the other side. We already know the guy and they figure we won't resist if he asks to come aboard for a friendly little chat. We open the door, and bang! There are a bunch of thugs with guns waiting for us."

"You're really so trusting, Matt."

"I learned how to be that way a long time ago," he announced.

"Well, what alternative do you have?" Tanya asked coolly.

"Let's just fire up and run for it."

"Yeah, right, Everett. Have you forgotten there are half a dozen ships picketed around us, and I dare say they're better at flying and fighting than we are."

"Don't write us off that easy, Leonov," Matt replied sharply. "Justin and I were damn good twenty years ago and even better now."

"She's got a point," Justin interjected. "We only figured out how this thing even turned by accident. There's most likely a lot more we don't know yet. I guess we're going to have to just hang out and wait to see what he does."

Matt sat down grumbling in his chair, cursing under his breath.

"While we've been debating this, he's damn near alongside," Matt finally said, "so I guess you guys have won, but so help me, if we're taken prisoner or killed I'll never forgive you two. Shit, if you hadn't of come back into my life I wouldn't even be in this fix now."

"Thanks for the confidence," Justin snapped coldly. "Look, I didn't ask for this, I got stuck with it."

"Well, screw you too," Matt growled.

"Will both of you shut the hell up, they're docking."

Justin felt the bump of a docking collar attaching to the side of their ship.

"So who's going to open the door and let him in, because I sure as hell am not."

Cursing, Tanya got out of her seat and went aft.

Justin looked over at Matt.

"We're kind of stuck with it. We'd better go aft."

"I just don't like my fate being in someone else's hands."

"We agreed to that the day we joined the Academy, or have you forgotten?"

"No, but that was different."

Matt sighed and finally stood up.

"The problem is, if it *is* OK then she was right, and I just can't stand that sometimes."

Justin, shaking his head, put his hand on Matt's shoulder and the two followed after her.

Bel Varna stepped through the airlock alone and saw the woman waiting for him, her two companions stepping up behind her. He could sense their tension, the hesitant, expectant look in the eyes of the two men. They were fighters, that was obvious, just by the way they stood poised and ready to spring.

"So how's the war going?" one of them asked.

A bit taken aback, he said nothing for a moment.

"We were able to watch one of your holo stations broadcasting the information," Tanya said, looking back over her shoulder with a flash of anger.

"Far too complex to even try to explain right now," Bel finally said.

"Are we your prisoners?" Matt asked, and Bel could sense that an affirmative would most likely mean that he would die.

"If you'll look behind me, you'll see no guards," Bel replied. "I am a diplomat and politician, not a jailer sent to lock you up. Is that what you expected?"

"If the situation was reversed, what do you think we would do?" Justin asked. "We're an unknown factor. From what little you told me it's best that we aren't allowed to go back to tell our people what's coming."

"It would have been safer for me if I did so," Bel replied, feeling somewhat put out. "But in all honesty you might be useful to us." Surprised at his own candor and without waiting for an invitation he went over to the table where he had shared their tea last time and sat down wearily. The events of the last two days were taking their toll.

"Can I get you something to drink?" Tanya asked. "Some tea, perhaps?"

Bel looked up at her and smiled.

"My thanks to you, yes."

Tanya pulled the steaming mug out of the microwave, hesitated for a second, looking over at Justin, and then reached into a cabinet down near the floor. She fished around in the back and pulled out the flask, then gestured to ask if she should put some in.

Bel watched her and saw the quick exchange of looks. So, the one with the name almost like his had a problem with drinking and his friends were hiding it. Yet of the three, he was obviously the one to whom the other two turned for decisions. Curious.

"Once I depart from your ship, you are to immediately turn around and leave for your home world."

Matt visibly relaxed.

"So that's it? Just get the hell out of here, is that it?"

His translator stumbled on the world "hell" for a moment, finally producing the Shun word for the torment of eternity without being assimilated into the one.

"Hey, five minutes ago you were set to fight if he didn't let us go," Tanya snapped.

Bel chuckled at the exchange and Tanya looked over at him, embarrassed by her outburst.

"In a very short time our system will be occupied by an advance guard of the Zollern Dynasty," Bel announced. "Supposedly they are here to insure transfer of our world to the Hive, though there might be a hidden game within all of this. All I can tell you for sure is that a balance of power that lasted for hundreds of years is unraveling, and it is safe to assume that this will soon involve you as well."

"So you're letting us go to pass the word, is that it?" Justin asked.

Bel nodded.

"Why?"

"Because I expect you to fight, that's why."

Tanya wearily shook her head and sat down.

"With what? What you called a raid damn near overwhelmed us."

Matt looked over at her in dismay for revealing just how vulnerable they were.

"Look, who's kidding who here?" Tanya snapped. "He downloaded our computer, so they can figure it out themselves. I'm not revealing something he doesn't already know."

"You weren't prepared last time, you weren't expecting it. This time you'll be ready."

"So why are you doing this?" Matt asked suspiciously.

"To put a thorn in the side of everyone, that's why."

"Are you going to fight them?"

Bel hesitated for a moment.

"No."

"Oh, I get it. You sit it out and set us up to do the deed," Matt snapped back angrily.

"You don't understand."

"So please enlighten me," Matt replied sarcastically.

"Our resistance would accomplish nothing more than a brief delay, and in the end we would be occupied, our merchant fleet confiscated, our world garrisoned."

He thought for a moment of telling them what an occupation by the Viceroy Avla would mean if he should become hostile but decided not to.

"Whoever comes your way, the Zollern, the Hive, they're not expecting resistance. Most of the systems are not even inhabited."

"What about these people called the Gar?"

Bel smiled. "I'll talk to them. Others might not even know what happened yet. Remember, news travels only as fast as the fastest ship. If the ship that pursued you survived it would only now be getting back to its home world."

"It took what only seemed like seconds from when we started to jump until we arrived here," Tanya said quietly.

Bel smiled. Could they really be that primitive?

"I would estimate that from your system it's five standard days. In the last instant before you achieve jump, you accelerate to light-speed. Time distortion sets in. Thus, just to get word across several systems might take fifteen, even thirty days or more. It could be a dozen ten-days or more before a response occurs."

"Just how does this damn thing work then," Justin blurted out, "because we sure as hell don't know."

Again he could see the exchange of angry looks towards Justin. So he had decided to be candid and the others did not approve.

Remarkable, simply remarkable, and Bel chuckled softly.

"You people amaze me. We'll worry about that later, I don't have the time to tell you how it works. For that matter, I don't think I can even begin to explain it."

"So we can get a response from someone, though, within a relatively short period of time. Oh, that gives us plenty of time," Matt snorted.

"Or we could just throw in the towel," Tanya said quietly. "It's better than getting annihilated."

"Throw in the towel?"

"A metaphor for surrender."

Curious turn of words and he wondered where it came from.

"As a primitive world—" and he saw them bristle. "Pardon me, but to the Zollern or the Hive that is how you appear. You will be occupied, space travel even within your own system will be denied. Your system will become a base to be fought over if the other side should ever launch a counteroffensive. Your people will be in the middle and you will lose everything. It is part of an historical process when more advanced cultures encounter ones that are more primitive."

He saw them bristle again and this time a touch of anger welled up.

"Stop your foolish display of pride," he snapped angrily. "I am simply speaking the truth. No matter what you think of yourselves, you have no idea of the powers confronting you. Each of the other empires occupies hundreds of worlds, they command fleets of thousands of fighting ships that are capable of extending their power against any who are not as strong. You sit wrapped in your conceit and yet you admit you don't even have a shadow of understanding about how your ship even works. Such things were mastered by others thousands of years ago. If you and your people wish to survive in this universe you must learn all that you can master. You must fight with cunning or quite simply you will die, your world reduced to a bone which others will fight over and then finally abandon."

The room was silent for a moment.

"So what do we do?" Tanya finally asked softly.

Bel reached into his pocket and slid a small lacquered box across the table.

"This ship is of Gar design. When you rebuilt it, did you change any of the computer systems?"

"No," Matt replied and then hesitated, "at least we don't think so."

Bel motioned for them to follow him forward. Stopping at an access hatch just aft of the forward cockpit he stopped, opened it up and peered intently inside. Bel opened the lacquered box and pulled out a small translucent cube, then slipped it in. He then went forward, climbed into Tanya's seat and ran his fingers across the screen.

"It appears to have fed in," Bel announced. "Remarkable, you mimicked the design almost exactly.

"I've loaded into your main computer technical knowledge related to the design of this ship and all systems aboard it. I've also included information on standard weapons systems, tactical and strategic doctrine, and various defensive countermeasures. You'll find a translator based upon the system used by this machine." He pointed to the small translator clipped to his shoulder. "Also, a weapons crew is even now mounting the latest Gar-designed anti-ship strike missiles onto the weapons pylons outside your ship. Please don't activate them while still in our system, as they're rather difficult to stop once they've been launched. Take them back, strip them down and build replicas. That should give you something to go on."

The three of them looked at him, stunned.

"You still haven't answered a key question," Matt said quietly.

"And that is?"

"Why?"

Bel chuckled.

"I have my own reasons and they are in part related to Cor. Slow the Hive down, throw their plan into disarray, even if only briefly. That will help achieve what I want and that is all I'm going to say. I'm also putting a certain trust here as well. Needless to say, if word should ever get back to the Zollern or to a certain Viceroy of my help, it will go poorly for me, so let us just say that this information was already aboard the ship, and the Gar pilot stupidly failed to purge his system before attempting to self-destruct. You'll find that your antimatter fuel tanks have been refilled as well. Now kindly leave here."

Without another word Bel climbed out of the seat, then turned and headed for the airlock.

"Thank you."

He turned and looked back. Tanya came up and touched him lightly on the shoulder. He felt a slight thrill, for after all she was a woman from a savage world and who knew what practices they might indulge in. He was even more startled when she leaned over and kissed him on the cheek.

"I doubt if we shall see each other again. Your chances are not all that good, and as for me, I am going elsewhere for awhile. Safe journey to you. Power up and leave once my ship is cleared."

The airlock slid shut behind him.

The three looked at each other in awe.

"We've just been given the universe!" Matt chortled excitedly, "Damn, I knew he'd do it."

Justin sighed, realizing what had just been done, feeling overwhelmed. He had hoped that once this mission was done he could get out. But there was no hope of that now. They had him, and deep down he knew as well that even if he was offered a chance to get out he wouldn't take it. A thousand years of struggle for knowledge had just been handed to them inside a small cube that could rest in the palm of his hand, and he had to find out what was in it.

✧ Chapter VIII ✧

Exuberant, Justin leaned over and slapped Matt on the back as he finished powering down *Prometheus*.

"We made it. Damn it all, we made it!"

Matt sighed and settled back in his chair, looking at Justin and then back to Tanya with a happy grin.

"The mad thing flies like a charm. Let's fuel her up and take her back out for another spin."

"Like hell," Tanya said wearily, shaking her head. "Look, guys, it's been great making history but one trip like that's enough for me. All I want to do is download the data and get the hell off this ship."

Justin looked back through the forward view screen. The light on the far side of the hangar went from flashing yellow to green, indicating that the hangar was now fully pressurized. Unbuckling from his chair, he started aft to the crew quarters to pack his few belongings and was surprised to find that Tanya had followed him.

"What are you going to do?" she asked, her voice filled with concern.

"You heard my orders. An official courier ship of the United Nations is docked on the other side of this Skyhook Tower and I'm to report aboard for transit back to Earth."

"Don't do it."

Justin laughed and shook his head. "I have to, it's orders."

"To hell with your damn orders. If it were a Corps ship that'd be one thing. This is the UN government we're talking about. Defect, Justin. Hell, you yourself admitted your sympathies are more with the Colonials now."

Justin smiled sadly and shook his head. "I promised Mahan I'd come back once my job was done. Well, I'm finished here. We test flew this bird and the damn thing works. I did more than I hoped to do and I've got to go back."

"She's right, Justin. The Corps no longer answers directly to the UN. The hell with them."

Justin looked up and saw the anxiety on his old friend's face.

"Now don't you start that with me as well," Justin said quietly while he finished packing up his flight bag.

"Look, Justin, I just talked to Seay on a secured downlink. He said that if you want to defect you'll have asylum here on Mars."

Justin laughed softly and shook his head.

"And trigger a major diplomatic incident? I'm sorry, I can't do that. Technically the service indirectly answers to the United Nations. Unless I receive a direct order from Mahan to the contrary, I have to go. Look, I really don't want to go—I'd rather stay here with you two and see what that Bel character gave us. But I gave a promise to Mahan to come back and I've got to live with that. Besides, there's a hell of a lot more riding on this. Someone has to tell those fools back there exactly what we're facing. Maybe they'll listen to me since I was out there and actually saw what was going on. We've got to get our act together on all sides if we're to stand a chance. That's why I've got to go."

Matt smiled. "That's exactly what Seay told me you'd say."

Matt shyly extended his hand. "Take care of yourself, roomie."

"You too, sailor."

Justin took Matt's hand and fought down the choking sensation in the back of his throat. As he let go of Matt's hand he turned to face Tanya, not sure of what to say.

She looked at him and he was surprised to see tears in her eyes. She tried to say something, then turned and fled back to the forward cockpit.

"Damn, first time I ever left her speechless," Justin whispered.

"That's a minor miracle."

Justin hoisted his bag, then went to the airlock door and punched it open. The hangar was already starting to fill up with the curious who stood about gawking at the ship. As he stepped out of the ship he felt the momentary tumble in his stomach as he left the artificial gravity of the ship for the zero gravity of the hangar, which was attached to the one Skyhook Tower still operational on Mars.

Pushing off, he floated across the open chamber, reaching the far door where a Colonial marine motioned him over.

"Captain Bell?"

"That's me."

The marine looked past Justin back to the ship.

'You really flew her to another system, sir?"

"Most certainly did."

The marine grinned and extended his hand.

Justin shook it, a bit surprised by the awe in the young man's eyes. Something told him that what he had just accomplished was historical, perhaps even as important as Armstrong and Aldrin, or Thorsson and his own grandfather going to Mars back in '25. But that was history. It was strange to think that his name might actually be remembered for this, and the thought comforted him. He could put the fear that he would be remembered only for the Bradbury Incident behind him.

"I've been detailed to escort you to the ship that's waiting for you, sir," the marine said, the look of wonder still in his eyes as he stared at Justin and then gazed back at *Prometheus*.

"Well, lead the way, then."

Justin followed him down the corridor, making their way past the crowd of people moving to grab a glimpse of the Gar ship. They finally reached an airlock door.

"They're hooked up on the other side, sir."

"Thanks."

The man looked at him closely.

"Sir. Good luck. I'm supposed to tell you that there are EDF people waiting for you in there."

"I know."

"Take care of yourself, sir. It was an honor meeting you."

The marine saluted and then drew back. Justin smiled—it sure was one hell of a change from the reception he had received less than two weeks ago.

Justin opened the airlock and floated through, the door closing behind him.

"Captain Justin Wood Bell."

Justin felt his stomach tighten at the sight of the black-uniformed EDF colonel waiting for him at the end of the airlock corridor.

Justin merely nodded.

"Captain Bell, you are under arrest on charges of treason."

Bel Varna looked up from his desk, startled by the man who walked into his office. He wanted to give a sidelong glance at his nephew for this complete failure of intelligence to find out beforehand who the visitor was, but to even break eye contact for a second would be a show of weakness.

The man drew closer, moving catlike, his imperial blue uniform shimmering. Falsin Zollern, nephew of the Viceroy of Avla, drew closer. He was atypical of the Zollerns: short, almost to the point of being considered abnormal, so thin that at first glance he might be mistaken for a holy ascetic. It was the pale, almost translucent eyes that gave him away, though. They were sinister, frightening. If the eyes were a mirror into the soul, Bel thought, then he was looking into a heart of death. Falsin stopped at the edge of the embroidered carpet that ringed Bel's desk and stood silent, imperious, as if waiting for him to rise.

As a Prata of the Assembly he knew that he should not stand and made a point of leaning back in his chair. The

old wood creaked, echoing in the silent chamber. He knew
this would annoy Falsin, who would expect groveling from
a nonroyal.

"I can tell by your expression that my arrival is unexpected,"
Falsin said, his voice surprisingly deep.

"I will not deny that," Bel replied, knowing it would be
foolish to answer otherwise.

He knew that the Viceroy's fleet was undoubtedly five
ten-days or more away and Avla's nephew, as commander
of the light squadrons of rapid attack ships, usually moved
ahead of the main fleet. Falsin had reputation for cold
cruelty unique among the Zollern. If the Zollern did engage
in cruelty it was usually inadvertent, the bungling of a
bureaucrat who let things get out of control. Falsin saw
it as a matter of policy.

What was disturbing was the knowledge that his uncle
was of the same cast, made worse by the fact that the
Viceroy had a cunning intelligence which Falsin lacked.
He was a good enough field commander, able to take orders
and carry them out ruthlessly, but to plan the attack? The
intrigue of court politics was beyond him—for that he
relied upon his uncle for survival.

"It is obvious you are not pleased by my arrival," Falsin
said.

"Oh, to the contrary, it is an interesting surprise. Might
I inquire as to the reason for your visit?"

"I have come in advance of my uncle to insure there
are no problems."

The latest intelligence, which he had received from a
light merchant transport arriving from the imperial world
only this morning, was that the Viceroy's fleet had not
pulled back from the Shun frontier until after the
alliance with the Shun had been finalized. To do anything
different would, of course, have been madness. At best
possible speed they would still have to cross through
fifteen or more systems to traverse to this, the far side
of their territory. A hundred days at least. The merchant
had taken twenty-one days to return, the war had started

fifteen days before his departure. It'd be another sixty days, more likely seventy before they would arrive.

"Would you care for a drink?"

"Of course I would care for a drink," Falsin replied, and without the slightest nod of thanks he took the goblet and downed its contents.

Bel wanted to wince with pain. The damn fool was drinking a rare Perjordin import more than a hundred years old as if it were swill brewed behind the barracks. Without bothering to ask, Falsin refilled his goblet near to overflowing. As he raised his cup some of the wine spilled onto the carpet. Bel wanted to scream at him for the insult. As a Zollern he must realize just how ancient and precious the carpet was. Falsin looked at him over the rim of his cup, and Bel realized that the spill had indeed been deliberate.

"My ship will dock here until the rest of my squadron arrives, which should be in thirty days' time. I expect my men to be treated with the respect they deserve as defenders of the Dynasty, and if there are any incidents you will be held responsible."

Tossing the goblet on the floor by the door, he walked out of the room laughing.

Bel breathed a sigh of relief and then motioned for Darel to send someone in to clean up the mess, though he knew it would be impossible to get the wine stain out of the silk-like material of his carpet. A hundred years of labor had gone into that carpet and now it was ruined. But even as he thought it, he smiled.

Justin Bell looked over at his commanding officer, Admiral Mahan, surprised at the vehement tone in the man's voice.

"You heard Captain Bell's reports . . . there's this Zollern Dynasty, a war on their border, and worse yet this race called the Hive. Procyon will be the flashpoint and we're on the border of that system. Unless we stand united in this and forget the differences of the past they'll eat us alive and spit out the pieces."

Lin Zhu, Secretary General of the United Nations, sat impassive, and Justin could sense that Mahan had somehow crossed over the line.

"Your idealism is all well and good, Admiral Mahan— perhaps *too* good for a military man, and that is why the last war was lost. From the report of your captain," and he paused and nodded disdainfully at Justin, "the Colonists now have the technology to face this threat and we do not. He failed in what he was assigned to do."

"What was he supposed to do, kill the other two who are his closest friends and hijack the ship? That was not part of the agreement when he went out there, and would have been a violation of his oath of honor."

"I'm sick to death of your damned oaths of honor," Zhu snapped. "The new government expects obedience, not moral philosophy, from its officers."

"You forget the long-range considerations," Ibn Hassan, the minister of defense, intoned softly. "Let us look at this logically. First, we are not even sure there really *is* a war out there. This report by Mr. Bell states they received their intelligence from observation of radio channels and uploading of data. Let us see that data and then we'll discuss this exchange requested by the Colonies."

Justin stood silent, staring straight ahead. Though he knew the deliberate withholding of information was in itself a crime, he sensed that to reveal the help by Bel Varna and the full technical upload provided by him might not be the most prudent of actions at the moment.

"We should make the offer anyway," Mahan replied forcefully. "The Colonial request is, I think, the logical one given the current considerations. All they want are certain key resources—just a small part of our stockpile of titanium alloys needed for the ships, which they simply can't produce fast enough, certain other resources and technical support, and some of our best pilots to be trained on the simulators they're setting up."

"And they still control the designs, the technology is withheld from us, and even our pilots will only be allowed to fly as co-pilots. They'll fly but have no understanding of what's inside the machines. I can't believe you're asking for this."

Justin, frustrated beyond words, slammed his fist on the table, causing the men and women gathered in the room to look over at him in surprise.

"There's no time to waste now," he snapped angrily. "I was out there, I saw it. There are forces marshaling out there that can smash us in a day and here we sit arguing. Even if we get a dozen ships online we'll be lucky to stem the first attack, and that's only buying time to build more and get ready for the next attack. Nearly all the best pilots for the Colonial service were killed in the final stage of the war. They need highly trained personnel and they need the materials to build the ships."

"And when they are willing to release all the technical data to us," Hassan said coldly, "then they will be saved. We can build the ships and train the personnel ourselves."

"They already have the team in place," Justin argued, "the personnel that built the replica of the Gar ship. The time needed to train Earth technicians to build the designs we were given would be wasted. I saw some of the plans; they aren't all that difficult, the basic components are the same. For us to start from scratch is madness, we'll be occupied before then. Making Mars the center of manufacturing is our only logical choice."

"And did you think to copy those plans?" Hassan pressed. "Bring them back here to Earth with you?"

"I promised Admiral Seay and Commander Everett that I would not. Those were the conditions I agreed to before setting foot aboard their ship."

"You are a traitor!" Hassan roared, standing up and pointing an accusing finger at Justin.

Hassan looked over angrily at Mahan. "I am outraged that you and your armed thugs met an official EDF ship when it touched down at Geneva and took this man from their control. I demand that he be turned over at once to the United Nations government for trial."

"He can not be charged for something that was not a crime," Mahan replied.

"Didn't you order him to get the plans?" Hassan asked, now turning on Mahan.

"No."

"This is incredible," Hassan snapped. "When I heard what you two were up to I told you that was to be part of his mission."

Startled, Justin looked over at Mahan, who extended his hand for him to stay quiet.

"I could not in good conscience order one of my officers to knowingly violate the military code of honor by giving an oath and then breaking it, even if it was to a former enemy. I sent Bell out there to try and gain access to the ship as ordered, to try and persuade the Colonial forces to share the ship with us, but nothing beyond that. I think he did his duty admirably. He was part of the first team to go beyond our system and he came back with invaluable intelligence as to the threat we are facing.

"The man should be commended and decorated," Mahan said coldly, staring at Hassan, "and not sullied by the obscene word 'traitor.'"

"He failed in his mission, as have you, Admiral Mahan," Hassan replied sharply, "and you are dismissed from this meeting."

Mahan stood up rigidly, slamming his computer notebook shut, Justin standing to follow him.

"I want charges filed against Bell," Hassan snapped, "and he is to be placed under arrest for dereliction of duty."

Mahan, saying nothing, turned and walked out of the room, Justin at his back.

Hassan watched him leave.

"The bastard," he snarled as the door closed behind Mahan.

"Don't press it too hard," Zhu said.

"Why not? He's under my orders."

"Not directly anymore, it has to go through the United States Government."

"To hell with the United States. If he even so much as sneezes the wrong way we'll place the Corps under direct EDF control."

"Not quite yet," Zhu replied. "The Earth Defense Forces are nowhere near ready to seize control. If there was ever a direct military confrontation the fleet would tear them apart."

"Then I want him fired."

"And have a rebellion? Because that is exactly what would happen. I think even that old fool Thorsson would call for it, and if he did this government would fall."

"I wish that old bastard would hurry up and die," Hassan replied. "He's half-senile as it is."

"Perhaps it might come sooner than you think," Zhu said coldly. "But there are other things to consider and foremost is how we can still turn this war out there to our advantage. I have no reason to doubt anything that Bell told us here today. He's one of those damnable Academy types and thus is honest. We have two ways of looking at this situation. One is a military solution, which seems to me to be the path of a fool."

Zhu looked around the room.

"And then there is the political solution."

Not a word was said between Mahan and Justin as they stepped into the hallway. Mahan was instantly surrounded by his heavily armed staff. Justin was still somewhat taken aback by the threat of force that Mahan had pulled off. An entire company of assault marines was arrayed in the corridor and out into the plaza. Facing them were several companies of EDF assault troops and the tension was near the breaking point, both sides armed and ready to fight.

Walking swiftly out of UN headquarters Justin followed Mahan and his staff, with dozens of marines closing in around them. Three heavy-assault copters were already warmed up in the parking lot. Justin went with Mahan into the lead ship, and the assault troops backed into the other two. As they lifted off four Tracer atmospheric fighters wheeled above them. The entourage winged out over Geneva and dropped down at the airport, where a USMC shuttle was waiting to take them back to Wallops. Again security was tight. Justin expected something to go wrong until the transatmospheric jump rocket was finally up over a hundred thousand feet and winging westward to safety.

During the two-hour flight to America, Justin briefed Mahan on the part of his flight that he had not revealed to the UN Council regarding Bel Varna and the information upload. Mahan grinned with delight and then went forward, leaving Justin to drift in and out of a nightmarish sleep.

Simply too much was happening too fast, Justin thought wearily. The flight back from Mars had been an ordeal. The EDF crew had barely let him sleep, grilling him eighteen hours a day during what was euphemistically called a debriefing but was more like an interrogation. He had almost cried with relief when the ship finally touched down at Geneva and Mahan, along with a heavily armed USMC ground assault team, was there to meet them and persuade the EDF team that Justin was now "USMC property." The humiliation and tension of having to endure a confrontation with the governing council before leaving Geneva had almost pushed him past the breaking point.

As the shuttle started into its final approach at Wallops he looked up to see Mahan coming aft.

"How you doing, son?"

"Beat to shit, sir."

"You did good, real good, though for awhile there I thought those EDF bastards were going to shoot all of us rather than let you go."

"Thanks for pulling me out, sir, but at that point I really almost didn't care anymore. Damn it, sir, here we are squabbling over this little piece of turf and the entire universe is at war. It makes our argument seem like a couple of children fighting in the sandbox."

"Madness," Mahan sighed, shaking his head. "How tough were they on you coming back from Mars?"

"It got a little nasty once or twice, but I guess they wanted me delivered intact."

"I threatened to start shooting the nearest EDF people I could find if they so much as touched you," Mahan replied. "I agreed to the bargain of letting the council meet with you, but it had me worried until we finally got out of there. Don't worry, you weren't really in all that much danger. They needed you intact, and after you got back they couldn't afford the incident I was willing to stage to get you under Corps control again."

"Thank you, sir, I wish I had known that at the time. They had me a bit rattled."

He didn't want to admit that the political officer had suddenly produced a bottle of rum halfway back home. He had resisted, but that was almost the worst torture of all.

The shuttle banked over hard and seconds later touched down, turning to enter one of the bunkers that lined the runway.

"I'm not sure how much clout my threat carried, but someone else was raising holy hell as well," and Mahan motioned out the window.

This time tears did come to Justin's eyes. Thor Thorsson, founder of the Academy and Justin's old mentor, sat in a float chair beside the plane, looking up. Thorsson saw Justin, and smiled and raised a hand in salute.

Stepping off the plane, Justin made his way through the crowd of military officers waiting for Mahan, barely hearing their congratulations. A small circle of green uniforms parted and Justin saw Thorsson in the middle. Coming to attention, Justin gave the best salute he had managed in years.

"Justin Bell, you certainly look like hell," Thorsson said, looking at him appraisingly, and then a smile creased his features. "My god, son, it's good to see you again."

Overcome, Justin could barely speak.

"I didn't know if I'd ever see you again," he finally whispered, kneeling down beside the float chair so that he was at eye-level with Thorsson.

"Kind of wondered myself at times," Thorsson chuckled.

"I know you're tired, but do you feel up to a little talking?"

Strangely, Justin felt suddenly wide-awake and he nodded.

"Come on, let's find a place to talk. I need to hear everything."

Thorsson turned his float chair and Justin walked beside it as Thorsson headed to a side door. Justin looked around and saw that only Mahan was following. They passed through the doors into an elevator that dropped them down to an underground shelter, which was empty except for two marine security guards. The guards opened the door into a small bare room and then closed it behind them.

"So three of my old cadets were the first ones to leave the system," Thorsson said, his face beaming with pride. "I had always hoped that I'd live long enough to see the day. How are Leonov and Everett?"

"Arguing, as usual, but they did a great job. We never could have made the flight without Matt, and Tanya handled the negotiations with Bel superbly. She also got a good handle on the navigation system, and her recording of the news broadcast gave us a lot of information. I was mostly just along for the ride."

"Tell me everything," Thorsson asked, and Justin reviewed the details of the flight, the meetings with Bel, and the return. When he had finished Thorsson sat in silence for a long moment.

"It reminds me of the Indians who lived here in America. They were crushed for two main reasons—the superiority of European technology, and their own inability to stand united. The English, the Spanish, Dutch and French all were at war with each other, as were the Indians, and yet it was the Europeans who were able to fan the disagreements of the Indians they met, pitting them against each other in turn, rather than the other way around. It's how Cortez took Mexico, using Indian allies, and the French and English were masters of it in the eighteenth century. Here we are fighting with each other and these empires will come and carve us up."

While he spoke Thorsson looked over significantly at Mahan, who simply nodded in reply.

"How did this Bel Varna strike you?"

"Shrewd . . . a politician, not a warrior. His world is one tiny power caught in a far greater power struggle."

"So why did he help you?"

"I think he's trying to draw to an inside straight. It's an insane move, a long shot for him, that we could organize and offer resistance. Maybe it was just purely to annoy somebody or perhaps even to have a fall back for himself if things get too hot."

"While he strikes a deal with someone else," Thorsson replied. "It's a grand old game that he's playing. Smaller powers like my Norway have been doing it for a thousand years."

"Can they beat us?" Mahan asked.

"Sir, even if we stood united, our chances are damn slim. Cor, Bel's world, has a fleet already in existence, and *they* caved in without a fight. One world doesn't stand a chance in the long run. We're talking about empires of hundreds, maybe even thousands of worlds."

"We have to play Bel's game," Thorsson announced. "Buy time, fend off the first attack. Since we stopped the first raid, we can assume that whoever it was will send more, but if we can build a response rapidly enough we might be able to break that attack as well. Then the trick is to get out there, to contact other systems. Build an alliance somewhere while also keeping ourselves from getting swallowed up by whomever we approach. It's an intriguing problem."

Thorsson smiled and looked at Justin and Mahan.

"You know, I kind of figured it might turn out like this."

"What do you mean?" Justin asked.

"The universe held only one of two possibilities. Either it was empty, waiting for us to take, or it was filled with life. Thanks to that first raid by the Trac ship—" He paused. "I guess we'll call them 'Gars' now, we knew there was something out there and it was hostile. If it was hostile, it meant there was war. The fact that nothing came back for years planted the suspicion that there were other forces in conflict delaying a return, a belief our Dark Eye project confirmed. That was one of the scenarios I had considered when I first established the Academy."

"How's that?" Justin asked.

"Did you ever wonder why I insisted that the Academy be established along military lines, when there was no one at that time to fight, since Earth and the Colonies were united?"

"For the discipline, since we were involved in law enforcement and also for preserving the peace on Earth."

"That's a bunch of shit," Thorsson said coldly, and Justin was surprised to hear the fatherly Thorsson utter an obscenity. "If that was the case it should have been designed as a law enforcement academy. I wanted trained and disciplined soldiers, that's why. I couldn't say that openly, but that was the bottom-line goal in my program. I wanted an elite, highly trained cadre, bound by all the finest in military traditions—a sense of duty, honor, and comradeship. That's why I turned to the old United States military academies for the model, since in their day they were the best.

"That was shown in the Colonial War. The men and women of the Academy became the military leaders in that war and they fought it using the traditions they had been trained in. That, more than anything else, is what kept it under control, the fact that beyond the issues you were fighting comrades whom you respected and in many cases loved."

As he spoke his voice was soft, filled with pride and sadness. "And even that war served its purpose as I hoped it would," Thorsson whispered.

Justin looked down at him, stunned and the old man nodded his head and smiled.

"Long before the war ever started I knew that historical dynamics would eventually lead us into conflict. It is part of an inevitable process that goes hand in hand with expansion and colonialism. There is always a point when colonies transcend the mother country and move to independence. I knew that in the end there would be a war between us and I wanted it to serve a higher purpose . . ." he paused for a moment, ". . . to train and prepare us for the next one."

"Damn it, do you mean you wanted the war?" Justin shouted, aghast at what he was hearing.

"Of course I didn't want it, but I knew it was an historical process that was inevitable, therefore I prepared for it," Thor answered.

He stared closely at Justin. "Don't look so horrified, Justin Bell. I was planning for the survival of our race against whatever it was we would eventually face out there. If one is to prepare for war, one must study it, and tragically one must participate in it to gain knowledge and practice. It was often said afterwards by those who fought in it that the American war with Mexico was the training ground of their Civil War."

"Do you know how many of your cadets died?" Justin asked coldly.

"You don't need to tell me," Thor said sadly. "You forget, Bell, that I never had children of my own. Each one of you was, in a way, like a child to me, filled with promise and hope. I bore each death as a sacrifice and unless you have children of your own and lose them you'll never know the pain I have known from it."

Justin stood silent, unable to speak, not sure if he was filled with rage at a man he had idolized all his life, or pain for someone he still loved.

"I know what the war did to you. I think you knew from the first time we met that you were one of my favorites. I always tried to tell myself not to become attached like that but I did. I taught your father, I flew with your grandfather . . . you were like my own. And there were so many others—Colbert, Kelly, Shoemaker, Wang, Faisal, Kochanski . . ." His voice trailed off. Justin realized that the names he was whispering were cadets who had been killed in action serving on both sides.

Justin felt a stab of pain as Thorsson looked up at him, his eyes bright with tears.

"War and politics, one and the same," Thorsson finally said. "I suspected that we were racing time, that the arrival of that first ship from those you tell me are the Gar was the warning signal. They had a means of translight and we did not. Our best people told me it might be a hundred years or more before we'd master it. I begged for a massive increase in military appropriations, building more space-based defenses, and was laughed down. Oh, there was a flurry of interest for a while after that first ship, and more after the second, but then interest waned. Their argument was that it was nothing more than a random threat and there were far more important things to spend our money on at home, like building entertainment parks, giving money to those who don't deserve it, or creating a new bureaucracy to oversee other bureaucracies. Damn fools! That's always been their argument, as if freedom is something you just find in the gutter and put in your pocket without charge.

"So I pushed for the Academy instead, training all of you to the old code, and waited for what I knew would be our final little war between ourselves. It was a razor-edged balance. If the war was controlled, we would not harm ourselves too much," and he paused again, "except for those who fought it. But at the same time it would stimulate the work that needed to be done. The research done in the last fifteen years would not have been equaled in fifty or a hundred without conflict. That is why the raid by the Gar went awry for them. If they had come twenty years earlier they would have defeated us in a day.

"You see it in the Colonial effort to rebuild that Gar ship. With a real threat breathing down on them daily, they saw their one hope in unlocking its secrets, and they did—just in time. We also trained our pilots and built at least the primitive weapons we might need, which did in fact work against these Gar."

"So that's why you resigned and founded the Bilateral Commission?" Justin asked.

"I knew that my cadets would control the fighting, though tragically there would be some mistakes. . . ." He paused to look over at Mahan, who said nothing, returning his gaze. "It was the governments I was worried about, their losing sight of what was being fought over, wishing to destroy everything, if needs be, for victory. In this conflict victory was not Colonial independence, victory was survival for our future."

Again he paused.

"Only I did not think it would go on so long, that so many of you would die. Now I know how Abraham felt, for I placed all that I loved on the altar, willing to sacrifice it in order to see those who lived afterwards *survive*."

Justin stood silent, unable to reply. He suddenly realized just how old Thor was; he had already been in his late seventies when Justin entered the Academy. Thor sat before him, bent over with age, his face heavily lined with wrinkles as if the skin were simply dropping away from the skull. He realized with a cold certainty that Thor was dying, and he felt a deep stab of pain. All the high promise that the man had dreamed of and once knew, the great leap into space, the first expeditions to Mars, the peace on Earth enforced from space and his creation of the Academy, all of that was now in doubt.

Thorsson looked back up at him and smiled.

"Don't feel sorry for me," he whispered. "I can't stand that look in someone's eyes."

And though ordered not to, Justin still felt pity, imaging the frustration this old man—and all old men—must feel, a realization was hitting him with a grim certainty. He himself was now in his mid-thirties and the surreal sense of immortality that all young men feel had been shattered in the war. Yet now he understood that if he did ever manage to survive what was coming, there would be a day when he would be like Thorsson, and all things would be in the past.

Thorsson reached out and took Justin's hand.

"You are so transparent, Bell, you never did master that fault. You couldn't reconcile what happened at Bradbury, so you tried to kill yourself by drinking. You look at me now as if I am already dead. Well, don't rush the mourning," he said with a soft chuckle. "I can still play one final game. And even after I'm gone I know the dream will live."

"I wish I could be so optimistic, sir," Justin said sadly. "I can't forget the image of that fleet. Tanya worked on a bit of the translation of the narrative. It belonged to the Golden Hive, and that was just part of one of five fleets. And I then come back and have to listen to those bastards in Geneva. With thinking like that we'll be squashed like a noisome fly."

"Damn it!" Thorsson shouted, his voice suddenly holding once more the deep baritone that could cause thousands of cadets to listen with rapt attention. "I didn't plan all the plans of these fifty years to hear you say it was finished.

"Answer me this, Bell, where did you, your father and grandfather come from?"

"America . . . Indiana."

"And how do you define what you now are?"

He looked over at Mahan.

"I guess still an American. Though the Academy was United Nations it was primarily funded by us and we were most of the cadets, along with the Russians, Japanese, and Colonists. Why?"

"Though Norwegian, I was on the mission to Mars aboard a ship mostly built by Americans. You people, after your second revolution back at the turn of the century, were the ones who got the space program going again. It was your revitalized belief in the Turner Thesis, that a frontier defines the character of a country, which motivated it to reach for the stars and pulled the rest of the world along with it."

"And now look at us," Justin said coldly. "Our leaders sell out to the coupist United Nations government, crawling rather than defying them. Hell, we finished the war on the wrong side."

"Both of you," and Thor looked over at Mahan and then back to Justin, "you fail to grasp a fundamental point. America is not a place . . . it is not Indiana, or Maine where you're from Mahan—it is an ideal.

"If it didn't exist, I would create it in my mind. It is not the land, it is the hearts of the people no matter where they are. It is a dream that existed long before Jefferson wrote the words and it will exist long after this planet is nothing but a burned cinder. That is what you must hold onto, both of you. It is not the government, and that is now the root of your problem as it was a hundred years ago. People too easily define what their country is by those they sometimes so foolishly put in power. It is the hearts of the people that are the country and the dream. America once existed here and maybe it will again, though at the moment the dream is darkened by those people they now call leaders who sit in Geneva, and their Gestapo of the EDF."

He smiled at the two of them.

"America, the Academy, all of that is what is inside of you and I think at the moment it is somewhere out there," and he pointed up to what Justin knew was space and the Colonies.

Thor cleared his throat noisily and smiled sadly.

"Now, young Justin Bell, I think it is time we got you the hell off this planet."

"What do you mean, sir?"

"Mahan here, along with a little help from some of my Bilateral people, managed to spring you from EDF hands, but I can assume that Geneva will try to put you under arrest again, or worse yet, just simply kill you."

"I was afraid we'd have to shoot our way out," Mahan replied.

"Admiral, do you have any *Glenn*-class fighters fueled and ready to go?"

"It just so happens we have one warmed up out on the flightline right now."

"Then I suggest you give Bell here the keys to the fighter

and send him on his way. I think his days with the USMC are finished for right now."

Justin looked at Thor and Mahan in confusion.

"Hell, Justin, if you stay here I'm going to have to arrest you."

"I thought I *was* under arrest," Justin replied.

"Bullshit. Get the hell out of here, Bell."

Justin looked back at Thor. "Sir, why don't you come with me. It'd be good for you to see space again."

Thorsson shook his head.

"I've got a little something to do here yet."

"The coupists are moving in against you. It'll only be a matter of time before they have you. You're still respected in the Colonies."

"Oh, don't write me off so easily, Bell. Just because these old legs don't move much anymore," and he lifted one of the shriveled limbs and let it drop, "doesn't mean I don't have a hell of a lot of kick left."

Justin feared he was saying good-bye forever. He came to attention and, facing Mahan, saluted. Mahan saluted in turn and extended his hand.

"Take care of yourself, Bell. Tell Seay what's happening here."

"How do you know I'm going to the Colonies?"

"There's a fight coming, this time a straight-up conflict, not like our last one. It's what you trained for and you won't miss it. Now get going."

Justin looked back at Thorsson and saluted, the old man returning the gesture.

He wanted to say something more, to thank him somehow, but all he could do was reach out and touch him lightly on the shoulder. Thorsson reached up and grabbed hold of his hand, squeezing it fiercely and then motioned for him to leave.

Justin walked out of the room and, minutes later was strapped into the fighter cockpit. Clearing the end of the runway he throttled it up, pointing its nose up to the heavens.

✦ Chapter IX ✦

"You heard the news?"

Lin Zhu turned away from his computer and looked over at Hassan.

"I know. They let the bastard go."

Hassan, his features dark with rage, sat down across from Zhu.

"I told you we should have kept him in our custody. A little persuasion and he would have finally talked."

"Don't be so damn primitive," Zhu snapped coldly. "What could he have really told us?"

"I think he held back."

"Held back what? He obviously wasn't stupid enough, or loyal enough, to have made a copy of the memory cube that this alien gave them. Therefore any information he might have had regarding technical details would have been limited merely to what he observed. Beyond that I think he gave us the truth at the meeting. Remember he's from the Corps. That means that he gave us a factual report since it's his sworn duty to do so. Torturing him would have revealed nothing of any real worth."

"The arrogance of the man, that's what angers me," Hassan said coldly.

"He's from the Corps, what else did you expect?" Zhu

replied absently. "Of course he's arrogant. To him and his kind we're usurpers and it goes against their grain that they're now stuck with us. It's always been an amusing problem for types like him to have to answer to types like us."

"We're the legitimate government of Earth," Hassan replied sharply.

Zhu laughed. "Don't give me that pious line. We saw the chance and we seized the power in the confusion after the war. By doing it we made it legal, but it was a naked power grab and the governments that could have stopped us were too gutless to try."

"Too decadent, you mean."

Zhu smiled nervously. Even though this man was on his side, Hassan still frightened him. He could not see this issue in an intellectual light, that the traditional powers of the United States, Russia, England and Japan had slowly been losing their edge. Diverted and drained by the resources required to fight the Civil War, they had not been able to combat the shift of power at home as other nations raced ahead economically to challenge them. Beyond that, they had grown complacent, letting the Corps become a power almost unto itself. Maneuvering the EDF into the vacuum had been easy enough to accomplish since the war ended.

Zhu could see that the defeat of the war had actually come as a blow to Hassan's ego; the man simply could not see it as an opportunity. He was also driven by a hundred-year dream of vengeance against the West, which he now had another thing to blame for . . . the loss of political control of space. There was room enough for vengeance—and that would come—but it was still all part of a vast and wonderfully elaborate game of power that should be the pleasure in and of itself.

"If I had followed your advice we would have had a rather ugly confrontation with the Corps," Zhu finally said.

"Good. Let them try it. We had Mahan here. Arrest him too! Shooting the bastard would be a pleasure."

"All in good time. We're not quite ready yet for that. Shooting Mahan would trigger war right here back on Earth. We might control the orbital bombardment stations now, but the Corps has nuclear weapons as well. By gaining the stations we gained the balancing chip to block them. But if we should ever use them, they'll use their weapons as well. Let us be realistic, Hassan, they could very well beat us."

"There would be precious little left for them to go home to," Hassan said coldly.

"I want to run a living world, not ashes," Zhu replied sharply.

Hassan stirred uneasily as Zhu stared at him. "Well, to hear this Bell talk, we won't have much left anyway before it's all done."

Zhu leaned back in his chair and laughed. "Do you really believe that?"

"You said he was telling the truth. If he was it seems like we'll be overwhelmed in the next attack."

"The Colonies might be overwhelmed," Zhu said quietly, "but why should we be?"

"Damn it, they have the weapons and we don't."

"Oh, yes, we do."

Hassan looked over angrily at Zhu.

"You heard him, there are five powers out there, all of them interested in us."

"The ones called the Shun do sound appealing," Hassan replied softly.

"They all sound interesting and I dare say that if we play the game correctly you and I will still be in power, and our goals accomplished as well."

Hassan slowly started to smile.

"So look what the cat dragged in," Matt quipped, looking up from his desk.

Justin smiled wearily and slumped onto an old beat-up chair that on Earth would have been decidedly uncomfortable. Here in the lighter gravity of Mars it was at least tolerable. Five days cramped in a fighter, twice now to Mars in less than a month, was getting tedious.

"So I guess you're a man without a country," Matt said. He hesitated for a moment, then reached into his desk, pulled out the decanter given to them by Bel, and tossed it over.

Justin held it for a moment and the temptation was all too real. Yet something about the meeting with Thor, and for that matter everything else that had happened, stopped him. He suddenly remembered the old story of a cadet back in the Academy who was a notorious teetotaler, had told about Stonewall Jackson. The famous general had experienced only one night with the bottle and the following morning announced that since he liked it far too much he would never drink again, a vow he kept until he was on his deathbed and the surgeon gave him brandy.

I like this far too much, but not now. He smiled, shook his head, and tossed the decanter back.

Matt grinned.

"So I guess you're cured."

"At least for the duration."

"But you're no longer with the old Corps, my friend."

"I have a fighter. Admiral Mahan told me to take it and get the hell off-planet, but he never said anything about returning it." He hesitated. "I thought I'd sign on with you folks—that is, if you'll have me."

"That's what I was hoping I'd hear," Matt replied enthusiastically. "I never could understand why you stayed with the service when the war started. You belonged out here with the Colonials from the start."

"The oath, I guess. Sometimes I'm not even sure any more why I did stay. I think it's because I believed in a unified government. Now, after all that's happened . . ." His voice trailed off.

Service to what? In the beginning it was for the United Nations and the Academy that was part of it. Then, as things started to go wrong there, it was still at least for the United States and of course the Corps. But now even that seemed to be going under, the coupist government with its EDF controlling everything, the only balance left being the USMC. He wasn't even sure how much longer they'd hold out. His grandfather had always said that the day the United States, Russia, and a resurgent Britain turned their military over to the UN was the day the world was finished. It was obvious that day was here.

Matt looked over at him and slowly extended his hand, which Justin took.

"You had me worried to death. When you agreed to go back to Earth with those EDF bastards I thought you were cooked. Hell, you should have stayed here with us—it'd have saved you the round trip."

"I had to go back. It was my duty, I'd given my oath that I would."

Matt wanted to make a sarcastic comment about giving oaths to traitors but held back, knowing that if the situation were reversed he would have done the same.

"You know Seay's been catching a load of grief over you. They kind of figured you'd head back out here. They want you arrested and returned along with your fighter. Hell, there was even a bit of saber-rattling involved in it, threats that'd it be, what did they call it, 'a serious provocation' if we harbored a wanted felon who had stolen a classified ship."

"And what was the reply?"

"Supposedly Seay told them in rather graphic terms to perform a certain impossible anatomical act. He's madder than hell as it is, what with their refusal to send the spun-titanium alloy. I guess you heard as well they've refused to release any pilots for training for service with us."

Justin nodded, having monitored the military channels on his flight out.

"You're not out here alone, though. Half a hundred USMC pilots have suddenly resigned, and should be out here in a couple of days."

"Who?"

"You most likely know some of them—Allison, Jeffreys, Ethell . . . you remember him from our class."

"Ethell, the best damn pilot who ever lived. Resigned! He was loyal to his oath."

Matt chuckled. "I think old Mahan arranged for them to volunteer."

"Something's brewing on their side. They can't be so stupid as to not realize the threat. If we don't stand united we'll get overwhelmed. Even as it is, we don't seem to stand much of a chance."

"Well, it's not entirely hopeless," Matt said quietly.

"What've you done since I left?"

Matt got up from his chair and motioned to the door.

"Come on, let's go take a look."

"Am I cleared for this anymore?" Justin asked.

Matt grinned.

"Hell, you were appointed a full Captain in the United Colonies Fleet two days ago and assigned to this project."

Justin looked at him dumbfounded.

"Seay figured you'd come straight back here. The paper work's already been run through—you can go through the formality of signing later."

Matt reached into his desk, pulled out two gold stars, and tossed them over.

"Your uniform's hanging in your room. Pin these on when you get a chance."

Justin looked down at the stars. Somehow it still didn't seem quite right that he was wearing the stars of what, in the back of his mind, was still the other side. And yet, now, who was the other side?

"Come on, Tanya and another old friend are dying to see you."

Matt led the way down the corridor and out into the main hangar area. A month ago the vast room had been empty except for *Prometheus* and the reassembled wreckage of the Gar raider. Now the cavern was swarming with activity, hundreds of technicians were at work, the room echoing with shouts, orders, machinery booming, and Justin looked at it with awe.

"We've got a full assembly plant going here, and three more are gearing up. We've already got the hulls of three more ships near completion on the floor here, and the zero-gravity foundry in orbit is pouring more. The problem is the spun-titanium hull. They've got the facilities back on Earth—we could triple our output if they'd only share it, damn them."

Justin noticed that Matt had said they, rather than you. Just the mere change in pronouns seemed so profound to him.

"Let's go back in the labs," and weaving their way through the cavern Matt led him to another corridor, which dropped down into a lower level. The last time he was here, Justin realized, he had not even been aware of the existence of this area and he suspected that he had been denied access for some very obvious reasons. The upper level was the assembly plant, but as he stepped out into the lower floor he realized that this was where the years of research work had been done to even get the first ship online. Before passing through the double airlock into the main floor, Matt pulled on a clean suit over his uniform and Justin followed his example, feeling slightly foolish in a white bonnet covering his hair and a respirator mask.

The spacious, brightly lit room was tomb-like and hushed in contrast to the bustle on the upper level, even though hundreds of personnel were gathered around in various work areas. Matt led him through the room and Justin saw teams working on newly fabricated machinery and components for what he assumed were the ships being assembled on the upper floor. Some of the equipment looked vaguely familiar, but most of it was a complete mystery. To one side of the room he saw what looked like an assembly area for ship-to-ship missiles.

"The Gar design," Matt said. "We stripped it down and found we could adapt the frame of our own Shrike ship-to-ship missiles to the internal components. We're turning out one a day now and the damn things are supposedly deadly, with weave evasion against laser counter-battery, and even a flechette counter-missile system built in."

"I'm glad I didn't mention that part to them."

Matt looked over at him.

"Hell, I only told what I had to. For all they know we went out, snooped around, uploaded some data and got the hell out. Bel, the missiles, all the rest is only known by the Corps and," he hesitated, "by our side now."

Stepping into yet another side corridor, Matt opened a door and ushered Justin in, then took his mask off.

Justin did likewise and then looked around at the banks of holo screens and flat two-dimensional displays. Two women, their backs turned, were hunched over one of the monitors.

"Hey, we got company, ladies!"

"Bell!"

The two voices were a chorus of joy and they left the monitor to rush up and embrace him. Tanya's hug gave him a wonderful chill and he pulled her in under his right arm. The sight of the other woman filled him with a flood of happy memories. It was Madison Smith, his first friend at the Academy and someone he had not seen since the start of the war. Her brown features were filled with a genuine joy as she reached up and kissed him loudly on the cheek, then stepped back to look at him appraisingly. Her head was cocked slightly to one side, a habit she still had and that he still found endearing.

"Tanya told me you looked like hell, too much of the bottle, but you seem to be on the mend."

"Well, that's the first halfway decent greeting I've had since this whole adventure started."

Madison seemed not to have aged at all. Her last vestiges of what could have euphemistically been called baby-fat had given way to a most pleasing feminine form. Her eyes were, as always, aglow with an inner happiness that seemed ready to explode out of her at any moment. It was good to see that at least one of his old comrades had not been scarred by the war. He noticed as well the ring on her hand. So she was still married to the xenoarchaeologist she had met while at the Academy and serving on Mars as an observer.

"How's Clarence?"

"Out there digging away," she said with a laugh. "The last war didn't stop him, and this little excitement he most likely isn't even really aware of. The kids are staying with him while I'm working here."

"Kids?"

Madison reached into her pocket and pulled out the obligatory photos.

"Four boys and heaven help me, all like their dad, noses glued to the ground." She paused for a moment. "Not a pilot in the set and their mom's glad of it."

They battered him with questions about his trip back to Earth and it wasn't until Tanya finally brought over a cup of coffee that he got to turn things around.

"So what have you found out?"

All three of them grinned.

"It looks like that Bel character gave us damn near the whole shop," Tanya announced excitedly. "We downloaded the computer into the main system here as soon as *Prometheus* was brought in. Talk about a lot of nervous techs worried about crashing the system before we got it unloaded! Right at the top of the list was the translator software. Once we got that, a little modification to one of our systems and the information just started to spit out. The software's adaptive as well. Feed a language into it, it starts running voice and print inquiries back at you, and within minutes it starts translating. We even tried to stump it with Magyar and Finnish and it crunched them right back out. The artificial intelligence is way beyond old Uncle back at the Academy.

"As for the ship, there were full CADs for every component onboard right down to the molecular computer chips and individual nuts and bolts. Damn, Justin, it's like taking one of our computers back to the Middle Ages and hooking it up and showing knights jet planes."

"Yeah, but chances are you'd get burned at the stake for your effort," Justin replied, "and no one would understand what the hell you were trying to show them anyhow. Beyond that, do we even have the infrastructure to make what they're showing us?"

"That's the amazing part as well," Matt interjected. "It's sort of like an encyclopedia in a way, walking backwards through technology levels. Not only are we shown the systems but also the machines to make the systems to start with. So if we can't manufacture what we need with our existing hardware and software, we can turn out the machine that then makes the machine."

"That takes time," Justin said quietly.

"Years, normally. We can't wait, though. Some of the stuff we're jury-rigging as we go, but fortunately fourteen years of war taught us how to turn things around quickly when we had to. If this stuff had gotten tied up in peace-time it'd be years before we got something moving. We don't have time for Parkinson's Law to take effect the way it does back on Earth."

"That's been a problem at times," Madison interjected. "Some of this stuff, particularly the tech material related to the engines, stands a lot of theories right on their heads. We've got a lot of Ph.D.s wandering around with steam pouring out of their ears . . . some of them ecstatic, others having fits since everything they thought they knew just got heaved on the ash heap and they're back in grammar school again."

"So how does it work?"

"What?" all three of them asked.

"The ship, for starters."

"I've had it explained to me, but I'm still not sure I've got it right," Matt interjected. "Gravity waves. When we're inside the gravity well of a sun, the gravity wave engine doesn't work, that's why the ships are rigged with antimatter drive. However the farther away from a gravity well you get the less the canceling-out effect the sun has on the gravity waves of the rest of the universe. It's bizarre, but apparently the engine works in inverse proportion to the strength of the gravity. That's why we started to accelerate the farther away from the sun we got, which didn't seem logical at first. One of the tech folks described it like a boat planing off a wave. You start to accelerate, there's a lot of resistance, and then you start to plane. The trick then is to find the transit points."

"Transit points?"

"Yeah, remember in the Academy we talked about Gate Theory, that there were gate points between systems, sort of like wormholes? Well, you have to hit the transit point— it's like a target floating out there. Achieve that and you're on your way to the next system."

"And if you miss it?"

"Well, it seems that you just keep going and then you have one hell of a long trip back at just under light-speed. It seems that's what kept us protected even with this Imperium damn near on our border. They had yet to find a transit point. Maybe the first Gar ship simply muscled its way here, or maybe poking around over at the edge of Procyon they found the transit and hit here. There seem to be two in our system—we hit the one to Procyon, and there's another one that the last attack force used.

"Thus, we have three different engine systems aboard— antimatter, gravity wave, and the one that interacts with the transit point, along with the inertial dampening system. The maneuvering is done by magnetic waves. The ship sets out a charged field, then whichever way you want to turn, that side is reversed in polarity in relationship to the field and away you go. You get a sideways jump, but with engines burning it actually works out into a banking turn. Again, the farther out from a sun or planet you are, the better it works."

"It sounds a bit more complex than the way you described it."

The three started to laugh again like school kids in on a joke that one of their friends didn't quite understand.

"Oh, there are only about a hundred-thousand pages worth of copy on it, most of it math beyond anything I've played with. The key thing is though, we can worry about the theory side later. Bel gave us a jump-start with the CAD drawings. We don't have to have it fully figured out yet . . . we just simply start turning the parts out and then master the technology. It's disquieting since it is a total reversal of the scientific process. The CADs we knew our machines could handle were loaded into our standard construction computers, the raw materials were fed in, and damn if we don't start having parts coming out. If we had the raw material, especially the damn hulls, which are the hard part, we'd be turning out a ship a day inside another month. Justin, the designs are elegant. It follows the standard curve on nearly any machine. When first invented it's pretty simple. Complexity, however, starts to take over as engineers keep adding new things in, until it is almost beyond understanding. Then finally, a stage is reached in which a certain elegant simplicity comes back as the machine reaches its final refinement. That's what we have here."

"There's something disquieting, though," Madison announced.

"There she goes again, worry," Matt said.

"What is it?" Justin asked.

"It seems like there's an upper limit on this."

"What do you mean?"

"On technology. All this stuff we're looking at, we're like kids in a candy shop, but when you get right down to it, if we had been left alone for another hundred or two hundred years I think we would have cracked it ourselves."

"Do I hear a troubled human pride?" Justin said with a smile.

"No, that's not the point. We were already into a basic grasp of gravity waves and the potential use of them, even the magnetic wave steering. It's sort of like this—consider, the tech jump from the Wright Flyer to an old Eagle F-15, which took just three-quarters of a century. Or from the F-15 to a Glenn Fighter, that's just about a century. However, the learning and advancement curve was even slowing there. Show the Wright brothers the F-15 and they would have been astonished. It would have almost been beyond them—CRT displays, infrared seekers, autopilot, global positioning technology; all of that would have been beyond their imagining. But take an old fighter jockey from the late twentieth century and show him a Glenn, and he'd sort of nod and say that he could see it and understand it."

"I'm not following you, Madison."

"Just that the learning curve, or should I say, 'progress curve,' was slowing down and we were sort of reaching the upper limit of capability. Well, all this stuff, Justin, they've had it for thousands of years and it's changed precious little. It seems we're looking at the pinnacle of scientific technology. There simply isn't any farther to go beyond this."

"Well, it seems like a hell of a jump to me," Matt replied.

"Yeah, I know, I'm wowed by it too, but it means that when we achieve this we're almost at a dead-end."

"Let's worry about surviving this particular dead-end," Matt said, "then we can get into some angst regarding progress."

"OK, I know, but anyway, regarding the other information—the societal and political stuff?" Madison said, shaking her head. "It's simply incredible."

"Say, how did you get into this project anyway?" Justin asked. "This seems like a long way from a dig."

"Not far at all. They wanted a linguist and they knew I was the best around."

"What about the political side, that newscast?"

"There was some history included in the data," Tanya interjected, "It pretty well matches up to what Bel said; however, since he gave us the information we have to assume it's biased. In this alliance of royal houses, reptilian was the dominant power. They're at war with other systems—one that might pass as humanoid, this one they call the Shun, and the Perjordin. Then there are these bugs, the Hive, coming up from the galactic core, that are maybe even the bigger threat."

"And Bel's race?"

"Weird, they actually do look Neanderthal. Some folks are speculating they might actually be Neanderthal for real, maybe borrowed from here fifty, a hundred-thousand years ago by some lost race that wandered through. We have those DNA fragments from the research on Neanderthal; when we can get a sample we'll run a comparison."

As Madison talked she pulled out a piece of paper and did a quick sketch of the Milky Way.

"As the old saying goes, 'we are here,' three-quarters of the way out from the galactic core," and she put a dot on one of the spiral arms. "If where we are is at twelve o'clock, the Dynasty occupies the area of space from twelve to two relative to us inward towards the center and above us. The edge of their domain, at twelve, is Procyon. The Shun and the Perjordin are in a band from ten to one above and below us while the Hive is an arrow coming straight out towards us."

"Outward beyond us?"

"According to what we've got, it seems like nothing major to speak of. No transit points located yet."

"So all these different powers are in a band inward and the Hive will be knocking on their door."

"Looks that way."

"And the Zollern, how do they run their show?"

"Each of the worlds has a certain autonomy and a ruling house. Some are what we would call feudal, land granted by the Emperor of this House of Zollern. Others are oligarchic, a few even appear to be republics, but more than a hundred out of the five hundred systems they control they rule directly. Politically it's a wild hodgepodge that must be a nightmare to control. As for the overall system of this Imperium, they're brutal to be sure, but at least there's some veneer of civilized behavior."

Madison paused for a moment.

"I guess that's what disturbs me the most. I mean, for hundreds of years we dreamed of making contact and most of us believed that when we did we'd somehow find something better. Justin, it's just as bad out there, in some ways even worse."

"So what else did you expect, angels?" Tanya sniffed.

"One could always hope," Madison replied sadly.

"Who hit us then?"

"Looks like this one house called the Gar, like Bel said. It's weird, they're semi-nomadic, fanatically independent-minded. Bel attached a memo explaining them. In a way he seems fond of them, says that out of the various families they have the best sense of honor."

"Cossacks," Tanya announced.

"What?"

"They remind me of Cossacks. The wild children of the steppes. Might raid you for the fun of it one day, drink with you the next. Respect bravery in an opponent, in fact even honor it, open-handed but God help you if you piss them off."

"What about the others? This Hive?"

"They're class-A bastards," Madison announced coldly. "They're a gray, faceless mass, far outnumbering the other groups. Militarily they aren't as sharp as the Perjordin or Zollern, but they make up for it in simple raw numbers. In combat they're fanatical to the point of suicide. Also, the other systems tend to fight against each other with at least a modicum of rules; for instance the use of nukes against planets is frowned upon. The borders keep shifting back and forth and the other sides realize that what belongs to the enemy today might in fifty years be taken and occupied, and who wants a strontium-laden world? When the Hive is done with a fight, the system, if it is not taken, is usually a radioactive wasteland. Apparently the fight that the Dark Eye project detected was one fought out between the Hive and some other force fifty years back. We were able to match it up with our observations. Whoever was on that planet is dead."

"What about the free states?"

"There are a scattering of them," Tanya replied. "Border worlds, especially between the major powers, which shift back and forth, both sides allowing them to exist as buffer states and also as convenient ports of trade for smuggling and privateering between systems that might at that moment be at war with each other. Cor, or Procyon, broke away when the Zollern Dynasty was too preoccupied elsewhere."

"So what now?"

"Continue to analyze the data, start training once we get the first simulators online, and hope that we have enough time to get ready," Matt said coldly.

✧ Chapter X ✧

"Our intelligence reports indicate that the system outward from Cor has obtained the ability to go translight."

Naruth Zollern, the Viceroy of Avla, looked up slowly and fixed Ambassador Holzan with his gaze.

"Go on."

"A ship of Gar design arrived at Cor two standard days before hostilities were declared. I found out about the arrival of the ship from my usual sources."

"Prata Norru?"

Holzan smiled.

"One must never reveal one's sources," Holzan said smoothly, surprised that the Viceroy would know of the internal politics of a minor world on the other side of the system.

"It is my job to know about where I will be stationed," the Viceroy said, as if reading Holzan's mind, and the ambassador found the response to be disquieting.

"And this ship returned to its system?"

"Apparently."

The Viceroy looked down at the holo display of the system beyond the frontier. The world in question was suddenly highlighted in red, a printout of information appearing to float alongside it.

The Viceroy studied the information intently and then finally looked back up at Holzan.

"What do you think they took back with them?"

"I have reason to believe that Bel Varna visited them once, perhaps even twice."

The Viceroy cursed softly under his breath. Holzan knew that the Varnas were a source of injured pride for Naruth. During the rebellion his grandfather had been defeated by Bel's grandfather in the one brief military action fought between the two sides, and in atonement he had killed himself.

"Have him killed."

Holzan shook his head.

"There are too many connections between Varna and some of the families in the Diet. Support for this alliance with the Shun is lukewarm at best; killing Varna might shake that support."

"Damnation to the Diet," Naruth growled, "let them whine."

Holzan tried to force a friendly smile. *Damn warriors, they understood nothing of the finer nuances of political interplay.* The Varna line had once been representatives to the Diet, and with Cor eventually being forced back in, chances were the Varna line would hold such a position again. Killing one of them could have repercussions that might be dangerous later. There was no sense in making a martyr out of Bel. There was no thought of even mentioning his personal attachment.

"Perhaps we can arrange an accident later, a year or so from now," Holzan finally said, figuring to offer some hope of revenge in the future. "If we kill him out of hand there'll be a rebellion . . . even an accident might trigger that. Remember, our agreement with the Hive is to turn the world over to them intact."

"A smoking ruin would be more to my taste."

Holzan shook his head. *Fool, didn't he see any of the long-term implications in all of this?* The Hive was the dark force at the back door, but Zollern policy was that it could be controlled and used to advantage. At his audience this morning with the Kaza that point had been reinforced.

Policy? Just how realistic was it, Holzan wondered, and what games within games that he was not even aware of were being acted out on other stages in this vast, elaborate play?

He could surmise one of the final intents here, to use the Hive to bring the more recalcitrant members of the Diet back into line. Granted, there might be some destruction, but it would be to the worlds whose leaders were increasingly difficult to control. The plan within the plan—but to even begin to discuss this with a semi-barbarian such as this son of the House of Avla was dangerous.

"What do you think he gave them, these barbarians?"

"I don't know. But they are only barbarians."

"Never underestimate a foe, even if he is lying on the ground and looks dead," Naruth said softly, his gaze still focused on the holo map. "Remember, there is the rumor about some Gar ships being lost. If it was these barbarians who did it, they have teeth."

"Is it really our concern?"

"It should be," Naruth snapped. "First, it means there is a transit point we knew nothing about. Perhaps the Hive does not even know about it, and that could be to our advantage."

"How so?"

Naruth looked at Holzan as if he were a fool. "If we know about it and they don't, we could have a force on their flank."

There was a point to that, Holzan realized, and he nodded in agreement.

"And besides, they are there. My crews need training; a barbarian hunt could be amusing and help my warriors to keep their edge."

Holzan stood waiting, cursing silently. Through his skill he had given this man the system of Cor without a fight. The Viceroy would have flattened it, killed tens of millions, and aroused the Hive against the wrong foe. Now he was talking about going off on a raid for the purpose of training.

The minutes seemed to drag by and Holzan waited, his anger slowly growing. Finally the Viceroy stirred and leaned back again in his chair.

"I want my rear area secured. It will still be thirty days before the main strength of my fleet arrives at Cor. Go back there, locate this transit point, and tell my nephew to advance across the frontier at once into this new system. If they resist they are to be annihilated. It's intolerable that unrepentant barbarians possess the knowledge of flight."

Holzan shrugged in acknowledgment, a slight that only a member of the royal line could dream of offering to the Viceroy of Avla. There was logic to his plan, though; a new transit point, perhaps unknown to the Hive, would be an advantage. Perhaps the Hive would even pass it by and then there would be a new colony to exploit. Beyond that, he suspected that if Bel had contacted these barbarians, whatever the reason, it undoubtedly held no advantage for the Zollern. So let the young princeling have his training romp, and after all, it was only barbarians who needed to be shown who was in control.

Thus is the fate of worlds decided, he thought with a sad smile.

Justin walked into the room and scanned it a bit nervously. The other officers sitting around the circular table had been men and women he had recently faced in combat. They looked up at him curiously. He recognized a couple of people from Academy days and nodded a greeting.

"I've invited Captain Bell to sit in on this session," Brian Seay announced, "since he was, after all, part of the mission. Also, I think we all know his skill as a tactician, and that is what this session is about."

Justin walked around the table to sit down between Matt and Tanya, and opening up his briefcase he pulled out and powered up his computer.

"Captain Bell, the floor is yours," Brian announced.

Justin stood up and looked around, not sure if he was feeling paranoid or if some of those present were less than pleased with his being in the room.

"Admiral Seay."

Justin looked across the table at a young woman leaning forward.

"Go ahead, Chelsey."

"I object to this man being here," she said coldly, staring straight at Justin. Justin recognized her as one of the original team whom he and Tanya had bumped from the test flight of *Prometheus*.

"That's not for you to decide," Brian replied sharply.

"I lost family at Bradbury. We're discussing tactical deployment and system capabilities here, and how do we know if this man might not switch sides again? I have no use for someone who jumps ship when things seem to turn."

"I lost family at Bradbury too," Matt said quietly. "Justin was once my roommate, and when I found out he led the assault I hated him for it."

A bit surprised, Justin looked over at his old friend.

"I got past that. It was war, Chelsey, and he attacked Bradbury thinking it was a legitimate military target. He resigned when he realized it was not, and I think he's paid a hell of a price since. As for jumping ship, every damn Colonial jumped ship when we broke with Earth, though I think you were a bit too young at the time to make the decision yourself."

"I still object," she said coldly, ignoring the less-than-subtle put-down.

"And you are overruled," Brian replied sharply, "and that's the end of it. I've known Bell for twenty years. I was his company commander at the Academy, he was part of my space-diving team and even when he was a plebe I was willing to put my life in his hands. Remember, he was the guy who led the mutiny against MacKenzie on the old *Somers*, and for a sixteen-year-old cadet he showed more guts than anyone I have ever known."

Justin looked over at Matt and there was a quick exchange of smiles. He had led the mutiny to save Matt from execution. Funny, in all the years since the two had never talked about it; the mutiny was to Justin an action to save a friend's life, nothing more, and to talk about it was an embarrassment.

"Now listen closely, young lady. I was the one who swore him into the service last month, and he's one of the best we've got."

The woman settled back in her chair and Justin could see that although she'd follow orders, it was obvious she hated him.

He looked around the room a bit nervously and again there was the faint tug to have a drink, or, if not that, at least to get the hell out. But there was no way out as he looked over at his old squad commander, who gazed at him as if ready to launch into a good chewing-out over a bed that was not made according to regulations.

He cleared his throat and then pushed a button on his computer to hook the signal in to the main display that filled the far side of the room.

"As of today we have only five translight ships online, along with one hundred and thirty *Corsair*-class antimatter drive fighters that might be capable of participating in the action.

"The key tactical problem is that an enemy fleet approaching this system will be impossible to detect until the moment it comes through transit and drops down from light-speed. Once it drops down, the attacking ship will start to rapidly decelerate the deeper it gets into the gravity well of the sun. We roughly know the transition line of this jump barrier, which is here," and as he spoke a schematic of the solar system appeared in the display field with a red line marking the transition zone, along with red circles marking the two known transit points.

"Approach time from this transition line is roughly forty-eight hours to Mars orbit and just under fifty-three hours to Earth, given current relative positions. A natural tendency and standard doctrine would be to establish a forward defense, thus engaging the enemy as far away as possible from the inner worlds. Unfortunately, given our resources I would rule that out."

"Why?" Chelsey asked, the suspicion in her voice evident.

"A number of factors," Justin replied, attempting to sound friendly. "First off, we only have five ships now that are roughly comparable to what we might expect; perhaps we might have twelve inside another month."

"We'd have twenty right now if Earth cooperated," she replied sharply.

"But they won't and I can't change that even though I tried," Justin shot back angrily.

He looked around the room coldly. "I don't care what Admiral Seay has ordered you to do but let's get this straight right now," Justin continued. "if you people don't want me here, then I'll leave. I did my duty as I saw it. I still live by that today, and if you people can't get past that, then there's no sense in my trying."

He fell silent, looking around the room. Finally one of them stirred, leaning forward and gazing at his comrades as if trying to gauge their opinion, and finally looked back at Justin.

"It's all right, Bell, get on with it."

Justin felt an inner sense of relief and nodded his thanks.

"As I was saying, we don't have the ships to cover a forward defense. We have a rough approximation of the transition emergence point of a ship coming in from Cor, as they call Procyon, which, from what we know, will be the staging area of attack. That still covers an area a thousand miles across. Unless they come through straight on top of us there's no hope of an intercept. Secondly, as they emerge they'll be moving at just under a fraction of light-speed and will hold above .9 light for several minutes. The speed bleeds off in a geometric progression; it'll be nearly a day before they're down to .1, and by then they'll be nearly inside the orbit of Saturn.

"The problem here is that we'll be standing damn near

still as they come roaring through and we'll have to accelerate in a stern chase. Quite simply, if we're out on the line we'll never catch them."

"What about positioning several hundred million miles in?" Tanya asked.

"Simple light-speed physics," Justin replied, and even as he started to answer she nodded, guessing what he was going to say. "Let's say they're ten million miles in front of you. If they're at .9 light, in fact they'll only be a million miles away before you get first sighting but still at ten million miles. In five more seconds they're past you. They'll be millions of miles ahead of you before you even start to accelerate. It's really not until inside the orbit of Saturn that we'd have enough advance warning to match their speed, and remember, that's matching speed with whatever ships we manage to have online when they arrive. Our .1 light-speed fighters really aren't any good until we're nearly into Mars orbit."

"That doesn't leave us very much to go on," Seay replied.

"In actuality, nothing at all," Justin replied. "We have to assume that they'll hit us with at least as much as the first attack, and this time they won't come in cocky, they'll expect a stiff resistance."

"What about attacking first?" Seay asked. "It might knock them off balance."

"I've considered that strategy, and it has some merit. However, I recommend against it. First off, who do we hit?"

"What do you mean?" Chelsey asked.

"Just that," Matt interjected. "The Gar were the problem before, but are they now? If they are, where do we find them? It might be the Hive instead, it might even be the Zollern wanting to take us. It could be someone else. All we know is that there's a major war out there. We're a third-rate power on the edge of it and it will spill over into our system in short order. Hell, it might even be two different powers fighting each other and we're simply their battlefield. We could jump through and find ourselves in a hornet's nest."

"There'd still be the element of surprise, though," Chelsey interjected.

"I'll grant you that, but frankly I think from both a strategic and political point of view, it might not be wise."

"Explain," Brian said quietly.

"They might not even know that we have translight capability and ships capable of achieving a good portion of light-speed. They assume we're primitives. Remember, we're but a very minor part of a full-scale war, a barbarian outpost to be seized as a base, and we're just a bunch of natives to be knocked off.

"For example, if Montezuma had had arquebuses and horses I think it would have been foolish for him to meet Cortez on the beach. The Spanish could have withdrawn to sea and the precious element of surprise would have been lost. Let him get inland, let him assume that everything is under control, then hit him and wipe him out and, even more importantly, let no word get back to Cuba and Spain about what happened. There's no sense in letting *this* Cortez know what he's facing or to warn anyone that we have something in our favor.

"Now to the second factor. We're used to what is nearly instantaneous communications within our system—no one is more than four or five hours away by radio. That no longer applies. News out there travels only as fast as the fastest ship, compounded by the time distortion created by relativistic speeds. Procyon is apparently a fairly easy jump from here, and yet it was still five days. From one end of the Zollern holdings to the other is, to the best of our estimates, almost four months with jumps through twenty different systems. So, it is sort of analogous to how armies and navies operated prior to radio and telegraph.

"Therefore, if we let them come to us and we manage to defeat them without a single ship getting back, it might buy us weeks, maybe even months before they realize what happened and vector a new fleet into this area. If so, it'll give us time to build, prepare, and gain a better understanding of just what the hell is going on out there."

"What you're saying here is that we don't even really know who the enemy will be or what his goals are," Brian interjected.

"Exactly, and that's why we should take a defensive stance until we get a feel for what's going on. Though I don't like to think it's true, we have to assume that maybe even Bel Varna is setting us up. Until we know better we trust no one out there."

"We're a border country," Matt interjected, "a third-rate, make that a *fifth*-rate power, and as such we can expect only one thing from the universe—the prospect of getting screwed by someone bigger than us."

Justin nodded slowly in agreement. How tragic it all was when he thought back to the naive idealism of his grandfather's generation, which assumed that if they contacted intelligent life it would be a wondrous, benevolent experience. Sad, but the history of expansion should have been warning enough regarding what happened when two cultures collided; in the end someone loses. He realized yet again that if he allowed himself to think about what might be happening a year or worse yet, five or ten years from now, it'd crush him. He had to stay focused on the moment, to get them through what might happen within hours, days, or at best weeks from now.

"We stay on the defensive then," Brian announced. "If we can trap them, we might get lucky and buy some more time."

"As for the tactical deployment," Justin said, glad that Seay was in agreement, "we muster just inside the asteroid belt region with our newer ships and use our antimatter drive ships for point defense against anything that breaks through."

"What about our Colonies out beyond that circle?" Brian asked. "You're talking about over half a million people."

"Saturn is now positioned near their probable line of attack; fortunately Jupiter is on the other side of the system right now. The only settlement there of any size is Titan, which numbers only several thousand people. Let's hope that they simply ignore it and are interested in bigger game. We're warning the Colonies and ships in the asteroids to stay low, turn off all transmissions, and hope they don't get detected."

"That's easy for you to say," Chelsey sniffed. "At least give them some defense, a couple of fighters."

"First of all we can't afford it, and secondly, by placing even one fighter there it just might draw attention to them. They'll come straight at Earth, and Mars will be the secondary target."

"What about defending Earth?" Tanya asked, and Justin looked over at her, sensing the chill in the room.

"They're on their own," Brian replied coldly. "Our own defense comes first. If we can repulse that wave and have resources left over to track the others down, we'll do it."

Justin wanted to say something but knew that anything he did say might very well jeopardize the small amount of trust in him that did exist at the moment.

"How do you see it, Bell?" Chelsey asked, and Justin hesitated, looking over at Brian, who nodded slightly, obviously interested in how he would answer.

"Our first concern is the protection of Mars. It's the center of resources for the Colonial Government; it's also where our facilities are located for building ships. We lose that and it's all over. After that our next concern is to make sure no one gets back to spread the word, and if that should include dispatching enemy ships moving towards Earth then I suggest we do it."

Chelsey looked around the room as if Justin's words had reinforced her position.

"In other words, defend Earth," she said coldly.

"We're talking about the possibility of genocide here," Tanya snapped angrily. "Of course we should try and stop it, damn it."

"The life of one Colonial isn't worth it," Chelsey said coldly.

"Enough on this," Seay interjected, holding out his hand.

"I accept what Bell's said here and he's placed our responses in the correct order. If by saving ourselves we save Earth as well, then that's the way it is."

Seay looked back at Justin.

"I've been in direct contact with Mahan on this issue and he is in agreement as well, though he is under strict orders to keep Corps deployments within near-Earth orbit. A tactical liaison channel is being established directly back to Mahan's headquarters so that we can keep him abreast of developments as they unfold."

"Is the UN government aware of this?" Justin asked.

"It is outside of government control. Mahan received strict orders that there would be no exchange of information."

"He's taking a hell of a risk then," Tanya said.

"Who isn't?"

"You realize what will happen if you are caught doing this?"

Bel Varna looked closely at his young nephew, sick at heart that he was sending him out on such a mission.

Darel smiled nervously and shrugged his shoulders. "It beats getting drafted into the fleet and serving under Zollern officers."

Bel smiled sadly. "Falsin's light squadron should arrive late today according to what Holzan just told me an hour ago. They were right behind him. If you encounter one of his ships don't try to run, even if you feel you can get away. Running will prove we're up to something, so if you're hailed let yourself be boarded. Remember, the chip containing the agreement and transfers of assets can be destroyed by simply pinching your skin where it is embedded. That will shatter the protective cover and your body will absorb it within minutes. Don't play the hero— destroy it! Your cover of being on a non-belligerent merchant trip should work for you, but they'll go over you and your ship from one end to the other looking for evidence to the contrary."

Darel tried to force a smile. Bel knew the boy was scared.

Most trade missions to the Gar were tricky enough even in peace-time. If they thought they could get away with it, they tended to simply "disappear" the ship. Darel would have to do some fast talking from the moment of first contact; that is, if he got through without being stopped by patrols.

"Now I've got other things to attend to. Safe voyage, boy."

Darel hesitated. "Come with me, uncle. There's no sense in staying here now."

Bel laughed and shook his head. "What, and run away?"

"It's not that at all. Chances are, once the Viceroy arrives you'll be arrested by him anyway."

"Holzan can't allow that. They have to keep up the farce that we've peacefully agreed to all of this, and I have to play the game to the end."

"You're just trying to play at being great-grandfather," Darel replied angrily.

"Look—Holzan, even if he is a Zollern bastard, is in some ways helping us, even if he isn't really aware of it. He won a lot of prestige by negotiating the treaty with us and he won't allow it to be shattered by the Viceroy. After all, he did get the use of our bases without a fight and he needs to keep it that way. He therefore needs me as well. No one will follow Norru. The power still rests on our side of the circle. I'll be all right. Now get out of here."

Bel was surprised when Darel stepped up and hugged him. Outward displays of affection were such bad form, and yet he found it pleasing somehow that the boy was worried about him to the point that proper etiquette was ignored.

"Out the back door, now," Bel said quickly and, breaking away from Darel, he shooed him to the door.

Bel returned to his desk and clicked into the pager on his computer. "Holzan, sorry to keep you waiting."

Holzan was obviously disturbed, and Bel had to suppress a smile. Making those who felt they were better than you wait was a wonderful part of the diplomatic game and

Holzan undoubtedly felt, and rightly so, that it should be Bel who waited now for him.

Holzan's image faded from the screen and seconds later the door opened.

Bel made a show of standing up and coming out from behind his desk, but also made it a point not to bow.

"Why did you keep me waiting?" Holzan announced. "When I called I told you it was urgent."

"A little family business, I'm sorry."

"Falsin has orders to meet his squadron after it comes through and then immediately proceed against the system that those new barbarians are from."

Bel said nothing, struggling to not let anything show. If it was true and Falsin succeeded in destroying them then all his plans were for naught. And the investment—what would the Gar do then? He was tempted to call Darel back, to drop his plan.

He knew Holzan was watching him. "Is that supposed to be a concern of mine?"

"We do know that you met and talked with them."

"Now where did you hear that?" Bel asked, his mind still racing. The barbarians had more than thirty days. If they were as cunning as he was beginning to suspect after examining their ship's computer log, they just might have a chance against a light squadron. A chance, but not much more.

"Was it my good friend Norru?"

Holzan looked at him closely and then smiled disarmingly.

"I really can't say, but we'll keep your little secret for now. Falsin will, of course, require the precise coordinates for the transit point into their system."

"Why ask me?"

"Bel. He will get it one way or the other. Your own military undoubtedly kept a record, so we can go that route, but I'd prefer to do this politely. I don't think you want the crew of your personal ship taken in by Falsin for his friendly method of questioning."

"I'll have one of my staff send the coordinates over to you. You can be the messenger and win Falsin's favor."

Holzan nodded his thanks, ignoring the taunt. "I also came to tell you that the Viceroy will be here as well within fifteen days, with his entire fleet. He was able to move faster than originally expected."

Yet more information, Bel thought, his stomach knotting. *More time, I thought I had more time.*

"We expect you to honor all aspects of the treaty. If there are no problems with the turnover to the Hive there will be no problems with the Viceroy."

"We'll observe every word of the treaty," Bel said evenly.

Holzan laughed and shook his head. "You free-thinkers are the shrewdest and most incorrigible liars in the universe, and damn me if I don't almost admire you for it," Holzan replied.

"We are practical business people. Both sides profit, but it always seems that when the other side fails to cheat us we're called liars."

Holzan, not bothering to ask, went over to the small cabinet that contained Bel's stock of precious Perjordin brandy and filled a generous glass both for himself and for Bel.

"Politicians like us should leave this type of bickering to others, Bel. It is a shame you keep putting yourself at odds with me."

"I protect the interests of my world, and those interests are best served by maintaining free-state status."

Bel took the glass of his own brandy from Holzan and sipped it, glad at least that Holzan was an obvious connoisseur who understood that brandy was best enjoyed slowly and not gulped. *It was interesting, the physiology is so different yet we both appreciate a fine drink.*

"It's too bad we're on opposite sides in all of this," Holzan said.

"You made it that way. Behind all the fine words I am an official of a system your family has chosen to occupy and then turn over to an even worse foe."

"That occupation can be done in a civilized way or by the mailed fist. It's up to you."

"I really don't think we have the power to decide that," Bel replied sharply, "not without the Viceroy of Avla."

He sipped the drink again, then shook his head as if bringing up something troublesome. "That ship you claimed was a Gar vessel. . . ."

Ah, here it is. Bel studied his brandy for a moment, taking a sip.

"Which ship?" Bel finally asked. "Dozens of them make port here every year."

"You don't seem to be hearing me very clearly," Holzan snapped. "I'm trying to make it very plain to you that if, when this barbarian world is crushed, Falsin finds any evidence of your contacting them, it will go poorly for you."

Bel nodded, looking closely at Holzan. Could it be that Holzan actually had a personal interest and was warning him? Holzan had never struck him as the type who would let his feelings get in the way of his career.

Bel returned to his desk and sat down.

"Let us suppose just for a moment that I did commit this act. Let me point out that if it did indeed occur prior to the signing of the treaty between Cor and the Zollern, then the point is moot. And besides, if they have come to *us* there is nothing violated, that is, if indeed such a fantastic thing did take place."

"The Viceroy won't see it that way."

He's warning me, Bel realized. *Yet the point was curious. It was evident that someone, most likely Norru, had found out and passed the word along. That word could have only been carried to Holzan, who returned to Zollern and spilled the information, then returned back here to warn me. A most curious game.*

"Simply a wild rumor," Bel finally replied.

"As I had hoped. There will be an investigation, though."

"Investigate all you want," Bel replied, glad that he had made certain that the central records regarding all incoming ships had been carefully altered.

"Anyway, if there were anyone I'd be concerned about

regarding this violation of contact with barbarians, I'd look towards the Gar. You know the rumors of their wanderings."

"Then nothing happened."

"Of course not," Bel hesitated, "and thank you."

"Fine. If you are free later this evening, do join me for dinner. I've brought back some wines from the Imperial vineyards you'll find delightful."

Surprised, Bel nodded an agreement. Placing his empty glass on Bel's table, Holzan bowed formally and left the room.

Bel sighed noisily and poured himself another drink.

Most unusual. Holzan sets me up with Avla and then tells me what he has done. Why?

There were so many variables and as Bel sipped his drink he realized that his head was in the noose. And yet, there was almost reason to laugh about what it revealed.

✧ Chapter XI ✧

"Captain Bell?"

Groaning, Justin opened his eyes and then squinted again. He snarled, "Turn off that damn light, will you?" and started to roll over. The realization hit him then and he sat up.

The young ensign looked down at him and Justin knew.

"They're here."

Falsin Zollern paced, pausing to look nervously over the shoulder of his intelligence officer.

The banks of screens were a scramble of information as the officer swept through the full band of frequencies. The computers inhaled the information, sorted it out, and came back with preliminary translations.

"Any sign of activity?"

"None yet, Sire. Most of the barbarian radio traffic appears to be centered in two primary locations around the third world and its moon, with a smaller cluster with the fourth world."

"Military traffic?"

"We won't know for a while yet. We still need the translations—we're not sure which bands are military and which are not."

"Give me a schematic of the system."

Falsin leaned over, examining the projection showing the relative positions of the planets and the thousands of radio sources.

The inner planet was producing emissions at nearly five hundred times the rate of the fourth one. The second had to be nothing more than a Colonial outpost.

Falsin cursed silently. It was impossible to monitor what their military was doing, if anything. The weapons they had might be capable of anything.

If the Gar had attacked here and lost, it meant these barbarians had some sort of serious capability.

Caution told him he should now wait, gather data for several days and gauge their reaction. But how would he explain that to his uncle—caution against savages? This system had to be secured, a refueling depot established, construction on fortress outposts started, antimatter refining initiated—then they could sit back to see which way the Hive turned.

A single knockout blow had to be made now to overawe these barbarians and bring them into line. The home world was the place to do it; he should not waste time on mere outposts.

"Signal the fleet. We move on their primary radio emission source . . . destroy that and the rest will come to heel."

"They're coming in."

Lin Zhu nodded, motioning for Hassan to join him.

Zhu studied the top-down projection of the solar system intently, the blips on the edge of the screen inching in. The reported positions highlighted in red were hours old, the orange course-projection lines showed them to be well past the orbital path of Uranus already and closing towards Saturn.

The image flickered for a moment as another radar sweep from Saturn came in, the signal well over an hour old. The course-projection lines shifted, turning several degrees from their former positions.

"The fleet's shifting course," Hassan announced, sitting down on the edge of Zhu's desk while staring intently at the screen.

A minute later another image came in, the projection lines shifting even more.

Hassan clicked the display computer's microphone and whispered a command.

Projection lines leaped out across the screen, all of them tracing straight to Earth.

"They're bypassing Mars," Hassan whispered. "This time they know we're the center and they're coming straight to us. A sound move."

"I'm glad you admire their logic," Zhu replied stiffly.

"It is the proper move. Mopping up Colonial outposts can wait."

"But that's where the real strength lies in this system."

"They don't know that," Hassan said with a smile. "It also fits perfectly into what we want to do."

Zhu nodded.

"Order the Corps Fleet to forward deploy for an intercept, and you damn well better be right on the rest of your plan."

"Oh, I most assuredly will be," Hassan said with an eager grin.

"Forward deployment is madness," Mahan snapped, shutting off the comm link to Geneva.

"Those are your orders. The Joint Chiefs have agreed to it as well."

Mahan looked back over his shoulder at the old man hunched over in the float chair.

"Their main force is coming straight here and will arrive in under twelve hours," Thor said. "it looks like they're deploying only one ship for a recon on Mars. The rest are heading straight here."

Mahan sighed and looked back at the plot board. "Should we ask for help from Seay?"

Thor sat in silence for a moment and then finally shook his head.

"No. Their only hope is point defense as they originally planned. If they show their hand now this fleet will turn on them and wipe them out. My hope was that they'd split up as they came in. Whoever's in charge on the other side is playing it smart, unlike his predecessor. By shifting Mars' forces, especially the new ships, it'll reveal our assets. Beyond that, if they come here first it'll give Seay time to get another ship, maybe two, online.

"If we're lucky they might get blunted here, but they will break through; there are simply too many of them even if Mars did divert them."

"You're condemning Earth, you know that."

Thor looked up coldly at Mahan. "Earth condemned herself a long time ago," Thor replied sharply. "Whatever hope we have now lies with the new worlds. We wasted a hundred years by not getting ready for this moment and the waste of the last forty, especially with all the warning signs, was criminal. I had hoped the Civil War would accelerate the process; given another ten years we might have reached parity. But we don't have ten years, we're down to days at best. It's the same old story and for right here, right now, the side of blindness has won. Made worse by those bastards in control.

"Look, Mahan, one system or the other was going to get it in this fight. Like I said, I had hoped they'd divide their fleet up but they didn't. Therefore either Mars or Earth would get hit first. If they had hit Mars, Seay would have put up a hell of a fight and maybe chewed them up a bit, and then just possibly Earth might have stood a chance. But that's not what I wanted, son, I wanted them here first."

He hesitated for a moment.

"I'm just sorry it had to be you."

Mahan nodded sadly.

"It's for the better. We lose Mars and we lose the future and any hope of survival. We lose Earth, and we simply lose the past."

"It's hard to look at it so cold-bloodedly," Mahan said softly. "This is home. The United States, home."

"The United States is dead, it died the minute it allowed the EDF to take control of things. The United States is somewhere out there; it just has a different name now, that's all."

Mahan looked back at the plot board. "I better get our fighters moving."

"Not all of them."

"You heard the orders."

"Whose orders, your so-called masters?"

Surprised, Mahan looked back at Thor.

"Fight the battle the way you see best, son. But I'd suggest just sending out a light screen for an initial probe. You'll lose some good pilots, but not all of them. We can analyze the defensive response. This sudden change of plan on Geneva's part doesn't fit somehow. There's something wrong."

Mahan smiled. "All right then." He hesitated for a moment. "Seventh Wing will do the forward, the rest will stand back as planned. Now then, let's get out of here."

"What do you mean?"

"I've decided to move my headquarters out into space."

"What?"

"Just that. I think out there is a better location for command and control."

"You'll get fried or cut off."

"We'll get fried here too, and I'll be damned if I'll be hunkered down in some bunker while the Corps goes into its last fight."

Thor smiled sadly. "Half a league, half a league . . ."

"Something like that. I've already arranged transport— we're pulling up stakes here in an hour."

"That's over a thousand personnel."

"Nearly four thousand counting immediate families for headquarters personnel."

Thorsson looked up at Mahan with a grin.

"You know, I've been a bit suspicious about all these Corps families leaving Earthside the last month."

"We've got close to fifteen thousand of them aboard

the Academy ship now and believe me, Thor, it wasn't easy getting them out quietly. It took a hell of a lot of money in some high places to pull it off. Thousands more have left for outer Colonies, or even for Mars, where Seay has been taking them in. It might not be fair but the Corps looks out for its own. If things go down with Earth I want my people to die knowing that their families were moved out of harm's way, at least temporarily. We've strapped a dozen *Orion*-class nuclear pulse engine tugs onto the Academy and it moves out of lunar orbit within the hour. We'll try and run them towards Mars or out to the asteroid belt. It's better than waiting down here for the end. That's where Headquarters will be for the rest of this fight."

Thor reached up and took Mahan's hand.

"Bob, I liked you thirty-five years ago when you were a pain-in-the-ass scrub. I like you even more now. Good luck, son."

"Don't wish it yet, Thor. You see, you're going with us."

"The hell I am! I still have a couple of things left to do here."

"And get yourself killed? Wake up, sir, the Bilateral Commission is dead and it's time to choose sides. You're leaving with me right now."

"Just try it," Thorsson snapped.

"I will," and he leaned over and punched a comm line open.

"Get that damn marine in here for our guest."

The door behind Mahan slid open and a graying Marine came through the door, dressed in his class-As, his left chest a rainbow of colors from forty years of decorations.

"Come on, sir, we've got a flight to catch," the marine growled, coming to attention before Thorsson.

"Sergeant Malady, if you touch my chair I'll have your stripes."

"You've taken them half a dozen times, sir, and you've always given them back. Now let's go, sir, or I'll carry you out of here, and we wouldn't want that."

Thor looked at Malady, the old hand-to-hand combat instructor at the Academy, and then back at Mahan.

"Leave an old man the dignity of choosing where to die," he whispered.

"Sir. The government wants you dead and now is the perfect time to finish you. The Corps still needs you and as of this moment I'm mobilizing you back in with the rank of Commandant. We want you in charge of the show again."

Thor looked at Mahan with surprise. "I'm too old to run the Corps again. Don't confuse your judgment with sentimentality."

"It's not sentimentality," Malady interjected, "just damn good sense, so stop bitching, sir, and take the job."

"I'm over ninety years old. My legs are useless and I'm dying by inches."

"Still young inside, though, and you can still think circles around most of us," Mahan replied. "I've got you, sir, it's that simple, so take over at least until we get out of this scrape. If you're worried about tactical and direct command and control of military units I'll still run that, but we need you for something far more than that and you know it."

Mahan looked at him closely and saw something start to reemerge that had been hidden for far too long. Thor finally nodded his head and then looked up at Malady.

"Come on, you lummox, get me aboard and let's get out of here."

A few minutes later Admiral Mahan walked out onto the tarmac, the late autumn sun rising off the Atlantic already warm with the promise of another humid day. Transports were lined up the length of the taxiway.

Mahan stopped to watch as the first transport nosed up then banked over to the southeast, rising higher and higher, pointing straight up, ascending into the heavens on a pillar of fire. Less than a minute later the next transport burst through the smoke, following its leader, and then another and then another as if the sky were on fire. The sun was darkened by the roiling clouds of smoke.

He walked over to the last transport on the line and turned to look back. Ground crews came running out of the hangars, while from the bunkers the launch and control crews emerged, racing to get aboard the last ship of the Corps leaving Earth. An ensign came running up to Mahan and saluted.

"Sir, EDF is raising hell. Their orbital monitoring is picking up our launch, they're onto us. I told them that we're deploying additional equipment and then cut them off like you told me to, claiming we were shutting down all links for security reasons."

"By the time they figure it out we'll be gone," Mahan said with a grin. "Now get aboard, young lady."

She turned and looked back across the field, ignoring the pulsing thunder of another ship lifting off, and Mahan could see that there were tears in her eyes.

He reached into his pocket, pulled out a tissue and handed it to her.

"Will we ever come back home again, sir?"

"Young lady, we're going home right now, so get on board," he said softly, and she went past him up the ramp into the transport.

He looked nervously at the taxiway. The next-to-last ship was revving up and turning out to head down to the end of the runway. There wasn't much time. At least the Gar attack had taken out enough of the orbital defense and surveillance grid that there was a hole preventing an immediate EDF space-to-ground strike, but they could still scramble something over here, and chances were they already had something on the way.

At last he saw them. Malady jogged alongside Thorsson's chair as they came out from beside the command bunker, and Mahan beckoned for them to hurry.

Thorsson slowed and waved Malady ahead into the ship. Malady hesitated until Mahan nodded for him to follow orders. Thor turned and looked back across the field and then up at the morning sky.

"Never thought I'd get sentimental about this planet,"

he said quietly, and Mahan saw that there was a small clump of dirt and grass in Thorsson's hand.

"Come on, sir," Mahan said quietly. "Space is waiting for us."

Justin Bell sat in silence, watching the monitor that was relaying the radar signal up from Mars C-in-C. The Zollern Fleet was fifty million miles away, aiming straight in on Earth and closing. Nothing was coming this way at all, absolutely nothing, the one Zollern recon ship painting them with several radar bursts and then turning about to rejoin the main fleet.

All the preparation, all of it seemed wasted. If only they had been able to coordinate properly there would have been a chance, but the Colonial government refused to release the fleet for an intercept and Earth made it clear it didn't want the help.

He could understand the Colonial government's caution. There was always the threat that they might somehow have stealthing capability and that the strike on Earth was intended to divert. But he knew that was unlikely. The main attack was going in and he now had to sit passively by and watch.

He looked over at his co, a young Colonial pilot.

"Wake me if anything changes."

Leaving his seat he went aft and collapsed on his bunk. More than anything he found himself wishing that he could simply go to sleep and wake up after it was all over. His old comrades and his Corps were about to die, and like all survivors the guilt was slowly eating into his soul.

Falsin Zollern settled into his command chair and nodded to his communications officer.

"Order forward ships to deploy to Tactical Plan One Four. Once we clear their outer defenses, concentrate on the primary world. Second wing to their moon. I'll personally open the bombardment."

He looked at his forward holo screen and shook his head

in disbelief. A thin screen of a dozen ships was moving in, positioning for intercept. Analysis was already showing that they had no steering capability other than thrusters—the engines were plasma and ion drivers, not even antimatter. It was pathetic.

The first ship attempted to engage by dropping a spread of missiles, which were dispatched within seconds. More missiles leaped out, and his ships turned to maneuver in for the kill.

Within seconds it was all over, the twelve barbarian ships destroyed, one of his slightly damaged.

"Sire."

He looked back at his communications officer.

"We have a signal from the barbarians' primary world and it's in our language."

Hassan could still feel the tingling in his hand from the recoil of the pistol and smell the acrid smell of gunpowder wafting through the room. He looked back over at Zhu's staff, who stood huddled in the corner of the room. The door behind him burst open and he did not bother to turn; they were his own men.

"Get his body out of here," and Hassan motioned towards the body lying on the floor, a pool of blood puddling out underneath him to stain the carpet.

A shame, the carpet would have to be replaced.

As they rolled Lin Zhu over Hassan looked into the now lifeless eyes.

You understood the path, he thought, *but you did not understand just how ruthless you had to be*, and he smiled. *Besides, we need a convenient scapegoat and you are now it.*

Hassan, still ignoring Zhu's staff, went over to the dead man's desk and hooked into the comm line.

"This is Hassan. That link that the secretary general ordered, has it been established yet?"

"Waiting."

"Hook it in."

Hassan looked over to the holo display screen and

seconds later it snapped to life. The image was grainy; apparently their video pickups' signals weren't compatible. He studied the image closely.

So Bell was right. They were humanoid but appeared to be of reptilian descent. The man he was looking at was pale, dressed in black except for what looked like traces of silver and gold thread on the shoulders and collar. There was no reaction. Hassan realized that the delay was still nearly thirty seconds or more each way.

"I am Ibn Hassan, director of my planet's government."

He ignored the frightened murmurs coming from the back of the room and the sound of the EDF guards dragging Zhu's body out.

The image moved, turning his head slightly, and then looked back at Hassan.

"Falsin Zollern of the Zollern Fleet. We demand your immediate surrender."

Hassan smiled.

"We would prefer to call it an alliance," Hassan said quietly, "but there is time to discuss that later."

He paused for a brief moment.

"There has been a change of government since the unfortunate incident regarding your last fleet and those responsible have been eliminated. I regret as well to inform you that our space-based military has rebelled and refused to surrender. If you would kindly dispatch them you will find no resistance on our part once you are inside the immediate area of space above our planet. Once you achieve orbit I look forward to meeting with you."

Hassan waited, standing still, not allowing his inner nervousness to show. By killing Zhu he could shift the blame and at the same time destroy the Corps. The question now was whether he personally would survive.

The seconds slowly passed and finally the return signal came in.

Falsin nodded, a thin smile creasing his features.

"I agree to meet."

❖   ❖   ❖

Admiral Mahan, his features contorted with rage, looked over at Thor.

"The bastard sold us out!"

Thor chuckled softly.

"A masterful move and the only way he could survive."

"What about Zhu?"

"Dead, that's obvious. It was the best way to shift blame and come out on top. Hassan knew that they wouldn't deal with someone who had humiliated them."

Mahan turned away from the screen and looked around at his staff who stood expectantly waiting.

"As of this moment the government of Earth has broken its remaining ties with the Corps. There is nothing more we can do here. I want all ships signaled to break off and make best possible speed for Mars. With luck most of us will get there. Our fighters are to maintain escort on the Academy—that's our weakness right now and I want those people moved to safety."

Mahan looked down at his left breast pocket, at the blue emblem of the United Nations that had betrayed them. He tore the emblem off and dropped it.

"Send a signal to Admiral Seay and tell him he has a new fleet on his side."

Hassan waited expectantly, though worried that nausea might overtake him. Space was an environment he had always hated and to vomit now because of the zero gravity would be a humiliation beyond bearing. They might think it was fear, and that thought tormented him.

He felt the nudge of the docking collar and a moment later the door opened. He stepped through and felt gravity return, almost as heavy as Earth's.

The suit he was wearing was cumbersome, a precaution that they had demanded. The door closed behind him and sound dropped away. Vacuum to kill any microbes, he realized. A moment later pressure returned and the door before him opened.

They were taller; that somehow bothered him and he

could sense that they were gazing at him as if he were a specimen in a zoo. With an attempt at haughty disdain he walked into the ship and tried to suppress his curiosity. Machinery was never of interest to him anyway and he focused instead on the two figures who stood before him. One motioned for him to follow and moved forward with a slow, steady pace down a broad corridor. They led him into what appeared to be an office or conference room, complete with a long table and a dozen chairs. Only one was occupied at the far end of the room. The man sitting before him leaned back in his chair with a show of arrogance.

So the game is universal, Hassan thought, and he waited, not conceding the opening move of speaking first.

"You were wise to surrender, barbarian."

The man's voice was soft, his words unintelligible, all but masked by the computerized translation that filled the room.

"As I said, I don't see it as a surrender, but rather as an alliance."

Falsin laughed. "A presumptuous barbarian, how amusing."

"Surrender means submission to a superior will or force and implies reluctance. I am willing to fully concede your superior force but I do so without reluctance."

Falsin sat silent for a moment, confused by the reply. It was hard to conceal that he was disappointed. He had hoped for a more forceful display and silently cursed the orders that bound him to seize the world and its space-based infrastructure with as little damage as possible. But still there could be some amusement.

"My intelligence officer informs me that you appear to have a number of different languages."

"We do."

"And does this mean that your world is divided?"

"It is."

"Pick a place on your world that you despise."

Falsin watched closely and saw the flicker of a smile

on the barbarian's face; he felt an instant liking for this man.

Hassan walked over to a display screen and pointed.

"This city was a center of defense against your last attack and was only partially destroyed."

Hassan watched as Falsin leaned over and spoke softly, and then sat back up and motioned for him to watch the screen.

A minute later a bright point of light flashed on the screen as Washington was destroyed.

He looked back at Falsin.

"I look forward to working with you, sir."

"Fine, but let me make it clear that if you fail in any way the next point of destruction will be whatever it is you hold dear and you will be there to greet it."

"Then I should inform you that you've only taken part of this system. A government in rebellion against our authority controls the rest of space except for this world."

Falsin nodded. So the system was torn with dissent. Typical of barbarians, he thought with disgust. He felt annoyed as well that all his ships had decelerated into orbit around this world. There was no real problem with fuel yet, though some of them had engaged in combat maneuvering. The situation was made worse by the hundreds of barbarian ships that were scattering in every direction. Some of them had been hunted down and destroyed, but most were still moving outward. He sat in silence, staring at the barbarian before him.

"One of my officers will interrogate you regarding the political and military situation here. Be truthful or you will regret it later."

"I wouldn't be so stupid as to lie to you," Hassan replied, letting a touch of disdain creep into his voice. "But I should tell you right now that the rebellious military force I mentioned is even now fleeing. If you pursue them immediately you can destroy them within hours."

Falsin slammed his fist on the table.

"Do you really think what you call a military is any

concern to me now, especially after their pitiful display? There'll be time enough to hunt them down; they have no place to hide."

Falsin whispered a command into his console and a door opened. His guards took Hassan out of the room.

The arrogance of the man, Falsin thought. He would not let this barbarian see his concern. There'd be time enough later to destroy what was left. Enough had been accomplished already within the last day. There was still the possibility that all of this could be some elaborate trap. Tomorrow there would be time enough to secure the rest of the system.

✦ Chapter XII ✦

It felt good to be out of the cramped quarters of his ship and Justin stretched lazily as he floated down the corridor of the Mars Skyhook Docking Station. The normally busy station was just about empty, all civilian traffic grounded except for the evacuation of nonessential personnel from near-orbit. The Skyhook Terminus was now strictly a military operation and even that was at a minimum. Only a dozen ships were currently docked, four of them the precious translight-capable ships.

It had been more than twenty hours since the shock of Hassan's capitulation had been broadcast throughout the system and with it the defection of the Corps to the Colonial side. Everything they had planned for over the last month and a half had been turned upside down.

No battle plan ever survived first contact, Justin realized, but this was a situation he had never even remotely considered. Stopping at the conference room, he cleared the security guard and floated in. He looked around the room and was glad to see Matt, who was commanding the original *Prometheus*.

Admiral Seay looked up at Justin's entry and nodded.

"I think we're all here, and besides there isn't time to wait. I'm changing our deployment."

"To what?" Matt asked.

"The Corps, as you know, has declared itself for the Colonies. They are evacuating near-Earth space. It's a miracle that the Zollern haven't launched a pursuit and crushed them by now. Hauling the Academy ship out of lunar orbit might be a wonderful symbolic and sentimental gesture, but it's slowing them down. They're barely two million miles out and committing everything they have to its protection. They can expect that at any moment the Zollern will strike them."

Seay hesitated for a moment.

"I'm therefore committing every antimatter *Grecko*-class fighter and our five *Prometheus*-class ships to a forward projection for a rendezvous with the Corps fleet. Our entire supply of Gar anti-ship missiles will be loaded onto the *Prometheus* fighters, with what's left over hooked onto the ships piloted by our best personnel. That's only forty-three missiles, so use them wisely, people."

Justin breathed an inner sigh of relief.

"Why, sir?"

Justin looked across the room. It was Chelsey again, Matt's co-pilot and he was finding her to be decidedly tiresome with her paranoia about Earth forces.

"That strips us to nothing here, sir. While we go off on this knight's errand we could be struck from another direction."

"Because it's a sound military move, that's why," Seay replied sharply. "If we can rendezvous with the Corps fleet before the enemy strikes we'll have a combined strength that just might match what they've sent out."

"Sir, it puts our fighters outside the defensive capabilities of this planet, and what the Corps has won't match that. We're stronger on point defense."

"It's an order and it stands," Seay retorted, "and that settles it. Man your craft—I'm ordering an immediate departure. Dismissed."

Chelsey looked around angrily, and shouldering past Justin she left the room. The rest of the assembled crews followed her out.

Justin floated up to his old squad commander and extended his hand.

"Thank you, sir."

Brian smiled.

"It's like the old days again, finally. The Corps is reunited and I'll be damned if I'll allow the families of so many friends to go down without a fight on my part."

"Chelsey had a point, though."

"Damn her, I know she did. But then again, an aggressive move on our part just might give us the edge. We have to fight them sooner or later and it might as well be now. The problem is that, given best possible speed for our *Grecko*-class fighters it's still a day to reach Earth. They could sortie and do the job in an hour. I know this goes against all logic. Sun-Tzu said that when you are weaker than your enemy, evade. We have no place to evade *to*; therefore audacity is perhaps our only chance. I hate to order this, but if the Zollern move and our entire fleet can not engage together you are not to commit our *Prometheus* fighters. All of you are to turn around and return here."

"You expect me to turn around and simply abandon them?" Justin asked softly.

"I don't expect it, Justin, I'm ordering it."

Falsin Zollern, barely able to suppress his rage, looked over at the plot board that showed the sortie moving in from the barbarian's other main planet. Long-range optical sensors had yet to get a quality fix on the hundred and sixty-odd craft to confirm what the groveling leader of the barbarians had claimed, but there was no reason to doubt it. The man was too shrewd to lie at this point.

He had thought of simply holding this world hostage, demanding the surrender of the Gar-design ships or the planet would be annihilated. That, however, was impractical and could cause problems with the Diet, who would object to the destruction of the world's infrastructure. Some would even be upset over the loss of life, something that he found to be illogical. It was, after all, war.

The briefings of the last day had made at least part of the picture clear concerning this system. The number of the barbarians was in itself troubling. The plague had not touched them and that threat alone could be an option he could later use and deny. At least they were divided, and their leader had seemed delighted with the prospect of destroying what he defined as rebels.

He looked back at the plot board. The barbarian ships were the antimatter drive type, and were accelerating rapidly. He'd let them get in closer, while the ships that were fleeing could get a little farther out from the gravity well of this planet, thus giving his own ships an additional edge with maneuvering that the other side lacked. The few barbarian ships of Gar design were equipped with magnetic coiling for maneuvering but it was doubtful if their crews had yet mastered them.

He turned away from the plot board and back to the memo he had just completed. There was more than enough evidence now to indicate that the barbarians had indeed gone beyond their system; chances were, to Cor. If so, the coincidence was simply too much to leave unattended. Bel Varna had to have had a hand in some of this. That at least could be taken care of immediately by the first courier ship back.

"Next ignition sequence in ten, nine, eight . . ."

As the alarm sounded Admiral Mahan cinched his shoulder harness in tight and looked at Thor to make sure that he was safely secured. His ever-present guardian, Sergeant Malady, double-checked Thor's harness and then quickly strapped himself in.

Mahan braced himself for the bone-jolting crunch from the nuclear pulse engines strapped onto the Academy ship.

The first jolt hit, surging up through several gees of acceleration, followed by a continued pounding as the dozen massive tug engines, which were nothing more than thermonuclear explosions detonating against coiled plating, pulsed and flared. Creaks and groans echoed through the corridors. The Academy, like all O'Neill cylinders, had not been designed for this type of pounding and already there had been numerous structural breaks resulting in the decompression of nearly fifty percent of the two outer decks. Fortunately the fifteen thousand passengers were deep within the core of the ship. The outer decks had been evacuated earlier since the protective outer coating of nearly three meters of lunar slag had been detached to cut down on the mass. Even with that gone they were still attempting to move nearly two hundred-thousand tons of ship and after thirty-one hours of running were still only two million miles from Earth.

The acceleration continued and Mahan rode it out, looking over at Thor, wondering how the old man was withstanding the high-gee stress—he seemed to be reveling in the power. Mahan smiled as he watched him. This was a man who had witnessed the last of the old United States Shuttle One launches, had been on the first expedition to Mars, had risen to found and command the Corps, and been the first commander of the Academy. His lifetime contained over two-thirds of the history of manned spaceflight and he had lived long enough to see humankind reach the stars. Even now he knew that the old man was plotting, still trying to find a way for survival, and more importantly, independence.

The alarm sounded again and seconds later the engines shut down. Since the cylinder was not rotating, weightlessness returned.

"Any sign of a sortie yet?" Thor asked.

"None."

"Curious. We're slow, especially moving the Academy ship like this. It's too damn bad we couldn't have lined up enough transports to simply get our people out that way."

"It would have been too obvious tying up that many ships. This was the only way."

"I wanted our fleet to get out intact. Instead they'll die defending this ship."

"There was no other way. We couldn't pull out beforehand. Our original hope was that if they broke through they would have been so chewed up that one more ship fleeing wouldn't have drawn notice. We never anticipated Hassan."

"I should have," Thor said quietly. "When I think about it, it was the only maneuver possible to insure his power and survival. It was almost elegant in its simplicity."

"So why are they waiting?"

"To secure their position on Earth. They'll want to occupy the Skyhook Tower, and some of the repair and construction bays in high orbit might be useful as well. Also I've been thinking about their tactics. Their maneuvering system . . . the magnetic coiling works better the farther away they are from a gravity well and any other magnetic disturbances. The farther away from Earth we get, the greater their advantage. It creates a paradox. Stay in close and we have some small advantage, but still not enough. Run, which we have to do, and their advantage increases. I thought he'd have made his move by now, just prior to our rendezvous with the incoming Colonial fleet. A good morale-breaker, to shatter us just short of safety."

"I already feel so damn hopeless," Mahan sighed.

"We still haven't engaged them yet in an open fight. The last time we were caught by surprise. Combined, we'll have four hundred ships to their forty-six. Granted, they have a dozen or more vessels of at least a thousand tons, but we still might give them a run for it. And if they close on this ship we do have a couple of arrows in her quiver as well."

Thor looked over at Malady, who grinned.

"I'd like to lead a boarding party myself," Malady growled.

"Admiral Mahan?"

Mahan looked up at the communications officer.

"Go ahead."

"Sir, the Zollern fleet appears to be moving to leave Earth orbit."

"Estimated time of arrival?"

"Hard to say, sir, since we don't have a very good profile yet on their ships' capabilities. Given what we know of the Gar ship design, it'd be less than thirty minutes."

"How long till the Colonial Fleet arrives?"

"They're already starting into deceleration. At least an hour, sir."

"Damn. So damn close!"

"Our enemy would have been a fool to let us join up. It had to be expected," Thor said quietly. "Now let's see just how good a fight we can put up."

Justin leaned over the holo screen, silently cursing as the leading edge of the Zollern fleet swept in and punched clear through the trailing edge of frigates deployed astern of the convoy. Flares of light snapped out as four of the frigates disappeared. *Glenn*-class fighters maneuvered to gain locks on the enemy ships, which easily turned out of the line of attack while the fighters, without any coiled maneuvering systems, continued on past their intended targets. Some of the inner line of ships, though, started to trade damage back before going under. They scored obvious laser hits on half a dozen ships, while one of the fighters simply rammed an opponent, both ships fireballing.

The first wave of the strike closed in on the Academy ship and Justin wanted to look away.

There was a blinding string of detonations and for an instant he thought the Academy was gone. Then the glare dropped and the wave of five incoming strike ships was no longer on the screen.

"They still have some fight in them!"

Justin looked over at his comm screen at Matt, piloting *Prometheus* off his port side.

"Area suppression, must have used a hundred or more nukes," Justin said gleefully. "Hell, they walked right into it!"

"Let's get a part of this," Matt replied.

Justin looked back down at the holo and then over at Tanya.

"We've got twenty minutes yet to close if we stay with the fighters."

Justin nodded. Mahan could pull his trick off against

the first wave, but the next attack would come in from all directions.

"Order the fighters to stop deceleration, that'll cut the time down."

"They'll streak right through," Tanya replied.

"So what? There's no sense in matching speed with the Corps fleet. If we blow on through chances are it'll shake up the Zollern, and it might split their attack. We're moving ahead."

"What about Mahan's orders?"

"To hell with the orders!"

Justin toggled his open command channel on.

"All *Grecko*-class fighters, stop deceleration, power up and go straight on in. *Prometheus*-class, maximum acceleration on my count. Five, four, three, two, one!"

Justin slammed the throttle forward, feeling the brief initial surge until the inertial dampening system caught up and took hold.

"We've got signatures on five Gar ships, Sire, moving ahead of the approaching fleet."

Falsin, still shaken by the annihilation of his first wave, nodded and turned to watch his main tactical display. Five flashing dots were detaching from the main body, moving rapidly forward.

The game was getting complex. The lumbering ships of the first barbarian fleet seemed little better than drone targets for gunnery practice. But it turned out they did have some teeth, and some were armed with lasers that were deadly at close range. The biggest ship, which they seemed so intent on defending, was going nowhere. It could wait.

"All ships to focus on the second fleet, follow my lead."

Admiral Mahan sighed noisily, turning away from the primary battle screen.

"They're breaking off, going after the Colonials."

"How'd we do?"

"Five kills on the area detonation, one, possibly two more."

"Our losses?"

"A third of our fighters, half our frigates, three destroyers."

Thor nodded silently.

"Get ready to drop first spread; ready, three, two, one, now! Break, break, break!"

Justin slammed his stick forward, the other four ships of his group spreading out into a starburst pattern as their load of Gar-designed warheads streaked forward. The starfield before him shifted, spinning as he dove underneath the approaching fleet. Space around him was crisscrossed with flashes of light and silent detonations.

Point defenses on the enemy ships opened up, gaining locks on most of the drone missiles while the ones with warheads jinked and wove. Flashes of light blazed.

"We got one, got one!" Tanya roared. "Direct hit. Others flaring; counting four, make that five hits!"

"Three ships turning in behind us."

Justin barely looked over at his co, a Colonial pilot he suspected was less than pleased to be assigned under him. Without waiting to be ordered, the Colonial initiated a preprogrammed series of jinking maneuvers to throw off laser aim and dropped another Gar missile, which would activate once pursuit had passed and then go for the nearest target.

Seconds later the round flared to life and one of the three pursuing ships disappeared.

It almost seemed too easy, Justin thought for a moment as he heard shouts of delight from his co and Tanya. But the other two ships closed remorselessly, the range dropping to the point that jinking would no longer be able to throw off the aim of a laser. He pivoted and pulled back up, cutting in behind another ship that had a lock on one of his comrades. Even as he fired on it with forward lasers, tearing the stern of the enemy ship open, the Colonial ship ahead of his target disappeared.

Was it Matt?

He banked over, dodging the return fire from the Zollern ship's rear gunnery turrets.

"Matt?"

"Still going, buddy, how the hell you doing?"

"Scared shitless, got two on me."

"Three here, hold on!"

Justin spared a quick glance at Tanya's tactical screen. It was a swarming confusion of dots, all semblance of control breaking down. A flash detonated in front of him, and he turned sharply, narrowly avoiding the mushrooming fireball.

This was nothing like the Civil War, with fleets streaking past each other in a few seconds and then sometimes taking hours to turn for another pass.

"The forward edge of our *Grecko*-class fighters is engaging," Tanya announced.

At the moment he barely noticed as he continued to twist and turn, attempting to throw off his pursuers. After several long minutes he found that each turn he made was slightly tighter than that of his opponents and that his ship had slightly faster acceleration coming out of the turns.

One of the two pursuers broke off and turned away, but the other attempted to hang on. Turning yet again Justin managed a momentary line-up and he held down on his firing button. The ship's computer calculated range and deflection and the twin guns mounted under the wings opened up, flashes of light slashing out across the port bow of the enemy ship.

Streaks of light came back and a shudder ran through the ship.

"Hit on port wing!" Tanya shouted.

Justin continued his turn, dropping in behind his opponent less than a kilometer astern, another shudder running through his ship.

Tanya toggled off their one remaining Gar missile. The weapon streaked forward and in less than a second it detonated against the stern of the enemy ship as Justin banked away.

More flashes of light winked across space as dozens of Grecko fighters dropped their single missile loads and then died as Zollern ships lined up for easy kills.

The exaltation Justin felt with his third kill died. It appeared as if they were being slaughtered.

Falsin watched the action unfold with stunned disbelief. The barbarians had Gar tracker-killer rounds of the latest design, something beyond comprehension.

"Our losses?"

"Fifteen ships gone, Sire, seven more damaged," and as he spoke the communications officer looked over at Falsin in stunned disbelief.

"Their losses?"

"Half of the smaller enemy ships destroyed, along with two of the Gar design."

He looked back over at his tactical. His ships were spread out, trying to chase down individual ships moving off in every direction. There was no tactical logic here, no mutual support, but there were so many of them! Even as he watched there was another flash as a tracker-killer dropped astern of one of his ships and destroyed its pursuer.

"Break it off! Order our ships to break off and pull back to the planet. Detail off one of the light frigates to make a run straight back to Cor! I'll send the signal up shortly detailing the situation."

His tactical officer looked at him in stunned disbelief.

This barbarian system was madness. His uncle had to understand that; it was madness and needed more than a recon squadron to subdue. He'd at least hold the planet that surrendered until help arrived.

"Break it off now and get that courier moving!"

"They seem to be turning away," Tanya said, her voice taut with excitement.

"They're definitely breaking away, turning back towards Earth!"

"Matt?"

"Still alive out here."

"Where the hell are you?"

"Where the hell are you?" Matt quipped in reply. "Remember, it's all relative."

"They're running!"

"I can see that," Matt replied, and Justin looked at his comm screen as Matt grinned like a demented child.

Justin toggled into his main comm line.

"All ships, all ships, form up screen astern of the Academy. Well done!"

Admiral Mahan exhaled loudly and leaned back in his command chair, then looked at Thor.

"Damnedest thirty minutes I've ever been through."

"Too bad we didn't win," Thor said.

"Hell, we're still alive aren't we? I thought we'd all be spaced by now."

"We didn't totally destroy them. I was hoping the Colonials would have enough of those missiles to finish them all off. That commander of theirs panicked. The damn fool most likely doesn't even realize we've probably fired everything we had. So he'll pull back to Earth now and use the EDF orbital bases as shields. Have any of his ships broken off yet to head back to the origin point?"

Mahan looked back at his screen.

"Half a million klicks out at full throttle, three escorts trailing astern." He hesitated. "Should I detail the *Prometheus* fighters to try an intercept?"

Thor shook his head.

"It's what they'd want. It would be a stern chase all the way and those three escorts will block them. If we chase he'll send more ships out behind them, box them in and destroy them. We can't afford it. Pass the word for everyone to make best possible speed to Mars. Let's get the hell out of here."

✧ Chapter XIII ✧

"This is monstrous, absolutely monstrous!"

Holzan Zollern stood in silence, almost ashamed to admit to himself that he was, in fact, afraid of the man before him. Naruth Zollern, his third cousin and the Viceroy of Avla, looked down again at the hard copy of the message sent back from the frontier. He crumpled the message up and cast it down on the deck, then turned and strode away, fists opening and closing convulsively.

Finally he spun back around and looked back at Holzan. "My nephew says that they were armed with Gar tracking rounds and there were five Gar ships in the fleet. I expect you to tell me how that could be."

Holzan looked around the Viceroy's cabin, trying to conceal his nervousness. Naruth was far closer to the throne than himself and he was obviously looking for someone to blame other than his nephew.

"They intervened, that's obvious," Holzan replied softly.

"But they're part of the Diet . . . that's impossible," the Viceroy snapped.

Holzan bristled angrily and then brought his rage back under control as he worked to analyze the situation. If the Gar were in the war, why only five ships? They would already have occupied the system in strength. Why provoke a fight and not have their full strength there? And for that matter, why provoke a fight at all; it would mean civil war.

And then the memory came back and Holzan felt a cold chill.

"The barbarians had a Gar ship and made contact somewhere," Avla said coldly, "and they either built more ships, which seems impossible, or help came in those additional ships along with a shipment of weapons. Too many things trace back here to this miserable system of Cor. I expect an answer and I want someone's head over this."

He paused for a moment. "And I mean that literally."

Holzan nodded slowly. "What are you going to do?" he finally ventured.

"Blot this flyspeck of a system out of existence. I'll sortie at once."

"With your entire fleet?" Holzan suppressed a smile. The loss of the fifteen ships by Falsin would be buried in the general casualty lists when the action was done. Amusing.

"My entire fleet arrives here across the next five days, then we move *en masse*. I never should have sent that idiot nephew of mine in there alone to start with. This time I'm going to finish it and then move on. Resistance or not, they'll be eradicated."

"Am I intruding, sir?"

Thor Thorsson looked over to the open doorway and smiled.

"Come on in," he said quietly.

Justin Bell pushed off and floated into the amphitheater. The room had always held a special place in his heart. It had been the site of so many gatherings of cadets, the hundred-meter dome overhead showing space in all its splendor. In his six years at the Academy it was where he had so often come to find peace, to float alone during the night watch when the ship was still, to look up at the heavens and dream. It was also the first place he had talked to Thor so many years ago when he was a scared cadet of sixteen. Thor had found him alone, thinking of quitting, and talked him out of it.

Justin looked up at the cold light of a million stars as Thor floated in the middle of the room. Drifting over, he reached out and touched a support beam and came to a stop by his mentor's side.

"Beautiful, always so beautiful," Justin said.

"And so cold."

He could sense the despair in the old man's voice.

The image above slowly turned, revealing first a brief glimpse of Mars, and then space again.

"I don't think we're going to get through this one," Thor whispered.

He looked over at Justin. "I tried to think of every angle, every contingency, and plan accordingly, but there was always one dominant factor I could not control—time. From the very beginning I sensed we were running a race. First a race to prevent our own self-destruction and then a race with whatever it was that we'd find out there, so that friendly or not we'd meet them on equal terms. All my plans of the last forty years have been predicated on that final point, being ready."

He sighed, the soft exhalation sending a cold shudder through Justin.

"Almost hard to believe," Thor said. "I've been such a damned incurable optimist my entire life. It was the only way I could get done all that I dreamed of doing. And yet now I think we've just about come to the end of all things."

"They might not come back."

Thor looked over at him.

"They have to come back. Earth, the poor damned bastards, has already been declared a territory of the Zollern controlled by the Imperial family. They can't occupy just half a system. They'll be back, and this time it'll be with everything they can throw against us."

"Then why did you push us to fight?"

Thor laughed softly.

"Tell me, should we have surrendered the way Hassan did?"

"Hell, no. I saw that in Bel Varna. The Zollern might not be the worst of them, but it's crushing nevertheless. I remember you teaching us about the colonialism of the past. When a superior culture meets an inferior one there is only one final conclusion, annihilation or absorption. In their eyes we're barbarians. Our culture would be destroyed, our freedom denied. And behind *them* is the Hive. Maybe they planned to turn us over to them, maybe they were going to use us as a base to secure their flank. Damn, we're just pawns in their galactic game. Six thousand years of what we are would have gone into the darkness. Fighting was the only alternative."

"Your answer described my reason for fighting. It was the only way. I feared before we started to find out what was out there. I thought we might face a monolithic power, though deep down I knew that was illogical. This galaxy is simply too big for one power to ever control. I had hoped that it would be us doing the finding first, then playing off one side against the other the way your friend Bel did, until we were strong enough to fend for ourselves. Three hundred years ago that was the only hope inferior civilizations had when facing the Europeans' technological advantages. It was, by the way, how America won its independence, by using France to block England. But we never got that chance."

"Are you suggesting we throw in the towel?"

Thor looked back at him.

"I'm simply not sure yet."

Justin was startled by the answer. For all of his adult life he was used to Thor always having a firm opinion on any question, and almost inevitably being right about it.

"Sir, we've got three more ships coming online within the week. Defensive systems are being beefed up around Mars, and there'll be nearly forty more missiles available. If they come in, we'll give them a hell of a fight. With

luck it might even be months before reinforcements come
from the Zollern; by then we could have dozens of ships,
maybe even enough to sortie out and take Earth back."

"I hope so, Justin, I hope so."

They floated in silence for several long minutes, and
Thor finally stirred.

"If they do come again, Justin, I'm giving you one final
order."

"Anything, sir."

"I'm having a historical log uploaded into the ship's
computer on Matt's vessel. You and Tanya are to transfer
over to his ship. Everything, a complete record of our
race's history, literature, art, music, all of it is there. If
they break through I'm ordering you to turn and run—
point yourself straight out away from the center of galaxy
and go. There's all of space out there for you to go to. All
of it to choose from. Maybe you'll find some place to go,
maybe not. But I want the record to survive. It's impossible
to think of the universe without special things surviving,
like Renoir or Beethoven's Ninth. I want you to have Matt
and Tanya with you as well. For a journey like that it'd be
best to have your friends along."

Justin looked over at Thor, startled.

"I can't do that, sir. My duty is here."

"I'm ordering you to go, young sir," Thor said in a fatherly
voice. "And don't try the argument that I should be the
one to go. I plan to stay right here, with my ship—it's
where I want to be. Now, do we understand each other?"

Justin could only nod his head in reply.

"So, Holzan Zollern, I think you come here on less than
pleasant business."

Varna got up slowly from behind his desk and went over
to pour two drinks, this time going into his finest and rarest
stock.

Holzan nodded his thanks as Bel offered the brandy
snifter. Holzan swirled the drink around inside the goblet
and sipped it.

"You've honored me with your rarest stock," Holzan said, looking up at Bel with surprise. "I always knew you had a couple of bottles of Tre '28 stashed away but you never shared it before."

Bel shrugged casually.

"This offer means something, I suspect," Holzan said.

"From your demeanor, which was quite evident on my monitor, it seemed as if you came with unpleasant news or intent. I thought to disarm you."

Holzan chuckled softly and went over to take a seat by the fire. He sipped meditatively on the brandy as Bel pulled up a chair to sit beside him.

"I've just come from the Viceroy's ship," Holzan said.

"I assumed as much. You left your quarters rather hurriedly just after they arrived. So the master beckoned and you came running."

Holzan stiffened slightly at the mild rebuke.

"Don't worry. I'd have done the same. He's been known to kill people when they don't appear promptly."

"He's a barbarian."

Startled, Bel said nothing. To hear a Zollern use the most crude of insults towards another Zollern was remarkable.

Holzan looked over at Bel and smiled. "I think that you, sir, can understand that."

"I said it all along, it's just that you couldn't allow yourself to admit it in public, though I suspected you felt it very much so in private."

"This whole war is a misbegotten adventure. The alliance with the Shun was his doing. This is no longer a game of balance of power, this is a stroke to try to destroy the Perjordin and in the process weaken the Shun, while at the same time bringing the other Houses of the Diet into line with the threat of the Hive. Madness! When the central order breaks down it will be chaos. The rules of war will be lost, a thousand worlds will be irradiated wastelands. It's almost ironic. It means that when the Hive does attack part of our system they won't stop. They will beat us because anyone that's left will at best be able to fight them with a club. I think even the Viceroy must sense that, but he'll smash countless worlds in order to build his glory on the rubble."

Holzan finished his drink and motioned for a refill. Bel passed the dusty bottle to him, then refilled his own glass as well, tossing the empty decanter into the fire.

"So what are you going to do?" Bel finally asked.

"Try to control it somehow."

"How?"

Holzan chuckled.

"I honestly don't know."

"You were never in favor of letting the Hive occupy Cor to start with, were you?"

Holzan looked over at Bel and smiled.

"You know, I had a hundred and twenty million invested in here. I couldn't move it out earlier, because it would have tipped off too many people. Then the banking house refused to move the money to another system, afraid that it'd draw too much attention to themselves."

"That's what you get for banking with the Norru clan."

"It was profitable to keep you independent. A little tax-avoiding for all of us, a little shifting of goods between adversaries to the benefit of both. That's gone now."

"But you did it anyway."

"It was my job to do it. And I protected you stiff-necked people from getting slaughtered by the Viceroy."

"And so masterfully sold us back to the Dynasty in the process, and then we get to be the breeding ground for the Hive."

Holzan smiled. "I guess I did do a good job, at that."

"There's something else you came here to tell me, isn't there?"

Holzan nodded. "I think there's going to be a little investigation."

"Into what?"

"I guess you haven't heard yet. A courier returned from the frontier yesterday and met with the Viceroy, who's waiting by the transit point for the rest of his fleet to arrive."

Bel tried to feign disinterest as he went back to the cabinet and pulled out a second precious bottle. He uncorked it and brought it back over, refilling Holzan's glass.

"Go on."

"The barbarians in the next system thrashed Falsin. He barely hung onto their primary world. A secondary world and what I assume are outer colonies are in rebellion. The damn fool lost nearly half his ships."

Bel chuckled as he took another sip. "I can imagine the Viceroy is not amused."

"He's taking his entire fleet in and plans to slaughter the rebels wholesale as an example. The primary world, which surrendered, is to be reduced to a state of slavery."

Bel said nothing. To show interest in the fate of barbarians who had insulted the Zollern simply wasn't wise.

"So why are you telling me this? After all, it is a bit of a humiliation for your family."

"The Viceroy is not my direct family," Holzan said angrily.

Bel nodded an apology.

"It's just that there was something rather curious out there. The barbarians had half a dozen Gar light transports and a number of the latest tracking antimatter rounds and detonators."

"The damn Gar, trading across the frontier. Incredible! You know the Gar though, no central authority, each clan doing what it sees fit."

"That's what I said," Holzan replied, "and that's why you surmise that once Cor is occupied the Hive will be given the go-ahead to move into their territory. My family has never had any love for them, but of course I never said that."

Bel knew what was coming but said nothing.

"It was the same design as the ship that came into this system half a dozen ten-days past."

"So? Gar traders come here rather often."

"And a Prata of the Assembly goes out to personally greet each one of them?"

Bel looked at Holzan and said nothing.

"I've been ordered to track down the source of the transfer of the tracking rounds. It might be the Gar. Regardless of who it is, I've been ordered to personally deliver the head of the man who instigated the transfer. I'm not speaking rhetorically, it was a direct order."

Holzan sat back in his chair.

"You know that the Norru family will say anything if the money is right. They'd even sell their own daughters if it'd turn a profit. I was going to head over there next to talk to them. I think they'll know who did it."

"Good luck on your quest."

"Also, orders are that no ship is to leave this system. I heard a rumor that even now your private vessel is powering up."

"Oh, they're just testing an engine, I believe."

"And is your Marshal Bathan testing all the engines on his ships as well?"

"Why, I'm just a politician, Holzan. I don't involve myself with the military's concerns."

"His entire fleet will be over there in six days time. I guess that will leave this system stripped," Holzan said shaking his head. "Curious move . . . I hope it doesn't create a problem."

With a deliberate slowness Holzan stood up, and Bel watched him warily.

"Good night to you, Bel Varna. Maybe someday we'll share that dinner that we've always promised each other."

Holzan started for the door.

"Holzan."

The ambassador turned and looked back.

"I forgot to mention something."

"What?"

"Oh, just that I arranged a little transfer of credit a while back. Seems that one of my innumerable nephews bought out a couple of minor banks that were part of a larger deal. Somehow a certain account wound up being transferred off our world the other day, just before the freeze ordered by your family took place. It was transferred to the Jorrin system's banks, if I recall correctly, with a rather nice accumulation of interest, I might add. The account number's still the same if I'm not mistaken."

A smile creased Holzan's beefy face.

Bel reached down and, recorking the bottle of brandy, tossed it over.

"To keep you warm, my friend. The last bottle of its kind in the universe. Enjoy!"

Holzan held the bottle up in salute and left the room.

Bel Varna, smiling, shook his head as the door closed. He returned to his desk and paged the crew of his private ship to request that they prepare for a little journey.

"Justin?"

Surprised, Justin sat up in his bunk and saw Tanya in the shadows sitting on the edge of his bed. He could sense she was scared.

"What is it?"

"Word just came in, a Zollern fleet has just entered our system."

"How bad?"

"Nearly two hundred ships," she whispered, her voice trembling. "Some of them are nearly the size of the Academy. They're heading straight this way, and we're expecting contact in less than twenty hours."

Two hundred ships. Then it was over, it was truly over. The nearly two weeks of stalemate, with Earth occupied but the Colonies holding out, was over. Mahan, Seay, and Thorsson had assumed that Falsin was waiting for reinforcements before pressing the killing attack. Two hundred ships was not just a killing attack—it would be annihilation.

"We just got orders from Thor. We're not to wait. The data's been uploaded into Matt's ship, and we're to pull out of here immediately. A new crew will be over here shortly to take this ship out."

Her voice started to choke up, and he leaned and hugged her.

"Thor wants to see us again before we leave. Matt's coming in to see Thor as well before we leave."

"I better get dressed."

"You have some answering to do."

Falsin, head lowered, stood silent before the image of his uncle on the holo screen.

"You disobeyed standard doctrine. You engaged with your entire force before knowing what your enemy had. It was the lowest form of crass stupidity."

Falsin, trembling with fear and yet feeling a mounting rage, looked up at the image in the holo field.

"We engaged their first fleet and brushed through it with ease. The main planet submitted then without a fight. I believed we were simply dispatching some remaining rebels to consolidate our position."

He waited the long minutes for the signal to reach his uncle, standing silently.

"I'll finish it, then," the Viceroy finally replied. "But I want an example made there. Don't destroy anything more on the main world. But make an example and let these rebels see it clearly so they know what is coming."

Falsin bowed low to the screen and then shut it off. He turned away and returned to his desk.

"Bring that barbarian in here and contact our destroyers orbiting their moon."

A moment later Hassan walked in and looked around nervously.

"I heard the news that a new fleet will be arriving," Hassan said. "I'm glad to see that we will finally have our vengeance."

"Our vengeance?"

"Precisely. I am part of you now. Your enemies are mine and by good fortune my enemies are yours."

"But you did not tell me of their improved weapons."

"As I told you, they were in rebellion. Why would enemies reveal what they have to their opponent?"

Falsin looked at the barbarian closely. The man was obvious too frightened to lie at the moment.

"Then let us show our enemy what to expect this time."

Falsin turned back to his command screen.

"Get me the *Ugara*, *Bacta*, and *Rapul*."

Seconds later the captains of the three ships orbiting the Moon appeared on the screen.

"Annihilate everything on the moon and the orbital Colonies as well, but preserve anything of military value."

Falsin switched screens showing a high-res image of the Moon. Several minutes later the first detonation rippled across the surface at Tycho Station. Within seconds scores of explosions flared to life. Bursts of light exploded around the Moon as more than a hundred orbital habitats disappeared.

Hassan watched the images, saying nothing, his eyes wide with excitement.

"You've just killed more than twenty million people," he whispered.

"It will only be the beginning," Falsin replied, not even bothering to look back at the screen.

"As of today all activity outside the immediate orbit of your primary planet is forbidden. All barbarians outside of that region will be annihilated. If there is one act of resistance your entire world will be exterminated. Do I make myself clear on that?"

"Perfectly," and Hassan smiled. "I and my government will be more than happy to serve you in any way that we can."

Falsin looked at the barbarian who stood before him, sensing that there was a brutality within that almost matched his own. The thought was comforting; it would make it easy to control them when their own leader was so eager to sell them out.

Thor looked up as Justin and Tanya came into the room. He smiled; as it was all too evident what must have just happened between them. It was so human of them, and that thought somehow gave him comfort.

"We'll be engaging within twelve hours. The Colonial

government was considering making an offer of surrender and I frankly had to agree with them considering the size of the fleet we're facing, but we just received a broadcast from Earth."

Thor paused for a moment.

"They destroyed everything on the Moon and all orbital Colonies outside of immediate Earth orbit. Falsin Zollern made it clear that no surrender will be accepted now. It is, quite simply, a fight to the death, and the outcome is inevitable.

"You can't run back towards the Zollern," Thor continued. "And from what you told me of their strategic goals, running out in the opposite direction would be futile as well; since they'll be going that way once," he hesitated for a brief moment, "once they've finished here. I'd suggest trying for that other transit point, the one the first Gar ship came through."

"Why there? That's hostile territory as well."

"It's the only other transit point we know of. It's either that or years of flying to heavens knows where."

"And then what?" Justin asked.

"Be Adam and Eve," Thor replied softly. "You'll have the total knowledge of mankind stored in your ship. Preserve it. Share it. I've seen to it that you have a supply of acid-free paper onboard. Write down everything. Basic materials on how to make things and survive are being stored aboard your ship in print form. And other things as well—Shakespeare, the Bible, Twain, and Tolstoy, Plato and Locke. The old game of what would you take to a desert island."

The door slid open behind them and Justin saw Matt come in, his co-pilot waiting out in the corridor.

"Bring her in as well."

Justin looked over as Chelsey followed Matt in.

"You sent for us, sir?"

"It's time the four of you left."

Matt nodded, saying nothing. Justin looked over at Chelsey, realizing that for some reason Thor had selected her to go as Matt's companion. She looked over at him warily and said nothing.

"Thank you, sir," Matt finally replied, "but Chelsey and I have been talking it over. We'd rather stay here and fight. Running away just doesn't suit us."

"You're not running away, you're running to something. Something has to survive, and with luck it will be you four that will do it and keep the dream alive."

"Us four?" Chelsey asked, looking over coldly at Justin. Thor chuckled softly.

"I think you'll forget your differences with time, and just maybe someone else out there will draw your attention instead."

Chelsey looked back at Matt, who looked at her nervously for a moment and then dropped his eyes.

"Oh, great, I'll be spending eternity with his best friend," Chelsey sighed.

"It could be worse," Matt replied casually.

Chelsey rolled her eyes and looked appealingly at Thor.

"Come now, young lady, it was Admiral Seay who told me you had an interest in Everett here, and I've always trusted Seay's judgment."

Chelsey blushed and lowered her head.

"The four of you get out of here. Be careful with your fuel and you just might have enough for that second jump. Now get out of here before I start into some long-winded speech and wind up crying and making a fool out of myself."

Thor motioned over to Kevin Malady. The old marine stepped forward and handed a small package to Thor. Thor motioned for Justin to take it.

"The Academy flag, the one that hung in my office. Take it. Maybe someday when we again reach for the stars and there's another Academy this flag will be there. You'll also find another keepsake wrapped inside the flag—a bit of dust from Earth to remind you of what was once home."

Coming to attention, Justin saluted, followed by the others, and he started to turn away. Tanya suddenly rushed forward, then leaned over and hugged Thor, tears streaming down her face. And with tears in his eyes as well Justin walked up and took his hand.

"We'll remember. Not just us, but afterwards, we'll remember."

Taking Tanya by the shoulder, Justin led her out of the room, not looking back, followed by Matt and Chelsey, who was crying as well.

Thor looked up at his guardian, who stood behind the float chair.

"Come on, Malady, we still have one last battle to fight."

✧ Chapter XIV ✧

"Are we being followed?"

Tanya scanned through her main nav screen, which was tuned into the relay station on Mars.

"Forty million out and nothing," she said quietly. "Their main fleet is still closing; nothing has diverted yet."

Justin leaned over to look at her screen. The Zollern fleet was still sixty million miles out and closing. They'd be in near-Mars space within another hour. He looked over at his own rear projection screen. Mars was now a barely discernible disc directly astern, receding farther with every passing second.

He looked over at Matt. "How you doing, buddy?"

"I feel like a bastard."

"Yeah, I know."

He turned to look aft. Chelsey was strapped into a pull-down seat against the far bulkhead, leaning back, her eyes closed as if lost in thought.

Though it was never spoken Justin felt as if he were somehow the leader of this group, that it was his duty now to divert the other three from the anguish they were feeling. But his own anguish was far too overwhelming. The urge for a really good drunk weighed heavily on him and he was tempted to ask Tanya if maybe a bottle had been added to the survival stores that filled the aft end of the ship. No, not now. Never again—and the words of the old song of the Academy hit him.

"It may be for years, and it may be forever . . ."

The Viceroy of Avla leaned back in his chair and yawned.

Hunting down barbarians was boring work, and such a waste. Precious munitions would have to be expended, and he'd most likely lose some ships as well; current computer analysis and projections indicated that at least twenty vessels would be lost in the upcoming action.

It was all so trivial—no glory to be found in the slaughter of savages.

"Sire?"

Annoyed, he looked back up at the main screen.

"What is it now? Are the barbarians doing anything yet?" His communications officer looked nervous.

"Go on."

"Sire, we just received a communication."

"From the barbarians? Ignore it."

"No, Sire."

"From whom, then?"

"Sire, I think you should look at this. Our last high-energy radar sweep of this system just came back in."

The Viceroy of Avla came out of his chair and stood in open-mouthed amazement.

"Justin, we got a request from Mars C-in-C coming in."

Stirred from his thoughts, he looked over at the comm screen. It was Admiral Seay, the message already ending.

"Play it back."

"*Prometheus*, request that you do a radar scan directly ahead of your trajectory at maximum power. *Prometheus*, request that you . . ." Justin turned the volume down and looked, over at Tanya.

"A signal might give us away."

"Hey, buddy, what the hell do you think is up?" Matt interjected.

"It'll give our position away, Matt, but you heard the orders."

Tanya keyed in the command and looked over at Justin. "Go ahead."

She hit the button and the pulse shot out. As the seconds passed he watched the screen intently, wondering what the hell was going on.

"Thirty million miles," Tanya whispered, "still nothing, thirty-one, thirty-two . . ." Her eyes suddenly went wide.

"Bodja moi!"

"What is it?"

He looked down at the reflected image coming back. Hundreds of blips filled the screen.

"Send that signal back down to Mars and keep pinging them."

He looked over at Matt.

"Looks like we're blocked by a second fleet. I think we better get the hell out of their way if we want to do this Adam and Eve party."

Justin looked back at the screen. It just didn't fit. It couldn't be a Zollern Fleet.

Gar, then.

Damn, they were caught between the Zollern and Gar.

"I'm getting an audio and visual signal from them," Tanya said. "It's aimed at the Zollern Fleet, but I think I can pull it in."

"Monitor it and patch it down to Mars."

The image on her screen was grainy, shifting in and out of focus. Half a dozen creatures who looked similar to the Zollern were on the screen, but their garb was different—flamboyant, almost garish, bright hues of red, yellow, green, and they seemed to be laughing.

"The language is different than the Zollern," Tanya announced, "I'm feeding it into the translator."

"All action in this sector will be viewed as an intolerable provocation and will be met by an appropriate response," and the speaker grinned, the group behind him laughing again.

Justin looked over at Tanya.

"Could you please tell me what the hell is going on here?"

"Look, Justin, I know just about as much as you do."

"Well, damn it, *something* is going on. You were the one doing the cultural and linguistic stuff with Madison. Who the hell are these people?"

"Why don't you go up there and find out," Tanya snapped, "and stop asking stupid questions I can't answer."

"Just what I was thinking," he finally replied.

He looked over at Tanya, realizing that though he still loved her, life with her was never going to be easy, whether it'd be for another fifty years—or more likely twenty minutes given the relative closing speed they now had with the incoming fleet.

The image shifted, disappeared for several minutes, and then came back in again.

"I'm getting a solid read on at least six hundred ships. Some of them are incredible," Tanya reported. "I estimate more than a kilometer long, habitat size."

Startled, she leaned back and then quickly shifted through screens.

"Damn, we just got pinged. A hell of signal! Shit, it almost peeled the hull off us."

"All right, let's break to my starboard, ninety degrees, and get out of here."

"We're getting hailed."

Tanya motioned over to the comm screen, which had been showing the ongoing signal to the Zollern. The image was now split, with a second smaller screen showing a crystal-clear image of one of the reptilian creatures.

"Identify, identify clan unit."

"Well, tell it who we are," Justin said. "What the hell, they know we're here."

"This is Earth ship *Prometheus*. Who am I addressing?"

The seconds passed as the signal traveled to the other ship.

"Barbarian! Are you the barbarians?"

"Damn it, I'm sick to death of being called a barbarian,"

Tanya snapped. "You and everyone else out there are the damned barbarians. We didn't start this bloody war, so drop dead!"

"You're a hell of a diplomat," Justin hissed.

"What the shit, Bell. Now we got two sets of bastards invading us."

Her reply finally reached the ship. To Justin's amazement their interrogator started to laugh and he could hear more laughter in the background as it turned away and apparently repeated what Tanya had said.

Their interrogator looked back at the screen and grinned.

"Shut down and prepare to be boarded."

"Eat—" Justin slammed the comm link off.

"Don't!"

"Look, it's finished, so let me go out my own way, will you?"

A smile crossed Justin's features then, and he leaned over and kissed her lightly on the forehead.

"All right, then."

Tanya turned the comm link back on, but before she could speak the creature on the screen looked over its shoulder and then moved away from the camera. A bulky form dressed in black sat down.

"Ah, my old friend with, how do you say it, tea. Would you care to share some with a friend?"

Justin could only shake his head and smile.

He felt the gentle nudge of the docking collar locking in place. Craning forward Justin looked up incredulously. The ship was huge, far bigger than the Academy, and apparently capable of going translight. The power involved was stunning, as were the concentric rings of what were obviously gun turrets studded along the ship's hull.

He got out of his seat and went aft, following Tanya, who watched the monitor by the door until it indicated an airtight seal. She pulled the door open and Bel Varna stood before them, grinning.

"Of all the people I never expected to see again," Tanya

gasped, "it was you," and she stepped up and hugged him, unable to contain herself.

"Such a greeting is worth the journey," Bel said with a smile as he came through the door and then bowed formally to Justin.

"Have I your permission to enter?"

"By all means, and the tea will be up shortly."

Bel stepped into the ship, and looking aft he saw the pile of crates stacked up and down the length of the corridor.

"A trade run?"

"Survival," Justin said quietly, and quickly explained.

Bel chuckled. He went over to the table in the galley and sat down, nodding his thanks to Tanya as she pressed a steaming mug of tea into his hands. He grinned at Matt and smiled a greeting at Chelsey.

"We must get her inoculated," Bel announced, and then he looked back at Justin.

"Just what are you doing here?" Justin burst out, unable to contain himself.

"Believe me, I would definitely have preferred to be someplace other than the middle of a war zone."

"With a fleet like the one out there, why didn't you stand up to the Zollern in the first place?"

Bel laughed and took a long sip on his tea.

"It's not our fleet."

"Then whose is it?" Tanya asked eagerly.

"The Gar."

"The Gar?" Tanya gasped. "Are they here to pick up the pieces, Bel? Just what the hell gives?"

"I don't get it," Justin sad, shaking his head.

"Just a little exercise in," he hesitated, "what would be the words, 'system politics.' "

"Geopolitics?" Justin finally offered and Bel nodded.

"I think you'll be pleased to know that just before I boarded your ship the Zollern Fleet stopped its advance and is now motionless."

"Why?"

"The Gar pointed out that a continuation of the action would result in a war."

"I don't get it," Tanya interjected. "Why should the Gar care?"

"I paid them to care."

"Then let me rephrase that," Justin said. "Why should you care?"

Bel chuckled.

"Because I'm at war with the Zollern. I don't want to injure your feelings. Though I rather liked all of you personally I would not bribe an entire fleet just to save you.

"The day you arrived in my system we were forced to accept a treaty with the Zollern that was tantamount to occupation and reabsorption into their empire, and then we were to be traded like pawns. That's why I armed you, to buy time. At the same time I sent my nephew to the Gar with a rather lucrative offer, the transfer of all our banking assets to their control, and believe me, that's more financial power than whatever your system could hope to muster. The Gar really don't care much for wealth, but it can buy them weapons and ships on the black market and that was appealing to them. We would have lost that money in any case under the Zollern, so I felt I might as well put it to good use elsewhere.

"The agreement was that they'd block Zollern advancement to Cor and this world. The Viceroy of Avla stripped his ships away from my planet to yours as I hoped he would. The timing was close, but I managed to leave my home world and link up with the Gar fleet at a prearranged rendezvous point with the latest intelligence. Even now Gar ships are moving into my system as well."

"Well, suppose the Zollern decide to fight? That makes our system and yours the battlefield."

"Oh, chances are it'll still turn out that way," Bel said casually, "but for the moment it won't. You see, even now the Gar are conveying a rather amusing bit of information. They know where the Perjordin Fleet is located. They now know where the Zollern fleet is as well. They'll sell that important bit of tactical knowledge to the highest bidder. I dare say the Viceroy of Avla will be the highest bidder. He'd be a fool to fight the Gar at this moment; there's no advantage in it, and besides, it would provoke an open civil war, something the Zollern must avoid at all costs if they are to face the Perjordin and keep the Shun in line.

"He's caught in a difficult spot. He'll make the high bid and then go after the Perjordin. They'll meet and fight. Maybe he'll win, maybe not. The result will be that the Gar will have an intact fleet, and if they wish to do so they could then take out the loser."

"But the Gar," Matt said, "are the bastards who attacked us in the first place."

"Oh, they do apologize for that. Actually it seemed that you were the victims of some youngsters out on," he hesitated, "now I remember your phrase, youngsters 'feeling their oats.' "

"Feeling their oats?" Matt shouted in exasperation. "They killed millions."

"Yes, unfortunate, and on behalf of the Gar ruling council I extend my humble apologies. Restitution will be paid in full."

"It still sticks in my craw."

Bel was silent for a moment as if puzzled by Matt's words. "It's time you grew up Matt Everett, you and your entire race."

"What the hell is that supposed to mean?"

"Look at the reality of what you are confronting. Take that first Gar ship that came into your system and the others that followed. The Gar have a tradition—when their young ones come of age they are sent out on a journey. It has a practical side, for often in their wanderings they find a new transit jump the way someone did yours. Some of those cubs were actually prowling for a transit right in our backyard and we didn't even know it. Often it's just a year-long debauch by their crew but at least the debauch is out of sight of their elders."

"So what the hell do you mean by growing up?"

"Disaster was already on your doorstep. Fortunately it was a few wandering Gar who opened the door first. Yes, they caused damage, but you took one of their ships and unlocked its secrets. When a group of them came you destroyed them. Paradoxical as it might sound, when I told the Gar elders about it, they weren't angry. They shook their heads at the folly of youth and actually expressed some remorse. Animosity and revenge didn't enter into the picture, they understood you were defending yourselves. Better that than a first visit by the Zollern, Perjordin, or, worst of all, the Hive."

"So why should the Gar help us now?" Tanya asked.

"I convinced them of what the Zollern were really up to, preparing to use the Hive to control the more recalcitrant elements within their realm. Granted it was a bargain that some, even in their own court, were leery of. The Hive would move from Cor into regions the Gar and others consider their own, that was evident. The Zollern hoped to use that threat as a lever to paralyze the Gar and bring them back into line. Instead I made sure it pushed them over the edge—that information, and one of the biggest bribes in the history of any race.

"This is a conflict that will go on for years. You have just entered into a terribly complex universe, and you, my friends, are by far the weakest part of it at the moment. If the weak are to survive they have to learn cunning. I have blocked for the moment the Zollern plot to turn over Cor, and parenthetically have saved you from annihilation. End result—the war here has been canceled for today."

Chuckling, he reached into his pocket and pulled out a small bottle.

"I had to leave home rather hurriedly, but I did manage to bring out a little of my best stock." He paused for a moment and smiled. "A good friend now has the rest and I'm certain he'll make use of it. In any case, would you care to join me?"

Justin, laughing, took the bottle as Bel uncorked it and, ignoring Tanya's angry look, downed the best drink he'd had in years.

"So I'm to stay here in this miserable backwater, is that it?"

The Viceroy merely looked at his nephew and said nothing.

"You have your orders. For the honor of the Dynasty I refused to concede that which we had already rightfully taken, and the Gar agreed. This system is to be split. You will control the primary planet for now, the Gar the outer Colonies. For the moment both fleets will withdraw, though the Gar will leave an occupation force behind in orbit around an outer planet. I now know where the Perjordin are and leave you in charge here while I go out to find and destroy them."

"This is absurd," Falsin growled.

"Damn you, those are my orders and they are to be obeyed," the Viceroy shouted. "If you had done your job right in the first place this never would have happened. You will hold your ground here. I'm dispatching a courier back to the imperial court for further orders. For all I know we might be officially at war with the Gar, or this could just be a whim of the moment for them. I have no authority to make any decision beyond the armistice here in this system."

He paused for a moment and then lowered his voice.

"Be thankful I've given you this assignment. If you were not of my blood I would have dumped your rotten carcass into space for failing me the way you did. Now control what you have until I can return to settle this issue. Exploit what you can of this system . . . I want a base here, and I want antimatter refueling plants running, repair and resupply facilities operational. These barbarians can build ships, so put them to work. If you fail me again, I'll personally cut your throat."

The image of the Viceroy faded from the screen.

Falsin turned away from the screen back to his command console.

"Get that barbarian Hassan in here now!"

"Bel Varna, I have the honor of presenting to you the commander of our United Colonial Corps, Thor Thorsson."

Justin stepped back and looked at his mentor. He felt a knot in his throat. The old man's eyes were alight with a fierce joy as Bel came up before Thor and bowed.

"I've waited my entire life for this moment," Thor said, his voice clear and vibrant. "Thank you for what you've done."

"It was profitable for both of us."

"I suspect," Thor said quietly, "that there might have been a little more behind this than mere profit. You saw kindred spirits in us, didn't you?"

Bel shifted a bit uncomfortably.

"It achieved a certain end for both of our systems, though we are not in the clear yet."

"At least now we have a start."

"The Gar find you all to be rather amusing. Pardon the term, but they rather like the idea of barbarians fighting a Zollern fleet to a standstill. They're offering technical assistance and additional weapons."

"We refuse."

A bit surprised, Bel looked at Thor with open curiosity.

"The capture of one of their ships and the missile technology you provided gave us the edge for survival, but for now that's as far as it goes. If they come in here now we'll die. What *we* are will be bled out and what *they* are will replace it. We didn't fight to simply lose in the end. Convey to them our thanks. If they want an alliance and for us to fight by their side we'll gladly do it, not only here, but elsewhere. That's our payback."

"You know they could take you just as easily as the Zollern," Bel said.

Thor chuckled. "I don't think you'd allow that. After all, I suspect that the fact that we received certain information from you is still a secret. With the Gar intervention in our system the Zollern, I suspect, believe that since we were flying Gar-designed ships and had Gar weapons that it was they who supplied us. That seems to be confirmed now and your tracks have been covered. Am I not right?"

"So far."

"I trust you can negotiate them into not occupying us. Otherwise the secret of the true source might be revealed."

Bel looked at Thor in astonishment. "After all I've done you'd still betray me?"

Thor looked up and smiled. "I think you can convey to the Gar that it's to our mutual advantage that we stay independent out here, though if they wish to position their ships nearby we'll be more than happy to loan them the space. Give us some room and we, a civilized people, will repay you. We happen to be damn good fighters who will never forget a favor. Occupy us and they have nothing because we'll fight them too if it comes to that."

Bel smiled slowly and then shook his head. "I think you'll be most interesting neighbors. I'll convey the message and I suspect, Thor Thorsson, that you and I will have much to talk over. You are, by the way, a frighteningly shrewd negotiator."

Bel bowed low and started for the door, then looked back. "Would you tell about my part in this?"

"I don't think we need to worry about that now," Thor replied with a smile.

Bel left the room, and Thor looked at Justin and Tanya.

"Well, Adam and Eve, I'm rather glad to see the two of you again. Where's Matt?"

Justin shifted uncomfortably.

"I think he and Chelsey are celebrating at the moment," Tanya said quietly, and Thor laughed.

"You realize that if it wasn't for Bel it'd all be over with now," Justin said.

"I know that."

"And yet you'd tip off the Zollern as to his part and perhaps destroy his world in the process?"

"Chances are they'll figure it out anyway; otherwise he would still be back there rather than here. But yes, I would. We can be destroyed in a number of different ways, and direct contact with a superior civilization is one deadly sure way. We'd be dependent on the Gar; we'd become their satellite and then we'd die—history is all too clear on that. They strike me as a perverse lot, and I think they're the only ones who would humor us on that. Give us some time to adjust and learn the other players in this game and we'll survive, but I want it on our own terms, not theirs. Maybe they can see an advantage to that, an ally that can fight and will remember the favor. I didn't spend seventy years of planning to lose it in the end like this."

He paused for a moment, looking around the room at Justin, Tanya, Mahan, Seay and Malady.

"I thought it was finished," he whispered. "Twelve hours ago I thought the chance had been lost. I'm sorry I was weak at the end like that."

Justin, fighting back his tears, stepped up to his side. He knelt down so that they were facing each other and handed Thor a small package.

"The Academy flag, sir," he said softly. I think it's time you hung it back up again—we've got a new Corps to train."